the Pool theory

ALEXA NAZZARO

TWO
PIGEONS
PRESS

MONTREAL

ISBN 978-0-9918161-3-2

Cover design & illustration by Sam van der Walde
Interior design by Jayne E Smith

Acknowledgements

For their help with this book, I wish to thank:

- Ricki Ewings, my editor, for her patience, insight and encouragement.
- Greg Willians for giving this book a last stamp of approval.
- Sara O'Leary and my classmates of English 412 for their early and valuable guidance.
- All the Loyola and Royal West students on the Vaudreuil–Lucien L'Allier train line for their antics that helped me shape Kye and his friends.

For just being there, I wish to thank:

- My father, who convinced me to type up my very first novel and try to get it published.
- My mother, who has always supported my quest to be true to myself.
- My sister, Tonia, for subjecting her friends to some of my earliest work.
- All the friends who have never let me give up.
- Justin and Ariane, for bringing the kid back in me.
- Stéphane, for everything.

For all the Kyes of the world.

The Beginning

(But it really
feels like the end)

Chapter 1

I wanted to see them, but she wouldn't let me get to her bra strap. Her hands pushed mine away, and her elbows kept jamming into my ribs.

I glanced up at the basement window right above the old television. The sun's glare revealed this thick layer of dust covering the coffee table. My mom would have been mortified to know that a guest could see how dirty the house was.

And this was no ordinary guest. She was Claudia Kemp, the cutest girl in my English class. And aside from feeling her tits, I had no clue what to do. She had her face buried in my neck, that spot that all the guys go for in the movies. The spot that *I* should have been going for.

I gently pushed her face away so I could try and kiss her just above her collarbone, but I ended up jammed somewhere between her chin and her ear instead. She giggled and pulled away, and I shrank to what felt like a point of no return. Some leading man.

"My grandpa used to always tickle my neck," she said guiltily, as though reading my mind.

This was getting better by the second. Next thing I'd know, she'd be telling me I looked like her dad.

I felt her hands at my T-shirt. I shook my head.

"Come on, you will, I will," she whispered. She took a breath. Her cheeks were flushed. Man, she was really winded. I almost felt embarrassed for her for being so into me. I did like her voice when she whispered, though. It was the first thing I had noticed when she tapped me on the shoulder just before Mr. Oertner started in on his welcome-to-grade-ten-English-this-is-going-to-be-hell speech. She wanted to know whether I had an extra pen. I did.

Now here we were two weeks later, and I was on the brink of having the best story of the year to tell Julian. He was my best friend. Well, one of them. Anthony was the other, but he wouldn't be as impressed with this. Julian would be floored.

Her fingers grabbed at my T-shirt again. Jesus, why couldn't it be evening? My scrawny excuse for a chest would hardly show under the dim light of the lamp standing next to the couch. Except it was only five-ish, because my parents were still stuck in traffic instead of watching TV upstairs. Not that they could have focused on CNN with me and a girl in the basement anyway.

I quickly looked around for something to cover myself with if the shirt was going to come off. There was this ancient blanket from the nineteen-eighties that was slung over the arm of the couch, but it must have been about the temperature of Dante's friggin' Inferno or something in that basement, not to mention the blanket was probably coated with my dad's jizz or something.

"What's wrong?" she asked.

"Nothing."

Her eyes looked sad, and her chin was all curled up like she was going to start crying or something. I took a breath and yanked off the shirt, like my pimply nonexistent pecks were meant to be this great comfort to her. She didn't look ready to make a wisecrack like Julian always did, but I couldn't be sure, so I reached for a bra strap.

When it fell, she pulled me to her in a long kiss full of tongue. My hands reached across to her back and tugged and pulled at the clasps, and she broke from the kiss long enough to help. Her grandfather comment and my dad's jizz were gaining distance as her tits rubbed softly against me, and I could feel myself getting hard again.

She stretched out across the couch, with me trying to lie next to her without getting this stale Frito chip that had been stuck in a crease of the sofa too close to my ass. I tried feeling her up and pushing down my pants at the same time, but this is tons harder than it sounds, especially considering that my jeans were glued to my skin and wouldn't budge. I was such a fail.

Claudia laughed.

"What's wrong?" I asked, my heart sinking.

"You're cute."

I threw my pathetic chest over the side of the couch and fished out my T-shirt from the pile of my dad's Time magazines. I felt so much better with it on, too, that I stood up and started yanking up my jeans.

"What are you doing?" Claudia asked.

"Nothing," I mumbled.

"Are you mad at me?"

Her chin was shaking again, and I thought that this time she would start crying for real.

"I'm a little cold," I mumbled, as I wiped the sweat from my forehead.

She got real quiet and stared down at the floor. I would have given anything to take those jeans off again, except that they were already past my knees, and we would have been there until Christmas for me to pull them down again.

I was sure she was going to get up and leave, but she just lay back down on the couch. Compared to me she looked like friggin' Marilyn Monroe.

Then she pulled her hands to her chest like she just remembered that her bra was on the floor.

"Your shirt's inside out," she said.

I shook my head. "Doesn't matter."

I sat back down on the couch, by her feet, and stared at her little pink toes, sort of like what flamingoes would look like from a plane or something. She had these crazy big spaces between them, and her legs were coated in soft hair, but none of that bothered me. I just wanted to be lying next to her again, even if we didn't end up doing anything, which sure as hell looked pretty official at this point.

Claudia picked up the Frito and looked at it, while I kept reminding myself of how badly I had just screwed up. And Claudia was tons hotter than Maggie Blake, whom I had spent all of grade eight pining after. Now, because of me, the only thing she was touching was a friggin' Frito.

Even screw-ups in movies looked better than this. I mean, take *The Godfather II*.

1. Shortly after the assassins try to kill Michael at his home, he meets with this guy Tom Hagen. As Tom enters the room, the table is empty, but only minutes later, Michael offers Tom a drink from a bottle of wine that has magically appeared.

2. When Michael and Fredo sit on a restaurant terrace in Havana there's a lady sitting at a table behind Fredo who switches seats back and forth.

3. In the scene of young Vito Corleone coming to America, his ship passes the Statue of Liberty going the wrong way.

And those are just some of the mistakes. Like I said, there are a lot more. But it's still the best movie ever made. This, on the other hand, was starting to look more awkward than that time I accidentally farted in math class.

Claudia pointed to the knitting basket sitting by the TV.

"Who knits?"

"My mom," I replied.

"That's cool."

She stood up, and I stole one last look at her chest. Her breasts were small and perky. The tiniest diamond-type stone on this thin gold chain hung halfway down between them, and it glimmered in the sunlight as she moved to put her bra on.

I sat back on the couch, the cotton clinging to my back. Man, when were my parents getting central air?

Claudia suddenly jumped up. "Oh shit, I'm leaking!" Her tits bounced a little, which was hot, but at that moment every brain cell in my head was focused on her underwear. They were massive and whiter than my T-shirt. How could I have missed those?

"Can you turn around a second?" she asked, looking a little irritated that I hadn't clued in on this myself.

I turned and faced the wall behind me. I could hear a lot of Kleenex being yanked out of the box on the coffee table. At least it was being used for something, even if I had put it there for a completely other reason.

"Where's your bathroom?" she asked.

"Upstairs."

She muttered a few swear words under her breath.

"Can you check the couch?" she asked.

I started rubbing at the couch around me, like I knew exactly what I was looking for.

"It's old," I mumbled.

It was also black, and I couldn't see a friggin' thing.

"Guys are so lucky," she moaned amidst tons of shuffling.

Sure as hell not all of them.

"Okay, you can turn around now."

She was standing there in her shorts and shirt, all busy with the million pockets on her knapsack. I watched her calf muscles flex as she leaned over and stuffed this small black case inside. A crazy web of veins ran along the outside of her thigh, and I got lost for a second in the blue and red.

I took my time looking back up at her face, trying to memorize what she looked like, what every inch of her had felt like against me. When our eyes met, she had this strange look of relief mixed with agonizing embarrassment.

"I'm sorry," she whispered, staring at the floor.

I felt bad for her, but if she wanted to take the blame for why we weren't still huddled together on the couch, then who was I to stop her?

A weird craving for Kraft Dinner was setting in, and my stomach made a few gurgling sounds. I thought about asking Claudia whether she was hungry too. I make a very good Kraft Dinner, but then I worried it wouldn't come out alright, although don't ask me how you can screw up something as simple as boiling pasta and adding some chemical-looking sauce to it.

I thought about just having an apple. I wouldn't have to cook that; those came from nature or god or whatever. But apples were boring, and I needed to offer Claudia something to erase the tortured look on her face.

"So what do you think of school so far?" I asked.

Nothing more exciting than all that small talk you make with grandparents at Christmas.

She shrugged. "I have Kearns for math, which really sucks." And she was going to switch English classes after this pathetic conversation.

She started playing with her nails, and I stared down at mine. They were all bitten, as usual.

Some dance song started coming from her knapsack. She ran over to it and unzipped the bag, the music getting louder as she pushed books and stuff away.

She pulled out her phone, took a quick look at it, and tossed it back in. I pictured her throwing the phone aside like that if she saw my number.

"My mom," she said. "She's convinced that if I'm not around to set the table and stuff, I'm going to end up in prison before I'm eighteen."

She rolled her eyes, and I laughed. She rolled her eyes pretty funny.

A sweet smile spread across her lips. She had a couple of slightly crooked teeth, but they were cute and not too obvious. And besides, she was friggin' smiling.

"I gotta go," she said.

"Right," I answered.

She climbed the stairs ahead of me and moved through the kitchen and den like she had been over a thousand times before. If only.

When we got to the front door, she turned to me. "I guess we'll see each other tomorrow?"

My heart started beating again. "Yeah, OK."

Her hand gave this little wave, and she took off down the driveway, her hair swishing around like in those shampoo commercials. No, Claudia Kemp wasn't cute; she was friggin' hot. And the best part was, she might still be interested in me.

Chapter 2

The next morning, Claudia wasn't in English, and I seriously started wondering whether things yesterday hadn't turned out as well as I thought. In the meantime, Julian needed a story. I had, after all, told him that Claudia was coming over yesterday. My other best friend, Anthony, on the other hand, was just looking at the schoolyard, bored out of his mind. He was anxious to figure out who was going to host movie night that weekend, even though Julian hated our movie nights. Girls were definitely more his thing. Hence the need for a story.

Never mind that this was the first big story of my entire life and I wasn't sure what to say. No way was I going to talk about anything super-private between me and Claudia, even though nothing happened. But I couldn't say that either.

"She's got white underwear," I finally said at lunch.

"What?" Julian set his Coke can on the grass in disbelief. He started laughing, and I joined in. Julian's laughs were pretty funny, and I kind of liked laughing with him. Anthony glanced at us both like we belonged in the Special Olympics.

"You know," said Julian, "not even my mom wears white underwear."

Anthony made a face. "How the hell do you know that?"

"It's called chores, idiot."

I didn't like when Julian called Anthony an idiot, but Anthony didn't seem to care. He held up the last bit of sandwich to his mouth, like he was getting ready to say something dramatic. It was sort of like how Julian paused before making big announcements. He'd take a big gulp from his soda or start playing with his phone, and you knew something big was coming. Anthony didn't do it right, though.

"I do chores, but I'm not touching my mom's underwear," he finally said. "No way; that's..." His eyes squinted as he searched for the word. "That's just nasty." He stuffed the sandwich in his mouth.

"It's not like I rub them against my face or anything," Julian muttered.

He threw his apple at Anthony's head and didn't miss. He never missed.

"I fold my mom's underwear too," I said.

Anthony glared at me, and I glared back. I kept hoping that someday he'd remember that Julian was the only good thing that had happened to us since we entered this stupid high school three years ago, and it was all because of gym class, which is kind of funny considering that me and Anthony aren't exactly going to win football scholarships.

But my luck turned last spring when Julian arrived from out west, landed in my gym class, and picked me to be on his softball team. I had never swung a bat. Ever. Then again, Julian couldn't see that, not even with his cool glasses, which were the first thing I had noticed about him.

He's the only guy I know who looks good in glasses. Like, Hugo Boss good. I don't know if it was because his eyes were the kind of exotic pale green that just kind of jumped out and grabbed you so quick that you didn't have a chance to notice the glasses. Or maybe it was because of the glasses themselves. They were purple, for chrissakes, but the kind of purple that only guys like Julian could pull off without being called gay.

Anthony's glasses, on the other hand, had those transparent frames that you usually wear because you already have a tendency to look like shit in glasses in the first place. He was cleaning them now, which he always did when he was pissed. I've known Anthony since kindergarten, when we fought over the same toy and were both put in a corner. We had known Julian since March of last year-six months.

"Dude, how many times do you have to clean your glasses?" Julian asked. He was getting antsy and bored, like he always did when me or Anthony didn't hold up our end of the conversation, which happened a lot.

"They get dirty, OK?" Anthony replied.

Julian stretched out his leg across the patch of grass between us and kicked my foot.

"Kye's the one who's dirty," he said with a laugh.

Anthony probably rolled his eyes. His head was too bent over his glasses to tell for sure, but that's my bet.

"Whatever," he mumbled.

I felt bad for Anthony, but at least Julian wasn't looking so bored anymore. Besides, if he wanted to think that my afternoon with Claudia was dirty, I sure as hell wasn't going to complain.

He and I took final swigs of our drinks, our ceremonious end to lunch, and stood up. Anthony was already ahead.

"She's in my math class, you know," he yelled over his shoulder as we all headed back to the school.

I ran to catch up to him. "You never told me that."

"Kearns," he replied, like he hadn't heard me. "That man's scary."

Julian wasn't listening, as usual; instead, he was checking out any hot chicks from the swarm of people in the hallway getting ready for class.

"Do you ever talk to her?" I asked Anthony.

Anthony grinned. "Your secrets are safe with me."

Julian's attention was back on us. "What secrets?"

My heart started pounding in my ears. I knew that Anthony's comment was payback for all the times this past summer that Julian came to my house and not Anthony's. Anthony kept saying how he had the nicer house, but that was only because his mom renovated the kitchen a couple of years ago, thanks to some money Anthony's grandfather had left her. Personally, if I had a bunch of cash, I'd fly out to California and camp out on Quentin Tarantino's porch. Who cared about kitchens?

Julian sighed and rolled his eyes. "So what secrets?"

I gave Anthony the hardest stare I could, and he looked down at the floor.

"Nothing," he replied.

I started walking before the conversation could go any further, and the guys followed. Normally, Julian always took the lead, but we had just passed Megan Astor, and Julian was more interested in her than in the rest of the planet put together, even if she always smelled like those perfume counters in department stores.

I got to my locker as fast as possible. I didn't like taking this way, mainly because there was a group of girls with their lockers just diagonal from mine. I didn't know who they were—I think the redhead was called Alissa or something like that—but they were pretty. I can take prettiness in doses, but a whole concentrated lot of hotness kind of scares me. But I couldn't send Julian through my detours. He'd think I was nuts. Besides, walking through the halls with Julian was easier, or at least that's what I liked telling myself. But not by that much, to tell you the truth.

I opened the locker door and immediately felt better, like I was protected or something.

"So, dude," said Julian. He was always calling me dude. Sometimes I wondered whether he remembered my real name, but who was I to complain? "Did anything else happen?"

"When?" I asked, distracted by some laughter coming down the hall. I wondered whether it was meant for me, and I got redder than the piece of pink gum stuck on the locker next to mine. It doesn't take much for me to blush.

Julian rolled his eyes. "*Yesterday.*"

I should have known he'd ask the question, and I could tell from his grin what was on his mind. I felt disgusted for a moment. Wasn't that stuff sort of personal?

"Helloooooooooooo." He waved his hand across my face. "Did you?"

"Did he what?" asked Anthony, looking from Julian to me.

I pulled out my math books and slammed the locker.

"Maybe," I answered.

"Maybe?" Julian glanced at Anthony like he was looking for back-up.

"There's no in between in maybe," Anthony said. "'Do or do not, there is no try.'"

Julian rolled his eyes. "One Yoda saying and he thinks he owns the universe."

"You probably don't even know who Yoda is," Anthony shot back, while Julian laughed.

"So tell me," said Julian.

Anthony took a deep breath. "Yoda is—"

Julian shoved him. "Not *that*." He then turned and stared into my eyes. His stares really freaked me out sometimes. His dad was some hotshot lawyer and wanted Julian to be the same. He definitely had potential.

I took a deep breath. "Yes."

Julian's eyes got wide. "Really?"

"More than once," I added.

Julian started laughing. "Shut up."

"Yeah, seriously, shut up," mumbled Anthony.

"We should celebrate," said Julian as the first bell rang.

"It *is* my birthday soon," said Anthony.

"January's like, four months away," I replied.

Julian smiled wickedly. "We can celebrate early."

I could have killed Anthony. Not that I honestly expected Julian to never find out, but having Anthony's birthday go by without Julian's knowledge wouldn't have been completely impossible. Until now. It was the first birthday since Julian started hanging with us. Mine's in February, and we didn't know when Julian's was. He kept changing it on us. It drove Anthony crazy, but I could tell it was just to kid around, and that he'd tell us when the time came.

I'm not going to lie, I'd already pictured Julian's birthday parties. They were probably like those beer commercials, with a lot of girls and loud music, even though Julian said he came from a smaller town. I didn't know how he'd react to the ritual me and Anthony had. I could tell Anthony was ready to tell him everything: the Godfather marathon, the bowl of Cheezies. Everything that Julian couldn't know.

Anthony glanced at me as though even he realized that would be too much information.

"We could watch a movie," he suggested casually, like the idea had just come to him.

"We're not sure," I quickly added.

Anthony's eyes widened like he had just found out I made out with his mom or something.

Julian looked from me to Anthony and back at me. "Do you guys do anything else?"

He didn't like movies half as much as me and Anthony. Then again, nobody did.

"We do stuff besides film nights," whined Anthony.

Julian laughed. "Holy shit, you have a name for it too?"

"Maybe Julian can think of something," I said, before I died from five heart attacks at once.

Julian shrugged. "Now *she's* hot," he murmured as some girl passed us in the hall.

Anthony rolled his eyes and started scratching his head like he does when he's bored. All I cared about at that point was hearing the second bell ring to save us all. And to have Julian completely forget about Anthony's birthday.

Chapter 3

Ask anyone else about Fincher High, and they'd probably roll their eyes and complain that the gym is really ghetto, with its bright-red stage and stained-glass windows that make you feel like you're in a church or something. Then they'd talk about the classrooms that all have this weird smell from centuries of people coming through them.

And of course, the mean teachers. The ones that you just know from their faces are out to fail as many kids as possible. Fincher has plenty of those. Like this really old lady who teaches English, I think, and she's all bent over, with these decorative handkerchiefs stuffed into the pockets of her blazers.

And then you couldn't bitch about Fincher without mentioning the cafeteria. It's pretty friggin' ugly. The benches are all this kindergarten blue, and the actual food section is just depressing. The cashier looks like she's been there since before Creation. And the lady that serves the warm stuff has a beard or something. I don't actually know that for sure; Julian told me. But why would he lie about that?

Thankfully, I don't have to go through the caf all that often, and I definitely never go during lunch. Way too many people. That's the other thing about Fincher High: lots of people, but there's not really any other option in Orion, where I live, unless you count Michael of All Angels. There's only, like, three hundred people in that entire school, which is amazing, considering that Fincher has about eight hundred. I would so have gone there, except that Michael is where all the religious freaks go. I could never put up with that Jesus stuff, even if I did just use the word Creation to describe that lady at the caf.

My secret dream is really to have a school all to myself. Well, for me and Anthony and Julian. But there's no way that will ever happen, so Fincher is an alright second choice, mainly because of all the hallways. It's amazing how many of them there are, which means I can avoid passing by most lockers. I've already had three full years of high school to rank the successful passing-by-locker experiences, and it boils down to a few things.

The obvious factor is age. Now that I'm in grade ten, passing by grade seven and eight lockers is pretty easy, except that I don't have any classes in those hallways this year, which sucks. The grade eleven lockers don't bother me much either, because those guys somehow seem too busy thinking about graduation and the future to even notice me. It's my grade and the grade nines that are the issue.

In my grade alone there's Damian Schofield, an asshole in the purest sense of the word. If I can avoid passing by his locker, that's half the battle right there. And I've been doing an alright job so far, thanks to this amazing tunnel-like hallway that takes you around the school and past the auditorium.

There are no lockers anywhere, and the auditorium is used, like, twice a year, for talent shows and stuff.

Sure, the detours take me a bit longer, but I spend the time usefully, mainly by running through Dr. Jacobi quotes. She's this phobia specialist down in Hawaii or something, and she looks like she could star in vitamin commercials. At least, that's how she looks in that picture you see on the back of every one of the gazillion books she's written. I've only read *Claim Your Fear and Live Your Life*. It's a lame title but a useful book, mainly because of the quotes. Every page has one, and I have them all pretty much memorized. I have the book stashed at the back of my closet in this box with all my stuff from grade school, like math certificates and marathon ribbons for running one friggin' block.

It's kind of funny that I have Jacobi all cozied up with tokens from shitty school, which is kind of responsible for getting me in this situation in the first place. But it's the safest spot. Hell, my mom doesn't even go that far back in my closet to vacuum.

I've never told Anthony about Jacobi either, even if he did live through all the same crap that I did. He looks like he's doing okay, though. I mean, sure, he probably does his best to avoid Damian and all the other jerks, but I doubt he takes detours like I do. He's kind of stronger that way than I am.

Jacobi says you should work yourself up to facing your fear, but I'd rather take part in one of those weird African ceremonial circumcisions I learned about in science class than walk by Damian and look him in the eye. I can't even see myself doing that ten years from now, or ever. So much for being cured.

In the meantime, though, I have my quotes, which I was going through in my head as I left French class on Monday.

Claudia hadn't tried contacting me all weekend, and now I was only two periods away from English.

I got stuck on one quote in particular, *Fear is nothing more than an irrational thought*, and for some reason I made a left towards the cafeteria instead of heading towards the usual detour on my right. My locker was really close to the caf, so I guess the move was rational, but it was also pretty big. Especially since French class that day was just before lunch, and people were already sitting on those blue benches, opening up their sandwiches or whatever else they were eating.

As soon I stepped into the caf, all my quotes turned to fizz, but I managed to get through it alright, even though I was sure everyone was looking at me as I walked by in a walk that I knew was nowhere near as cool as Julian's.

When I got out of the caf, I could already see that my hallway wasn't too busy yet, except for a few people. Like Matt Miles, who always had a ton of people around his locker and who just kind of intimidated me in general. Matt was only ever in one of my classes in grade eight, but with a name like that, how could he have been anything but a jerk?

I took a big gulp of water from the fountain that was right beside me, and almost whacked my teeth out on the metal spout when this chick bumped into me. Her long, blond hair fell off her shoulder and brushed the floor as she scrambled to pick up her books. Mine almost slipped from my hands when I saw her face. Claudia. Shit. From her look of surprise, I knew she hadn't planned the run-in. It was all just one big happy coincidence, and now I had to come up with something brilliant to say. Shittier.

"Hey," she said, smiling.

"Hey," I mumbled. "Your hair—"

"My friend dyed it on the weekend."

So sitting around with chemicals in her hair was more appealing than calling me. This was promising.

"It looks good." My cracking voice must have really been doing it for her.

She shook her head. "I am so going back to brown again."

"Okay," I said, like she was asking my permission. I wanted to say that I hadn't seen her around much, but figured that might make me look desperate. I passed.

"Well, uh, I have to meet my friends for lunch," I said.

"You always eat under that tree, huh?"

"Except in winter."

She giggled then, as though I had said the funniest thing in the world, even though I'm about as funny as that Russian dude Stalin that my dad's reading about. But it actually made me feel kind of good.

"The cafeteria feels so gross and sticky." She rolled her eyes.

I stared down at my feet. "You can join us if you want."

"Okay."

I looked up at her, hanging onto the last syllable of that answer. Did she look excited? Or polite, like she was doing me a huge favour? Hard to tell.

"Uh—I was heading over to my locker to get my lunch now," I said.

"Mine is just upstairs from yours," she replied.

So she had scoped out my locker. I had scoped out hers too, but I did my best to look surprised. The hallway had filled up a lot in the last couple of minutes, but all I noticed were Claudia's freckled arms and the little hairs that brushed against mine every so often as we started walking towards my locker. She also had these long, narrow fingers, and her wrist bone poked out of her skin in a crazy way.

"I just happened to see where your locker was once," she added quickly. "I'm not going *Fatal Attraction* on you or anything." She laughed.

I nodded. The movie reference was really sweet, and Anthony would have given her bonus marks for picking something from the eighties, but I didn't let it show. Too much.

From the looks on their faces, I wasn't sure if Anthony and Julian were pissed as hell at me or grateful to me for bringing Claudia along at lunch. They just acted all weird and shit, with Julian jumping Anthony non-stop and punching him in the arm. As long as they didn't make any white underwear comments, though, I couldn't complain.

"I don't know about you, but I'm already dying for Christmas break," Claudia said at one point, between teeny bites from her cheese sandwich.

"You've got a long way to wait." I laughed at my own stupid joke, but at least my voice wasn't breaking.

"Hey Claudia," Julian said suddenly in the voice that he always used when some brilliant idea hit him. "Can you help Anthony here with his homework? He's a bit learning disabled."

Anthony didn't say or do anything, and I wished I could have leaned over and kicked Julian on his behalf or something, but I didn't know how Julian would react. Besides, my aim would have been all screwed up.

"Ignore him," I said to her under my breath.

She smiled a smile that I couldn't read, then stood up and made her way over to a garbage can off to the side.

As soon as she was out of earshot, Julian leaned over. "What's with her teeth?"

"October's going to be eighties all the way," announced Anthony.

Movie nights would normally have been the last subject I would have touched with Julian and Claudia around, but it sure beat Julian making fun of Claudia's teeth.

"The eighties are cool," I said.

Julian rolled his eyes. "As long as I don't have to sit through *St. Elmo's Fire* again."

"What's your problem?" Anthony asked.

"Demi Moore doesn't even have tits in that film."

"Yes she does."

"Her hair's short."

"No it isn't."

"What's wrong with short hair?"

Claudia had come back and plopped herself down beside me. I liked that she chose to sit closest to me.

Anthony, Julian, and I kind of looked at each other, speechless.

"Nothing," we all said together, more or less.

"I was thinking of cutting mine off," Claudia said.

She pulled an elastic band out of her pocket and put her hair up. She looked really good in a ponytail. I imagined us again in my basement and me tugging it, and felt myself blush.

Julian suddenly stood up and tapped Anthony on the shoulder. "Let's leave these guys alone."

"Why?" asked Anthony.

"Because I said so."

Anthony sighed but stood up.

"Now, don't go skipping the afternoon or anything," Julian said over his shoulder as they walked away.

Claudia giggled, and I smiled back, even though I had no friggin' clue how I was going to fill the rest of the lunch period without boring her out of her mind.

Just then, her eyes narrowed, and she started squinting. "Who's that?"

I followed her gaze to the sidewalk, where some girl was standing. She had on these big Paris Hilton sunglasses and a baseball cap.

"Do you know her?" I asked.

"No, but I think you do," said Claudia.

The girl started waving like mad, and it was pretty clear she was waving to me. Her baseball cap suddenly fell to the ground, and she scrambled to put it back on, but not before I saw all her hair spill out across her shoulders and down her back. Annie Cooper was the only girl I knew who had hair like that—curly and wild. But what was she doing here?

"I don't think she wants to come over," said Claudia.

I knew she was right, but I also knew that I didn't want to risk walking away from Claudia and never talking to her again. The lunch hadn't exactly been a smashing success, but it wasn't a total fail either, and I knew I still had about twenty minutes or so to turn it into something better.

Claudia nudged me. "I'll wait for you."

I smiled back, stood up, and headed off in Annie's direction. She was now standing with her legs crossed, like she had to pee really badly. As I approached, the only other details I could make out were a big flowery-type ring on her finger and the freckles on her face. She had more of these than I remembered—dotted across her cheeks and down her neck, before slipping under the pink of her T-shirt. I tried remembering whether they crept down her legs too. I had, after all, seen Annie in a bathing suit nearly every day that past summer at the city pool, even if she had spent a lot of that time in the lifeguard's chair.

"Hey," I said.

Annie looked from me to the sky to the sidewalk. "I took the bus here," she said. "My school's not that far."

I had almost forgotten how raspy her voice was, like she smoked a cigarette a minute or something. Today it had an edge to it, and it made me uneasy.

She pulled off her glasses and stuffed them in her pocket. "I tried calling you."

"When?"

She shook her head. "Holy shit, denial already."

My heart was thumping, even though I had no friggin' clue what was going on. I quickly looked over my shoulder. Claudia was still where I had left her, picking random pieces of grass while looking at us. Still, something told me I had to be careful, especially when I looked back at Annie and saw her eyes filled with tears.

I stuffed my hands deep into my pockets. "What's wrong?"

Annie's eyes got wide, and a tear that had been hanging by an eyelash dropped onto her cheek.

"What's wrong?" she repeated. "Are you fucking serious?"

A couple of kids nearby stared at Annie like they had never heard the f-word before. I had never heard it like Annie had said it, so angry and mean.

"We can talk at the park across the street," I said.

Annie snorted. "No thanks."

Without thinking, I took her arm and pulled her away from the school. She didn't fight at all, like she had forgotten about her big swimming shoulders that were always bulging under the straps of her bathing suit. I remembered how they used to flex like crazy when she laughed, usually about something that Julian would say near the snack bar. He was always making her laugh, while the best I could do most of the time was stand under her lifeguard chair and look up at her with squinting eyes.

As we crossed the street, I clung to that image of Annie's water polo shoulders shaking as she laughed. Like the way

I obsess whenever I misplace a DVD, and I run through all my favourite scenes in case I never find the movie again. Sometimes it's hard to do because of all the background noise invading my memory, and suddenly some unimportant thing that my parents are bitching about interrupts whatever scene is going on in my head at that moment.

In this case, Annie was crying so loudly by the time we reached the park that it was friggin' impossible to picture her *ever* laughing, so I gave up.

Instead, I just watched her lower herself on the bench by the monkey bars and crumple into this sobbing mess I could barely believe was possible. Not even my mom could cry like that.

I pulled out a Kleenex from my jean pocket and handed it to her. It was pretty crummy looking, like it had already been used a hundred times even though it was still new. Not that Annie seemed to care. She took the tissue and dabbed her eyes with it, her head bent so that all I could see was this teeny grass stain on the top of her cap.

"You never came to the closing party," she said after a while, her head still down.

"Sorry."

She didn't answer, and I knew she was giving me a second to follow up my pathetic apology with an excuse. Not that I could have told her the truth. That Julian hadn't wanted to go for some reason and I was too scared to go alone. I couldn't tell her that.

"It was a good one too," she added.

I started feeling jittery and wanted to move the hell away from the international ranking of city pool closing parties, and find out what Annie was doing at my school.

She looked up at me, as though sensing my impatience. "Did you ever like me?" she asked.

The question was so honest it almost made me lose my balance.

Then, just as suddenly as she had asked the question, she put her hand up. "Forget I asked."

I tried making out the scribble on the inside of her palm, but she dropped her hand in her lap and continued crying. I looked around the park. Except for a swing swaying in the wind, the place was dead.

"I'm pregnant."

My head snapped back to the bench where Annie was sitting, her arms tightly crossed; where I was standing on feet that couldn't feel the ground anymore.

Annie started rocking back and forth like she was going to have a seizure. "Did you hear me?"

I couldn't speak. I tried, holy shit did I ever, but nothing came out. Not even a grunt from the back of my throat, or one of those forced coughs I tend to do when I'm nervous. And this was so beyond nervous. I should have been friggin' screaming or something. But scream what? I couldn't think of any words. Hell, I couldn't remember my own friggin' name at that moment, or where I lived.

The bell started ringing across the street like it was calling me, even though I knew that all it was really doing was signalling the end of lunch. Still, I could start making some things out. Like my name was Kye Penton; I was in grade ten; and this girl Claudia was probably taking off for her locker now, leaving me and her picked blades of grass behind her.

Chapter 4

Annie wore a purple bikini that night we all jumped the fence of the pool. Well, it was pretty dark at that point, so I can't say for sure it was purple. I can't even say we jumped the fence. More like unlocked the gate, since Annie had a key, so it wasn't this huge dare, and Julian had been teasing her about the idea for weeks.

Annie was the only reason we went to the pool as often as we did that summer. Normally, I would have been happy staying in to watch three or four movies a day, but Julian wanted to see Annie as much as possible, so we'd catch one movie in the morning and then get to the pool by noon, when her shift started. I didn't mind that much. Annie was the cutest lifeguard there.

She usually wore these plain, red, one-piece bathing suits, so you can imagine how happy we were to see that patch of skin between the two pieces of her bikini that night. I can still remember the way she smiled as she opened the gate. She didn't smile much on duty, except a shy grin in my direction every once in a while. If it pissed off Julian, he didn't let it show. He was the better swimmer anyways, and wasted no time that night diving into the pool and showing off his friggin' butterfly or whatever it's called.

I jumped in right after him and we raced, if you can call it that. It took me forever to reach the deep end, and when I did, Julian was already there, laughing at me and splashing my face. Annie begged us to stop, all paranoid that a neighbour would hear and call the cops, so we did, especially when we saw her silhouette slowly climbing into the shallow end.

I swam towards her and grabbed the hand that was brushing the surface of the black water.

"It's so cold," I remember her whispering, before I gently pulled her away from the ladder until she was closer.

As close as she was to me right now. Just a couple of inches away at the most. If it was summer again, I'd be smelling the suntan lotion on her body, and the chlorine in her hair. Now, all I smelled was faint vanilla.

I kept staring across the street at the tree in front of the school. It looked so still, like Claudia had never been there at all.

"How can that be?" I asked.

"Do I need to spell it out for you?"

"Are you—" I gulped so hard it hurt. "Are you sure?"

"I've spent the last two days looking at lines on a stick," she replied. "I'm positive."

I rubbed my eyes really hard, trying to get lost in the blackness. When I opened them again, though, Annie was still there, madly chewing on a fingernail.

"So much for your stupid theory, huh?" she asked.

When I didn't say anything, she shoved me.

She was stronger than I expected, and I fell back onto the bench and landed with a thud.

"*You can't get pregnant in a pool.*" Her arms were flying everywhere, like one of those crazy homeless people that panhandle in front of the downtown mall.

"Would you calm down?"

"I don't give a shit who hears."

Of course not. It wasn't *her* school within earshot, *her* fragile reputation at stake.

"How many other girls have you used that on?" she asked.

I tried catching my breath but I almost choked instead. "None."

"Aww, I'm touched," she practically spat.

I bent over and put my head between my legs. It's a Dr. Jacobi move I had never tried before. It was supposed to relieve anxiety and whatever, but it had always seemed like a such a weird thing to do. Until now. I was hoping that maybe some of her quotes would come to me too, but no such luck. Not that they would have been exactly useful, but my body felt numb, and I needed all the help I could get.

"Stuff your face in your crotch all you want," said Annie. "It's still yours."

I sat back up. "How do you know?"

"Sorry to disappoint you, but I'm not a slut."

I sighed and felt an ache through my rib cage. "I never said that."

"Well it sure as hell sounded like it."

"It's just—"

Annie crossed her arms. "I don't know what Julian told you."

"Why would Julian say anything?" I replied.

"Because he was an obnoxious jerk?"

"He liked you."

Annie's face crumpled for only a second before she caught herself. It reminded me of the looks she would give me and Julian at the pool whenever we acted like jackasses to catch her attention. An expression that would last just long enough for us to know she had noticed us before her eyes snapped back to the surface of the water, on the lookout for any looming danger.

"Whatever," she replied.

She sat down next to me on the bench, our thighs touching. The last time our thighs touched it had been pitch dark. Under the sun you could see all the weirdness between us.

"I was a virgin," she finally whispered.

"Me too," I mumbled.

And then the two of us got quiet. I had spent all summer trying to find ways to talk to Annie Cooper, but now being quiet with her felt like the best thing.

That only lasted until the wind started picking up. Then Annie gave this loud, disappointed sigh, pulling her leg away from mine and folding her arms, like she meant business.

"So what now?" she asked.

Her eyes were focused. Huge.

"We'll talk," I mumbled.

"When?"

"After school."

I tried picturing my grey locker back at Fincher, and the two afternoon classes that were still ahead of me, not counting the one I was missing, but no clear image came to mind.

Annie shook her head so hard her cap fell off, her hair flying everywhere. "Why not right now?"

I leaned over and picked up the cap and put it back on the bench. Heartburn had set in. It had been a daily symptom back in grade school, but it would usually go away once I was safe back home and I had gotten through the whole "School was fine today" lie with my parents. This pain felt permanent.

"Let me get my stuff," I finally said.

"How do I know you'll be back?"

Annie's eyes scanned my face, finally settling on my mouth as though waiting for some magical answer to escape from there. What the hell could I say? Finally, I kicked a stone across the grass and mumbled the only thing I could think of.

"Trust me."

* * * *

My eyes skimmed over my vomit covering the juice boxes, half-finished lunches, and gum wrappers stuffed in the garbage can. It was a good thing I had found one by the side door of the school, where no one could see me. The hair on my forehead was soaked, and my T-shirt clung to my back. I was still hunched over the garbage can, watching this long snake of spit sway back and forth from my lips. I wiped it away.

After quickly cleaning up in the washroom, I made a beeline for my locker. I was probably running super late by that point and didn't want Annie coming to the school and getting psycho on me. Thank god everyone was in class and I didn't have to take the good ol' detours.

Somebody was waiting at my locker. I slowed down a bit until I saw who it was. Claudia. I had completely forgotten about her—about her little arm hairs and freckles, or the way she pushed her juice up the straw of her drink box like I did. As I got closer, she smiled widely, like I was a friggin' rock star, even though I had just had the barf of the century.

"Hi," she said when I got to the locker.

"Hi." I looked down, hoping my breath wouldn't reach far enough to kill her.

"Are you feeling okay?" Her face looked all serious, and a big frown had formed between her little eyebrows.

No, I just hurled my friggin' brains out.

"I'm fine."

"I skipped art history to make sure," she whispered with a giggle.

I wanted to be grateful for her sacrifice, but I wanted to get the hell out of school more. I grabbed the lock and stared at it. What the hell was the combination again?

Out of the corner of my eye, I saw Claudia leaning against the locker beside mine, playing with a strand of her hair like she was thinking of something. "So, uh, what's up with that girl?"

"Nothing."

On any other day, I would have been embarrassed by this obvious lie, but this wasn't a normal day. Those were over, and I still hadn't figured out my friggin' locker combination. Shit, why the hell couldn't I focus?

"I have math next," Claudia said, gripping her stomach. "I could so throw up."

30-18-57. Finally. I opened my locker and brushed the top shelf with my hand. Two sticks of burn-your-mouth mint— there was a god. I kept my back to Claudia as I yanked off the wrappers from both and stuck them in my mouth. Then I grabbed my schoolbag.

"Where are you going?" she asked.

"Home." The two pieces of gum hadn't softened yet, making it hard to talk.

The bell rang, and students started pouring into the hall. I kept my head down and pushed as many books into my schoolbag as I could. When I looked up, she was still there, looking at the wad of gum twisting around in my mouth. She probably thought I was an unfeeling creep for not offering any.

Claudia's eyes narrowed again. "Look, I know it's none of my business and stuff, but is that girl bothering you?"

No, she just came by to tell me she was pregnant.

I shut the locker. "I'm just not feeling well."

Her eyes took on that look that girls get when you tell them a story about a homeless cat or something.

Then they brightened up. "Hey, you wanna go to a movie Friday night? My mom won tickets from the radio station."

I didn't say anything. I wasn't sure what to say. And Annie was waiting.

"I can't remember the movie," Claudia added, talking really fast. "It's probably a lame one." She laughed a shaky laugh, and I felt like crap for her.

"Okay, sure," I replied.

How did you tell someone that life as you knew it would be over by Friday?

Claudia blushed. "Yeah?"

She looked really cute when she blushed, and it just made me feel worse about everything. But then the second bell rang, and I knew it had already been too long.

"I gotta go," I said.

Claudia nodded and smiled before turning, her hair flickering against her face as she disappeared into the thinning crowd. I really liked it blond.

I took off for the side door. Hopefully Annie wouldn't be freaking out. Hopefully she could just hold on.

Chapter 5

Everything after that point felt really fast. I got off the school grounds pretty quickly, at least for someone who had never skipped class before. When I passed the lunch tree, though, I didn't see Annie anywhere. As I crossed the street I could tell that not even her cap was sitting on that bench anymore. It was bare.

I started looking anyway, like I was going to discover secret rabbit holes in the little forest nearby or something. I started panicking. What if she was in the school looking for me? Going from classroom to classroom calling my name; sitting in Mrs. Wentwood, the principal's, office, giving her the whole story while Wentwood, shaking her head sadly, dialed my parents?

My heart started beating until it was the only thing I could hear, louder than all those birds in the park chirping away or the city bus that was coming down the street. I contemplated taking it, but realized I had no change. I considered telling the driver that I had a pregnant nut job on my back and could he give me a break, but he looked like a real prick, so I didn't bother and just threw my fifty-pound knapsack over my shoulder and started walking.

When I got home, I raced to the kitchen and gobbled down the rest of the chocolate milk straight from the carton, something my parents can't stand, and somehow managed to get to my room without my stupid older brother, Adam, poking his head out of his bedroom to torture me about being home so early. Maybe it was because his girlfriend, Rebecca, was over; I could hear her giggling. Normally I would close my eyes and imagine what they were doing, but all I cared about was getting Annie on the phone before she called me.

When I searched her number on the Internet, only two possibilities came up. I couldn't believe my luck and thanked god or whomever for not forcing me to call Julian. I was pretty sure he had her number, but I also knew he'd have a ton of questions.

Things looked even better when the first number gave me an old lady's answering machine. I took a deep breath and dialed the second one. My hands were trembling. Rebecca was laughing like a friggin' hyena in the next room. Man, these walls really weren't soundproof, which could be a problem.

I pulled back the sheets from my bed and hopped in. Within seconds of covering my head, I needed air, but the phone was already ringing. It didn't exactly help that I was still drenched in sweat from the last couple of hours. I could feel the muscles in my legs twitch like they do when I'm super nervous about something.

And then a click.

"Where the hell were you?" Annie's voice was pretty level, but her tone was beyond pissed.

"How did you know it was me?" I asked.

I could practically feel her rolling her eyes at the other end of the line. "It's called caller ID."

The thought of my identity being spelled out on Annie's phone got me nervous, and I came friggin' close to hanging up.

"I was at the park," I finally muttered.

God, did my breath stink.

"Bullshit."

I held the receiver tightly to my ear. I couldn't trust one sheet and a blanket to muffle her voice.

"You promised you'd show."

"I cut class to meet you." That mouthpiece needed a good dose of Lysol, with the way I was spitting all over it.

"At least you won't have to give up your education."

I wasn't so sure, at the rate that things were going. I wanted to remind her that I still didn't know that it was mine, but that sounded like a loaded statement, even in my desperate state.

"Do you have my cell?" I asked instead.

I didn't give anyone my cell number, not even Anthony, and especially not Julian. It was a very sad looking hand-me-down that Adam had used two centuries earlier, with this ring tone that sounded like the music from a prehistoric Nintendo game. I hardly turned it on, which drove my parents crazy, but I guess now I'd have to. Still, anything was better than Annie calling my house.

"I need a solution, not another fucking number!" Annie screamed into the phone.

She asked me for it anyway, and I gave it to her, wondering with every digit whether this was the right thing to do. Then I imagined having to permanently disconnect my home line and trying to explain *that* to my parents.

"So what do we do?" she asked.

"I'll have something by Friday."

"Like what?" Her voice sounded edgy, pleading.

My hand pushed the sheet away from my mouth. Man, was it hot under those covers. "Is it Friday?"

"If you're lying...," her voice trailed off, leaving me to imagine the consequences. The picture wasn't pretty, and for a second I felt like I hadn't puked enough that day.

"In the meantime, don't tell anyone," I cut in, trying to break her momentum.

She laughed a sad laugh. "Yeah, like that's going to happen."

"I mean it," I said a little too desperately. "Especially your parents."

This made her laugh for real, and I caught the words "fucking insane" as I pulled my head out from under the covers to inhale. That's when I came face to face with Adam.

He was standing by my desk with this look of self-satisfaction that I would have beaten out of him had I actually been the stronger one between us. The whole room kind of started spinning, jumbling up my thoughts so badly that I couldn't even straighten myself out enough to ask myself key questions like *How the hell did he get into my room without me hearing?* or *How much had he actually heard?* I felt numb all over, and the only thing snapping me back to reality was the shrill voice from under the covers.

Adam stared at the bed like it was possessed. "You might wanna get that."

I went back under. "I'll talk to you Friday."

Annie burst out crying and hung up.

I popped my head back up, half praying that it had all been a dream and that Adam was still in his room feeling up Rebecca's breasts or something. Or that at the very least he had slipped out to spare me more agony. But the look on his face practically said *Why would I miss out on this?*

"Who's that?" he asked.

I couldn't peel my tongue off the roof of my mouth to answer him, so I just shook my head, like that was any better.

Adam's smile broke, and he just stared at me like he already knew I was doomed for life and there was nothing he could do but feel sorry for me.

"What's going on?" he asked.

I kicked the covers off my legs, not sure how to answer that, but I knew that Adam was going to sit there till midnight if I didn't come up with something that sounded a little more important than homework, but not as unbelievable as a baby. The thing was, what the hell could that be?

"I'm helping someone in trouble," I finally mumbled.

"Uh-huh," Adam replied.

"She just did something she shouldn't have," I continued, digging my grave a little deeper.

Adam's eyes narrowed until his eyebrows came together into one long fuzzy line. "She?"

I decided to skip over the fact that I virtually had never spoken to any girl on the phone before. Coming up with an idea for what this girl had done was tons more critical at the moment. I knew a teeny bit about shoplifting because Julian's brother apparently stole some envelopes from the dollar store over the summer. Smoking wasn't enough of a biggie, even though I had never tried it, and my knowledge of drugs was less than zero.

"I'm waiting," Adam said, looking like he was ready to jump me.

Rebecca appeared in the doorway, holding a tall glass of orange juice and some school textbook.

"What's up, little brother?" she asked.

Rebecca had decided a couple of months ago that I was her little brother. It annoyed me to death.

"It's okay, Beck," said Adam.

Rebecca's eyes got a little wider, and for the first time I noticed they were grey, and not green like I had always thought. She held her glass a bit closer to her chest and slunk away.

Adam turned back to me. "So?"

"I was tutoring her in math," I said.

"You suck at math."

I looked out the window. "She..."

This seemed to give Adam some hope of a real answer, because he pulled out the chair from my desk and sat down. He leaned forward, and all the muscles in those shoulders and chest that he'd been working out at the gym looked like they would burst through his T-shirt.

"Her parents are fighting a lot," I said.

"Everyone's parents fight a lot."

"This is really bad," I replied.

"How bad?"

I paused for a split second, waiting for a movie that had a lot of parental fighting to come to me. I couldn't think of any.

"She just needs my help," I finally said.

Adam laughed the kind of laugh that adults give when they aren't impressed. "From under the blankets?"

"Can you just leave me alone?"

"Hell no," Adam replied.

Jesus Christ, I wanted to kill him. The thought had crossed my mind plenty of times before, but this was different. I could almost see myself doing it. But then again, Adam was even bigger than my dad, and all muscle, so burying him would be a friggin' problem and a half.

I threw my head under the pillow. "It's really nothing."

"Bullshit," said Adam.

I wanted to cry; holy shit I really did. Just start sobbing like Annie.

I heard Adam get up from the chair, and in a matter of seconds he had flipped my whole body over and was standing over me, his hands locking down my arms so that I couldn't move. "Get the fuck off of me," I said.

"Who was that?" asked Adam.

"Nobody."

"Why did you skip school?"

"Because I felt like it," I said.

Adam shook his head. "Because you're in some deep shit."

I couldn't bear to hear those words. "No I'm not," I said, almost to myself.

He held my arms a little tighter. "Then tell me."

His muscles were clamping down on my lungs until I could barely breathe. I somehow brought my hand up to his face and pushed it into his cheek until his face looked like pizza dough.

But he still didn't let go.

"Tell me!"

"She's pregnant, OK?" I blurted out.

I wasn't sure how loud I had said it. I tried desperately to listen to any signs of life on the other side of the wall, like Rebecca gasping in the next room, or the front door opening downstairs followed by my parents talking about work or what to make for supper. But the house was quiet. Too quiet.

Adam climbed off the bed and stared at the opposite wall. The way his shoulders were hunched over, I could tell that for the first time in my life, I really had my brother stumped.

"She *might* be pregnant," I mumbled.

Adam turned around. "Is it you?"

He was staring down at his hands. Like if it *was* me he wouldn't be able to look at me ever again.

I shook my head hard. "She's not even pretty. Plus she's fat."

Annie was far from ugly, but the fat part wasn't a complete lie. At least in a few months it wouldn't be. If she was pregnant.

"Then whose is it?" Adam asked.

I turned over and stared at the wall, the covers pulled up to my chin. "I can't say right now."

I could hear Adam sigh. "If you don't tell me, I'm going to assume it's you."

I threw my head against the pillow in frustration. Why was he being like this?

"Kye?"

"It's Anthony, alright?"

"Anthony?"

I so should have stuck to the shoplifting story.

"Has he ever even copped a feel?" asked Adam.

I sat up, my mouth parched and my gut filled with a ton of emotions; anger towards Annie, frustration and hate towards Adam, and jealousy at Anthony's innocence.

"Anthony's pulled some shit, you know," I said.

"Like what?"

Adam leaned over, waiting for me to fill him in.

"Stuff."

"You can't just leave it at that, Kye."

It was the millionth time he had used my name since entering the room. He didn't believe a word of any of this crap, and wouldn't until I said more. I just wanted to close my eyes and go to sleep until high school graduation.

I took a deep breath. "It's not like I'm going to help her forever."

Finally, something that was the truth.

Adam didn't say anything, so I threw him my pillow for some kind of reaction. A pretty good shot too. He should have thrown it right back, but instead he kept the pillow in his lap and patted it like it was some kind of puppy.

"Do you believe me?" I finally asked.

The question sounded worse than I could have imagined.

To make it even worse, all Adam said was, "Get yourself out of this mess."

Then he walked out. With that kind of an answer, who knew what he believed?

Chapter 6

The following day at lunch I barely ate, and whatever appetite I had was cut whenever I looked over at Anthony. So I stared at either the grass or Julian the whole time, which was a bit awkward, since Anthony was pretty much the only one talking.

"Okay, so *St. Elmo's Fire* is out."

Julian's jaw dropped in the way it did when he made fun of us.

Anthony sighed. "I've thought it over and—"

"Hold on, hold on." Julian put down his sandwich as though he had to think about what he was going to say next, even though he always seemed to know exactly what to say.

"You have a chance to broadcast Demi Moore's non-existent chesticles and you're passing?" Julian hit my foot. "Kye, help me understand this."

"I don't know," I mumbled, even though I had a pretty good idea that Anthony was excited about something much bigger than Demi's teeny chest. I could tell from his smile, which was getting really wide. He was on the verge of pissing his pants from the anticipation. Man, I had known him too long. I took a bite of my sandwich, and it just lodged itself in my right cheek, like I was a friggin' hamster.

"I was thinking of *Ferris*."

Anthony emphasized the last word like we were retards. He locked eyes with me, looking right past Julian, who I could tell had no clue what Anthony was talking about.

Me and Anthony had watched *Ferris Bueller's Day Off* one weekend in grade seven at a sleepover at his house, and we loved it. I should have been excited, since I hadn't seen it since, but I couldn't even manage a fake smile.

"Please tell me this isn't another one of your ancient films," begged Julian.

Anthony stopped drinking his soda long enough to say, "Eighty-five."

Julian slapped his forehead. "Do you guys have something against the twenty-first century or something?"

Finally, a wisecrack to distract me from the guilt I was feeling looking at Anthony transform himself into a giddy five-year-old. I laughed as hard and as long as I possibly could without embarrassing myself.

Anthony looked like he was going to cry. He could be such a baby sometimes.

Julian let out a big sigh and started watching a group of seniors play football on the field, but Anthony wasn't done with me yet. He had tossed aside his lunch and was leaning into me, all serious and stuff. Not that I was scared. Anthony was the one person on the planet that I knew I could take down any day.

"You love *Ferris*," he said.

"Leave me alone," I replied.

"What's wrong with you, dude?" Julian asked.

"I'm just stressed."

I wrapped up the last bit of my sandwich and tossed it into the garbage can nearby. I usually didn't even try that stuff in front of Julian, because I never got it in, but today I didn't care. Sure enough, the sandwich hit the rim of the can and then landed right beside it with this miserable plop. I ignored it.

"What does he have to be stressed about?" Anthony mumbled. "I'm the one who has Kearns." He started playing with his unpeeled orange like it was a basketball. He was catching it too, even from high up in the air. God, was he annoying.

I glanced at Julian, hoping for another joke or story, but he was staring at me. One of those scary stares, too, like he already knew everything about Annie, including stuff *I* didn't even know yet. I looked down at his phone to check the time. Five minutes until I'd have to face Claudia in English. The way Julian was looking at me, I almost wished I was already there, even though I still hadn't found a way to get out of the movie on Friday. There was no way I'd have a chance to dream up an excuse during Oertner's lecture either. He forced us to participate in every class, smiling and nodding at us, like what we had to say was so important.

We all stood up. Anthony was officially pissed off at me, and just to make sure I got the hint, he refused to look at me. It bothered me that he was angry, but the person I *really* worried about was Julian. He was acting all quiet, and staring at the ground, the way he did whenever he thought about his dad. Julian hated his dad. It was the only thing about his family he ever really shared with us. I started wondering whether he hated me too.

"Annie was here yesterday," he said, playing with his cell as we walked towards the school.

So he *had* seen her. Shit.

"Annie?" I asked.

"The lifeguard from the pool, remember?"

"Oh yeah," I said, like it was just coming back to me then.

"What was her last name again?"

"Cooper," mumbled Anthony.

"Right."

Anthony shook his head. "You only spent all summer flirting with her."

"No I didn't," I replied, glancing at Julian. Normally he would have been peeved at the idea of me flirting with Annie, but I could sense that he had more important things on his mind. "Does she have friends at Fincher?" he asked.

I shrugged. The school doors seemed so far they might as well have been on Mars. I decided to take an intense interest in a paper cut I had gotten in history class that morning.

Julian started laughing the way he does when he wants you to feel small. "She didn't come to see you, right?"

"Oh crap, I gotta go," I replied, like I suddenly remembered something.

I took off, not exactly sprinting, but pretty friggin' close. We were inches from the door anyway, and soon I wouldn't have to hear Julian's comments on my oh-so-obviously pathetic escape. It was just a matter of seconds.

Anthony wasn't catching up to me, but I was so happy to get rid of him that I wasn't even pissed off. Besides, I probably would have stayed behind with Julian too.

* * * *

A minute left before Oertner closed the door and started rambling about *The Great Gatsby*, and Claudia hadn't shown yet. I started feeling relieved. Maybe a grandparent had died or something. Maybe I could toss aside all my stupid ideas I had come up with for why I couldn't go to the movies on Friday.

Claudia, I can't go to the movies cuz my parenting courses start Friday.

"Kye!"

Claudia was running towards me, but not in a dumb and desperate way. Nothing Claudia did was dumb, it seemed. Except be interested in me.

"My mom is using her prize movie tickets tonight with my dad." The words rushed out in this long stack, like she had rehearsed for hours. She smiled apologetically. What did she have to be sorry for?

"Okay," I replied trying really hard to not sound relieved.

Claudia sat down at her desk behind me and pushed a few strands of hair behind her ears. "At least now we can pick the movie we want."

Crap. But I smiled like I couldn't wait. Meanwhile, up at the front of the class, Oertner shut the door and started jingling the change in his pocket. He played with his change every friggin' day, but no one told him to stop, probably because we couldn't figure out how to pronounce his name. It's German or something like that, and no one's gotten it right so far.

"So, what can someone say about Gatsby?" he began, pulling the book out of this crummy leather briefcase that every high-school teacher seems to have.

"If he calls on me, I'm dead," Claudia whispered.

I didn't want to turn and look at her, but it was hard not to. She was covering her mouth to stifle a giggle that I was sure would have sounded cute.

I turned back and stared down at my desk. It was going to be friggin' impossible to get out of this movie date without Claudia having a bunch of questions that I couldn't answer.

I opened my notebook and gripped my pen, holding good ol' Gatsby with my other hand so that it could at least look like I was following along. When Mr. Oertner had reached the other side of the class, I looked down at the empty blue lines of the paper.

Dear Claudia, I started, then stopped. This wasn't a love letter for chrissakes. I scratched it all out. *Claudia,* I tried. That sounded way too formal. I scratched it out again as Oertner's voice got closer. I casually looked up to see him standing in front of my row.

"We see in this scene how Fitzgerald yet again is commenting on the American dream," he said, then turned and walked to the chalkboard, the seam down his ass stretched by his hands dug deep in his pockets.

Sorry, can't make movie. Grounded. Hope ur not mad.

I scribbled it all insanely fast and turned to toss it onto Claudia's desk. When I turned back around, Oertner was looking right at me.

"Kye, what do you think about Gatsby?"

Now, the only reason I didn't freak out was because I had caught the movie once at, like, two in the morning, which is when they show all the movies that twenty people in the world watch. Mia Farrow was crazy good in that film.

"Uh— Gatsby is lonely?"

Did Claudia hate people talking in questions as much as I did? For a second I forgot that that didn't matter.

Oertner dug his hand so deep in his pocket, it must have been nano-metres from his balls. My dad loves that word, nano. It means small, like miniscule. Like the size of a tadpole.

Or Annie's baby. My heart stopped.

"Why do you say that, Kye?"

My voice was definitely a little shaky as I scrambled to remember the movie. "Well, because he's throwing all these parties all the time, but he never seems to be a part of them. It's like he's making things happen so other people have a good time, but he kind of stands back. It's almost like he already knows it all doesn't mean anything."

Oertner looked at me for a moment before turning and going to the board again. I didn't know whether that meant that my answer was so good that it just kind of wrapped up *The Great Gatsby* and every other book on the planet, or that I was totally off. My money was on the second guess. A balled-up piece of paper suddenly flew over me and landed on my notebook. I opened it up to see a pretty, bubbly handwriting.

Talk after class?

I sighed and scribbled *OK* before passing it back. I had no clue what there was to talk about. The truth was, unless it was to tell Claudia how hot she looked today, and every other day, I didn't want to say anything at all.

When the bell rang, Oertner was hollering some reading homework as everyone scrambled out. Everyone except me. I stayed behind a second, straining my eyes to look as far to the back of my head as possible, but I didn't see Claudia anywhere. I gathered my stuff and walked out, spotting her by the water fountain across the hall. She didn't look happy, and I was pretty sure it had nothing to do with the pain her breasts must have been in by how hard she was squishing them against her books.

"You're grounded?" she asked, when I reached her.

"Right through until the weekend." I rolled my eyes like I was as annoyed about it as her.

Claudia leaned in close. "Because of us?" she whispered.

Oh my god, why hadn't I thought of that before?

"Yeah, sort of," I replied, my eyes suddenly fixated on the water fountain.

"But nothing really happened," she whispered, her eyes getting bigger.

I started fidgeting with my books. "My parents are kind of religious."

"Do they know about me?" She sounded terrified.

I shook my head. This was the first bit of truth I had spoken in 48 hours, and I stared straight at her for added effect. "They just sense it." My eyes fell back on the fountain.

She started biting her lip. I wondered whether that was a habit when she was nervous or pissed off or something. I wanted to know her habits.

"I have to go," she said.

Then she took off, like the memory of that day in the basement was as mortifying for her as it was for me. At least I had gotten out of my date with her. Maybe Dr. Jacobi was right. Maybe every cloud did have a friggin' silver lining.

Chapter 7

Friday rolled around, and still no big, foolproof plan to unveil to Annie. I had tried everything, mainly running through every movie I had ever seen for inspiration, which is something I always do. Usually it works, but I just kept thinking about Claudia, and then I started thinking about actors and their nice, California lives. Ungrateful bastards.

I was stuck in Orion, with nothing but a mall, an annoying older brother, and Annie. Oh, and parks. There are a lot of those in Orion. I picked the best one to meet Annie at that afternoon—smack dab between our two neighbourhoods, but far enough from anyone that I really knew.

When I got there, Annie was already sitting on a bench. My legs felt as heavy as my knapsack and my whole stomach did this flip when our eyes met. She looked unimpressed, like she was already in on my non-existent plan.

This was going to be worse than that time last year I blanked out in the school play. I know it's weird to put those two in the same sentence. I mean, how can I even compare a school play to this nightmare? The thing is, I can.

I only did the school play because Julian had dared me to do it, and because it was supposed to be a non-speaking role. Oh yeah, and Melissa Carlisle was in it. She was pretty cute, especially for someone with glasses.

Anyways, a week after I found out I had been accepted, the stupid guy who wrote it—some hotshot who had graduated from Fincher—decided to give me a couple of lines. I was ready to quit, but Julian kept bugging me about it, so I stopped eating and somehow managed to live to opening night. Melissa smiled at me backstage when it was all over, but I am pretty sure it was just gas or something, unless she had a thing for cadavers. Besides, she moved to Wisconsin that summer. At least, that's what I heard.

Annie wasn't going anywhere though. She barely moved as I walked towards her.

I put my knapsack down on the bench. "How are you doing?"

She cocked her head to one side. "What's the plan?"

I tossed these three pebbles between my shoes. It felt almost nice to be able to control something.

"What's the fucking plan, Kye?"

"Maybe it can just kind of disappear."

Annie laughed like this was friggin' hilarious. "That sounds awesome."

"Seriously," I muttered.

"And how do we make *that* happen?"

The word *happen* was almost muffled by Annie's hand as she covered her mouth, taking in what I had suggested. Taking in what I was still trying to understand myself.

After a second, she managed to whisper, "You mean..."

I said the word. The word that I could tell from her face she'd never ever be able to say. I kept my eyes to the ground as I said it. The pebbles seemed to take it well; when I looked up at Annie, though, her face was twisted in agony.

"Excuse me?" she stammered.

As funny as it sounds, it had never really crossed my mind as even a possibility. Now that I thought about it, it seemed like the obvious choice. Annie looked like I had just tried prying her heart out.

She pointed to her stomach. "This is a human being."

"It's small," I mumbled.

"I can feel it inside me."

I shook my head. "No you can't."

"Oh, I'm sorry, are you the one waking up every morning sick and fatter?"

"And what's so great about all of that?" I asked.

She paused and looked up at the sky, like the benefits of feeling like crap were going to come to her any second.

"That's what I figured," I mumbled.

A minute passed in silence before she spoke again.

"Have you ever even seen one?"

"Have I ever seen what?"

"*You* know."

"What kind of a question is that?" I asked. "Have you?"

She looked hurt. "What kind of a girl do you think I am?"

"What kind of a guy do you think *I* am?"

"They vacuum the baby up." Annie made this sucking sound. "Everything goes. Heart, skin, hair."

I snorted. "Like it already has hair."

She turned and stared into my eyes. "It does."

"But it's all really small, right?" I asked after a minute.

Annie shrugged. "A heart's a heart."

I sat down on the bench.

"And if the kid is already too big to be vacuumed up," she added really quickly, "they just take it out whole and throw it in a dumpster somewhere."

"That's bullshit."

"I've seen pictures."

"Don't believe everything you see on the Internet."

Annie kind of pouted here and kicked the leg of the bench. "They're real."

So she *had* been looking.

She looked like she had read my mind, because she shrugged. "Whatever."

A silence settled over us. It felt good to not have to say anything, at least for a couple of minutes. I closed my eyes, but knew that was dangerous with the amount of sleep I had had in the last few days. Besides, we couldn't stay like that forever, frozen in time. The thing already had a heart.

I opened my eyes again, squinting them against the light. "You could get your life back."

So could I, but this wasn't about me. At least, not right now. I had to focus on Annie. As far as she was concerned, I was just the creep who gave her this problem.

"You won't get fat," I continued.

She glared at me, but I could see her thinking about the shitty life she was having at the moment. I was on a roll.

And then her eyes got darker, like she had just remembered something important, and she clutched her stomach. "I can't."

This feeling of incredible desperation suddenly passed through me.

"I'll get the best one there is," I said.

Did the best abortionists have the number of procedures they had done engraved on some kind of trophy? Maybe they took out big ads. I could only hope.

"You mean the best baby killer," Annie snapped back.

I stood up. "Well, that's the only plan I have. You wanna keep the baby, go ahead. See if I care."

She started crying.

"But don't get mad at me when you have to tell your mom," I added.

"You have to promise me it won't hurt!" she blurted out, wiping a hand across her nose to wipe away the snot, just like a little kid.

"Tons of girls do this every day," I said, creating my own statistic.

"I mean the baby," she cut in, hugging her stomach. "It can't hurt the baby."

"It's an abortion, for chrissakes."

Annie bent over and picked up a blade of grass. "If you can prove it won't feel a thing," she said softly, like she hadn't heard me, "I'll do it."

I sighed and ran my fingers through my hair. "Fine."

I had no clue how I would pull this off, but it wasn't the first time this week that I was making a promise that I probably couldn't keep.

Chapter 8

I spent that night holed up in my room surfing the web for some sort of proof that an abortion wouldn't hurt Annie's baby, but all I came up with were stupid pictures of chicks standing on some beach with friggin' wind in their hair, looking all sad and pensive. I kept checking the time at the bottom right of my screen, and picturing what I could have been doing with Claudia instead. Now we would have been sitting through all those movie previews, and the lights would have gone low. Low enough for me to slip my hand into hers.

I refocused on my mission to find actual descriptions of the procedure and stuff, but who the hell would actually talk about that anyway? It was kind of like when you come across a handicapped kid at the mall or something, and you pretend that their legs or arms aren't messed up. I wonder if deep down that sort of stuff bothers handicapped people. Maybe one day they'll all band together and give us hell for acting like idiots all this time.

At eight thirty, I finally found this:

> *In the first 12 weeks, suction-aspiration or vacuum abortion is the most common method. Manual vacuum aspiration (MVA) abortion consists of removing the fetus or embryo, placenta and membranes by suction using a manual syringe, while electric vacuum aspiration (EVA) abortion uses an electric pump. These techniques are comparable, and differ in the mechanism used to apply suction, how early in pregnancy they can be used, and whether cervical dilation is necessary.*

Okay, so the word "vacuum" showed up a lot. But I didn't see the word "hurt" anywhere. Maybe there was hope. I moved along, and landed on a picture of what looked like a baby in a garbage can.

Holy fuck. I pushed my chair away from my desk, and closed my eyes real tight, the word *tadpole* running over and over in my mind.

Then the doorbell rang. Probably Rebecca for Adam. He had been pretty much ignoring me the last couple of days, but I still would have been happier with him out of the house. You just never knew when he would pounce again, and knowing it wouldn't be tonight would have been cool. I could maybe actually try and relax and watch a movie. Something lighthearted. Like *American Pie*. I even thought about inviting Julian and Anthony over, but neither of them had really talked to me much since Wednesday. Even Anthony had been acting weird.

"Kye!" My mom's voice boomed from downstairs.

I froze. Had showing up at my school not been enough for Annie?

When I got downstairs, my parents were both at the door, smiling a smile that worried me. I squeezed between them, almost pushing my mom out of the way, to come face to face

with Claudia. She had on this tight pink T-shirt, and her hair
was loose and falling around her face. The light from my front
porch made her face look shiny and nice.

"Hi Kye."

"Hi," I replied, stepping outside, my hand on the knob
behind me. I could hear my mom say something like "nice to
meet you" as I slammed the door shut. Claudia leaned against
the porch railing.

"I wanted to see you," she whispered.

"That's nice," I replied lamely.

Three quarters of my brain was still in the house with my
parents, whom I had left on the other side of the door. Were
they already upstairs asking Adam questions? Claudia smiled,
and I realized she was wearing lipstick.

"Hold on a sec," I mumbled, opening the door again.
I poked my head inside. The hallway was empty except for
my dad who was walking to the living room with a book. He
removed his glasses.

"Is everything okay, Kye?"

I nodded and closed the door again before he could ask
anything else.

Claudia looked like she felt sorry for me. "We can just
hang here for a bit."

"Yeah, sure." I had completely forgotten about the grounding thing. "You look nice," she said cautiously. I was wearing my old gym shorts from grade eight, and I had about five
drops of spaghetti sauce from dinner spattered across the
crotch area. Still, it was a better lie than any of the ones I had
come up with lately.

"You look nicer," I answered.

She folded her arms and giggled. I relaxed a bit. It felt like
I had been holding my breath for a century.

"Hey bro."

I looked up. Adam. Poking his head out of his bedroom window. He only called me bro when he was trying to act cool, which was only when he wanted to annoy the hell out of me.

Adam gave Claudia a little wave. "I'm Kye's brother."

"What do you want?" I asked.

"Can I borrow *Ronin*?" he asked, his eyes staying on Claudia.

"Yeah, sure."

Normally, I hated lending Adam any of my movies. He put his fingers all over the stupid CDs, even though I've told him a kajillion times to hold them by the tips. But tonight, he could have thrown *The Godfather* into a bonfire for all I cared. Besides, he probably had no intention of borrowing any movies. He just wanted to see Claudia; I could tell by the way he was staring at her, not in a guy-girl way, but in an are-you-the-knocked-up-chick kind of way.

"Alright, nice meeting you." He gave another lame wave at Claudia and disappeared from the window.

"Your brother's funny," she said.

"He's up for adoption."

She giggled. "Could you go for a walk?"

Anything that involved leaving my house sounded good to me at that moment, even going for a walk, which was usually something only old ladies with blue hair did.

Our arms brushed each other at least twice as we made our way down the driveway. I thought of holding her hand, but mine felt gross and sweaty. I wiped them against my shorts instead when I thought she wasn't looking.

"Hey, wanna go for an ice cream?" I could feel enough change in my pocket for two cones.

Claudia grinned. "Sure."

So we turned on Morgan and kept walking until Elm Grove. I knew the way like the back of my hand. Me and Anthony had been going to Safari's since we were, like, ten. It's the best ice cream in the world, hands down. I also knew that I wouldn't have to worry about getting shit from Anthony for bringing Claudia, since he wouldn't be there. Anthony didn't go to Safari's alone. Neither of us did. We had made this crazy promise to ourselves that we'd never bring anyone else to Safari's. Not even our parents or a sick grandmother. Or even, let's say, if either of us volunteered with a kid with cancer and we wanted to take him or her for their last ice cream ever. We weren't allowed. When we made promises, we meant business. I mean, we hadn't even told Julian about Safari's.

It was really quiet for a Friday night. Claudia and I ordered our ice creams and took one of the picnic tables outside. We sat across from each other at first, but I eat ice cream like a four year-old, and I didn't want Claudia to laugh. So I got up and moved to the other side, which made her smile really shyly. It felt pretty good to know I had put that smile on her face, and I decided to enjoy the moment.

"So, do you think it'll be a hard year?" she asked.

If only she knew.

"Nah," I replied, "my teachers are alright."

Claudia shook her head. "I hate my teachers," she said, "Especially—"

"Kearns," I said. "I know."

We looked at each other and laughed.

"Do I talk about him a lot?" asked Claudia.

I shrugged. "Not tons."

She laughed again and took a few spoonfuls of her sundae.

"Your parents seem nice," she said.

"Can't complain," I said.

Then I remembered that I was supposed to be grounded.

"Motherfuckers," I mumbled.

Claudia laughed. "Did you just call them motherfuckers?"

My heart almost stopped. "No."

She laughed harder. "That's hilarious."

"Why?"

I could feel my cheeks burning at the same time as a brain freeze set into my skull.

"You just don't seem like the type."

I wanted to ask her what type she thought I was, but my gut told me I wouldn't like the answer.

She got really quiet and kept spooning out small bits of her sundae, probably thinking about how to get up and leave without looking like a bitch.

"My dad was some guy on my mom's softball team," she said suddenly. "They slept together after their first game."

I nearly dropped my cone into my lap. Claudia suddenly had this faraway look in her eyes, like the picnic table we were sitting at and Safari's were gone, and there was nothing but something in the distance, something only she could see. I fixed my eyes on this dot of ice cream running down her forearm.

"I never knew him," she almost whispered.

This was probably a good time to say something impressive, but all I could come up with was, "Oh."

"Now *he* was a motherfucker." She gave a small smile. I tried my best to smile back, all the while wondering how close I was to being some guy on a softball team.

I pointed out the ice cream on her forearm as a change of subject and she brought her whole arm to her mouth and licked it. It was pretty sexy.

"When's your birthday?" I asked.

"November twelfth. Yours?"

"February fifteenth."

She nodded. I wondered whether she was trying to remember my birthday as much as I was trying to remember hers. "So what do you wanna be when you grow up?" she asked.

I jammed the rest of the cone into my mouth, the cold hitting my teeth. In the meantime, Claudia waited patiently, like whatever I was going to say after that last morsel of cone went down my throat would be life changing or something.

"I don't know," I finally answered.

"You don't have a clue?"

"No."

"What do you like?"

"History's cool," I replied.

Claudia rolled her eyes. "What do you *really* like?"

"Books," I said. "And movies."

Her eyes got big, like I had just told her my IQ was higher than Einstein's and Da Vinci's combined.

"Maybe you can make movies someday."

I laughed. "And live under a bridge in a box?"

"That would be cool," she said, giggling.

Only if she was willing to live there with me.

Claudia pulled an elastic out of her pocket and put her hair up. "I wanna be a teacher," she said. "I love little kids."

I swallowed hard. My stomach was starting to hurt, and I wondered whether I had eaten my ice cream too fast.

I forced a smile. "You always have elastics in your pockets."

Claudia laughed, and covered her face, which was a shame, since I liked looking at her face. Especially her eyes.

"I guess we should get going," she said after a minute.

Especially if I wanted to keep up my story of being grounded by parents who had miraculously let me leave the house to begin with. She got up and pointed over my shoulder. "I'm taking the 121."

We took off down the street towards the bus stop.

"I cannot *wait* to get my license," she said, rolling her eyes.

"Me neither."

I was actually dreading driver's ed. The idea of some stranger judging me on my stupid parking and stuff. Not that I would admit this to Claudia, especially as she seemed to be inching closer to me with every step we took.

I was wondering how I could put my arm around her without tripping over my own shoes, or without touching her skin with my sticky fingers.

By the time I had a strategy played out in my head, we were at the bus stop.

She turned and looked at me, folding her arms across her chest, suddenly looking unsure of herself. "You don't have to wait with me."

I shrugged and sat on the bench. "No problem."

Our arms and legs brushed each other as Claudia sat down next to me. After thinking it over about a million times, I finally put my arm around her. Her shoulders were a little bony, and I could feel the warmth of her skin through her jeans. She suddenly pulled the elastic out of her hair, and a couple of strands caught my mouth and chin. I started feeling the best I had felt in days.

Then her bus came around the corner. It stopped at a red light, and we looked at each other. I knew that red light would probably last a couple of minutes at most. The wind was picking up, and she looked almost freezing.

Without thinking, I leaned in to kiss her, a wisp of hair getting caught on my lips. I could taste some fruity lip gloss or something. I don't even remember anymore if she was kissing me back. To tell you the truth, I just remember thinking how funny it was that I was giving her this quick kiss after trying to ram my tongue down her throat a couple of weeks ago. Dr. Jacobi always talked about moving forward, but maybe sometimes going in reverse was okay too.

The bus pulled up to the curb, and Claudia smiled. I smiled back. Then she climbed on the bus and the door closed. I remembered then my mom telling me about my first day of kindergarten, and how she watched me walk all the way across the schoolyard before she went back home. That's how I watched the 121 drive away; like I was seeing it for the last time. It was only when the bus turned the corner that I began the walk home.

Chapter 9

Brian Chadwick lived in what must have been one of the biggest houses in Orion. It sat perched on one of those hills that looked like it was just made to hold a mansion. Only an asshole could live in a place like that. This was a pure hunch, since I didn't know who the hell Brian was. The only thing Julian had told me on the phone earlier that Saturday afternoon was that he went to another school and he was a senior.

I was so happy to hear from him that I didn't ask any other questions. After all, he was inviting me and Anthony along to a party. After last night's kiss with Claudia, I started thinking that this was going to be the best weekend I'd have in a very long time.

As we made our way closer to the house, though, a lot of questions started popping into my head, and my stomach was all in knots. It took every ounce of self-control I had to stay quiet, but Anthony couldn't shut up. Nerves did that to him, but I was worried that Julian would pick up on it and decide to turn around.

"How did you get invited to this party again?" asked Anthony as the mansion came into sight among all the other ones we were passing.

I rolled my eyes. Julian didn't say anything, but he didn't have to. Lights were on all over the house, and we could see people in every window. So the place was packed, a mixed blessing. It was obviously an open invitation, which meant Damian or anyone else from Fincher that we were better off avoiding could be in there. I stared into the windows, trying to make out the shadows and profiles. Anthony looked like he was doing the same, and Julian was staring at these girls in tiny skirts and jackets standing at the foot of the long driveway.

"Does Billy know anyone from our school?" asked Anthony.

"Brian," corrected Julian. "And would you relax?"

I tried catching Anthony's eyes to reassure him, but he hadn't looked at me much in the last week. He was still peeved about the whole *Ferris* movie thing, I could tell.

We walked past the girls and up the driveway towards the noise that seemed to vibrate through the house like it was a boom box of high-school hell. Nobody had seemed to notice us so far, but there was still a bunch of guys standing around the porch that we had to get past.

I took a deep breath and glanced at Anthony, who was looking almost terrified under the garage-door light. Still, it was either go through with this part and whatever humiliation went along with it, or risk losing Julian forever to guys at parties like this one. It's not like we had a choice.

Julian rang the doorbell and a couple of guys on the porch started snickering. Julian said hi to them like they were our best friends, while me and Anthony just stared into the front door, ignoring everything. It seemed like forever before the door opened and a girl with the whitest hair I had ever seen appeared. She sort of smiled and walked away, leaving us standing there like idiots. Julian walked in first and we followed.

As we made our way through the living room, I could practically see the little smile building on Anthony's face, and at least twice he turned to look at me to prove I was right. A couple of beers and he'd be pulling some shit that could drag our reputation back to grade seven. I'd have to keep an eye on him. So much for relaxing. I tried focusing on all the faces, but there were so many of them. There was no way I would ever spot Damian.

"Let the night begin, boys," said Julian as we entered the kitchen. I cringed. Why the hell did he have to talk so loudly, especially since the kitchen seemed busier than the living room.

There were almost as many people as there was liquor. Every inch of the counters was covered with beer and a whole bunch of other bottles that I didn't recognize. Chips, salsa, and used napkins were strewn everywhere, and what looked like wet paper towels were stacked in the sink. Some guys and a girl were sitting at the kitchen table throwing chips at each other and using their phones as shields. Whoever Brian was, he was going to get into some major shit with his parents.

Something cold poked my rib. It was a beer offered by Julian. Anthony was already sipping his. He hated beer as much as I did, but he faked way better. I just knew how to hold the bottle in a cool way, like movie stars do—between two fingers, really loosely, like it could just slip from your hand at any second but it doesn't. If it sounds easy, it isn't.

Anthony took a long swig from his bottle, and some guy bumped into him and almost made him hack. Then Julian turned to me, and it was my turn. I brought the bottle up to my mouth, and that disgusting piss-like smell crawled up my nostrils. I took a gulp that looked bigger than it was. It seemed to satisfy Julian, though, and he turned and started making his way back to the living room like he knew the place, me and Anthony not far behind.

The music was crazy loud, and Anthony started covering his ears like a little girl. I kicked him and he brought his arms down again, and when we turned the corner, I ran into some six-foot-tall dude. That's all I could notice about him, and that he smoked, because my forehead had brushed against what must have been a pack bulging out of his shirt pocket, and he smelled pretty bad.

"Fuck," he yelled and put his beer bottle down on the coffee table. Some of it must have spilled on him, even though it was too dark to know for sure. I stood there for a second like a total loser, not saying a friggin' word.

Then I walked off. I might have mumbled *sorry*, but I honestly don't remember. I could feel my heart pounding with panic as the thought of the guy coming back with a bunch of his best friends to beat me up crossed my mind. Still, the house was packed, and hopefully he wouldn't find me. He was probably already half-gone anyway. Besides, I wasn't alone. I looked over my shoulder for signs of Anthony or Julian, but everyone suddenly looked the same. Hopefully the guy couldn't tell anyone apart either.

I went back into the kitchen, where the chip warfare had intensified significantly. There were more guys standing around the table now, and the chips were flying at an ever-quickening pace. I found a spot with some other people and pretended to be as fascinated with this stupid game as they were. I silently prayed that Julian and Anthony would come looking for me.

Then someone decided to turn on the light that was right over the table, and I got nervous all over again that Six Foot would see me. I slipped away from the table and decided to try the doorway at the other end of the kitchen. It led into the main hallway, and within seconds I found myself at the staircase, where two girls were making out on the bottom stair.

To somehow make things less awkward, and since it was the only place in the house I felt safe, I decided to start studying the family pictures on the wall. One of them was of a little boy with a bow tie, probably Brian. So gay. I noticed the glass was cracked right at the corner of the frame, and this made me smile for some reason.

I suddenly felt a tap on my shoulder. Julian and Anthony, thank god. I spun around and came face to face with a girl. She had dark-brown hair that barely touched her shoulders and small glasses. She looked like the kind of girl in movies that never gets the guy. Cute, but not that cute.

"Are you alright?" she asked.

I just nodded and looked at her, trying to figure out how she could know me. I was pretty sure she wasn't in my grade, and she looked too nice to be friends with someone like Brian, but then I realized she probably knew him as much as anyone else here. She seemed more comfortable with that than I was. I looked down at her dark green fingernails wrapped around a beer bottle. She had this tattoo on her left hand, but I couldn't make out what it was. It looked familiar even if it was in a very vague sort of way.

She pointed to my bottle. "Drink up before it gets warm."

I nodded and took a long gulp that tickled my throat on the way down. I smiled like I loved the stuff.

She giggled and grabbed my hand. Hers felt cold against mine, but I was probably sweating like a pig like I always do. She didn't seem to mind though, and pulled me towards the living room. I scanned the place quickly for Six Foot or for anyone else who looked like they'd want to beat me up, but saw no one. We stopped at a spot right by this huge fireplace like you only see in palaces, and she grabbed my beer and put it down on the mantel with hers.

I could feel the music vibrating through the floors as she began to dance. She moved well, her hips doing that little shake that always looks hot. She lifted her eyes towards the ceiling for a second, and when she looked back at me, her face was flushed and her glasses were a bit fogged up.

She hit me playfully. "Dance, already!"

I danced for a whole ten seconds until I caught a couple of guys nearby whispering. Maybe they were looking at me, maybe not. Dr. Jacobi says we have to verify our fears, but it was too dark in that living room to verify anything. I froze in my tracks and just stared at the floor instead, fixated on these two or three peanuts that someone had dropped.

The girl was still dancing when I looked back up. She was holding her hair away from her neck with her tattooed hand and waving the other one in the air. She looked kind of funny, to tell you the truth, but she didn't seem to care. When the song was over, she took a sip from a beer off the mantel. I didn't know whether it was mine or hers. I don't think she did either.

"Didn't like the song?" she asked.

I shrugged. "What's your name?"

"Tammy."

I nodded.

She placed the bottle against her collarbone and looked at me with this weird intensity. "You're Kye."

"Yeah," I replied. "Wait, how do you know that?"

"I heard this guy call you."

"Was he really tall?" I asked, my eyes scanning the room for the millionth time.

She shrugged her shoulders. "I don't remember, but you were too busy staring at that picture to notice. Or was it them?"

She nodded at the two girls sitting on the stairs. The brunette looked like her tongue was scraping the blonde's stomach lining.

Tammy winked, and I could feel myself blushing. A new song was starting up, and she set her beer down. She was doing her whole hand-in-the-air thing again, and I decided to offset my feeling like a total retard by studying the tattoo, but this was kind of hard, and I just ended up feeling like a retard anyway.

I started shuffling my feet in some kind of lame two-step. Tammy slid her glasses up on her head, like grandmothers do, and took a good look at me. I was expecting her to find something on my face to laugh at, even though she was the one who looked shitty without her glasses on.

I almost felt sorry for her, so I reached over and pushed her glasses back over her nose. Much better. She giggled and started dancing again, the space between us getting smaller. She yelled something at me, and our noses almost touched. I thought I could feel myself getting hard, even though Claudia was way hotter.

Claudia.

That's when I stepped back. Tammy did too, almost like she had read my mind. The song wasn't over, but she wasn't dancing anymore, just watching me with a strange mix of guilt and embarrassment.

She breathed in deep before turning around and walking back towards the staircase where we had met. I picked up both beers from the mantel and followed her, even though I wasn't sure that this was what she or I wanted. I got even less certain when I finally made my way through all the bodies and found her sitting on the stair where the lesbo couple had been. She gave me a smile that looked pretty forced, but I sat down next to her anyway.

"I'm not interested in you, you know," she said suddenly.

I was relieved but a little offended too, I have to admit. And not surprised.

"How did you get invited to this party anyway?" she asked, looking straight ahead.

"My friend," I replied. "You?"

She shrugged her shoulders. "The same, I guess."

She brought her hand up to her forehead, and for the first time I noticed a red streak running up her arm. A rash or something. It made me depressed for some reason, and I just wanted to get the hell away from her. I wondered what the Dorito score was back in the kitchen.

"There's a girl," I blurted out.

She grabbed one of the beer bottles from my hand and took a long gulp. Her hand was shaking.

"I know," she said, passing the bottle back to me.

"What?" I asked.

She dropped her head in her hands, like it weighed a ton. She had let me see something that I wasn't supposed to, and my hunch was that it wasn't the rash on her arm.

"What did you say?" I asked again.

"Nothing," she replied shifting around on the stair awkwardly.

I just let her lie dangle in front of me, thinking about how to take a swing at it. I had been doing all the lying recently, so it felt kind of weird to have someone else bullshitting me. It freaked me out, to tell the truth, and I just wanted to get the hell out of that friggin' house. With or without my friends, not that it looked like they needed me much anyways.

I looked towards the front door. Big and white, with long narrow glass panes running down either side. Even if I couldn't unlock it, I could always jump through one of those windows. I pictured morsels of glass scattered on the carpet and on the porch outside, and every one of these losers wondering who that was that just jumped through the window. Maybe some of them would even run down the driveway after me to get my number or autograph, or just to give me one of those man handshakes and tell me how cool I was.

That's when Tammy mumbled, "I know about the girl."

I tried remembering whether I had seen her hang out with Claudia at school. Maybe that was why the tattoo looked so familiar.

"How?" I asked.

"I just do," she replied.

"I like her."

It sounded so stupid once it came out, I was half hoping Tammy hadn't heard it, but her head snapped up and she looked like she was ready to cut mine off.

"No you don't."

My heart skipped a beat. "What are you talking about?"

Tammy shoved her hair behind her ear. "If you liked her, you'd be helping her."

"Is she in trouble?"

"I can't believe guys like you can breed. I feel sorry for the baby already."

I almost choked, and I couldn't feel my legs in my jeans anymore. If I stood up, I was pretty sure they'd be wobbly, like they were any time I had to pass Damian in the halls, which didn't happen that much anymore, thanks to all my detours. I had almost forgotten what it was like, that feeling like you're walking on quicksand and any second you'll get sucked through. I had almost forgotten about Annie too, at least until now.

Suddenly, the music that had been giving me a headache seemed to have been put on mute, and nobody in Brian's house was talking, even though their mouths were still moving.

"You know Annie?" I asked.

"Whoa, you're good."

"How?"

She folded her arms real tight. "We grew up in the same neighbourhood."

If that was the case, then she probably went to Annie's school. Feeling the teeniest bit encouraged, I tried again to move my feet, but it felt like the salsa, dropped peanuts, and whatever else was coating the carpet had me glued.

I finally sighed. "I didn't know—"

"That she had friends?"

"That she sent them to spy on me."

Tammy rolled her eyes. "Oh please."

"Go ahead, give me shit," I said. "That's what you want, isn't it?"

"I actually fell for your dance moves," she replied sarcastically.

I pushed myself as far away from her as I could, which was maybe like, an inch, before my shoulder jabbed against the stair banister. It's hard for me to say how long we were quiet after that. The silence couldn't have lasted more than a few seconds, but it felt like a friggin' eternity.

Then a few guys arrived in the hallway and started pointing at the pictures on the wall and giggling, probably at Brian's bow tie. It kind of broke the tension for me, so I decided to continue talking.

"How did you know what I looked like?"

"I was at your school," she said. "That day at lunch."

So she *didn't* go to Fincher.

I took a sip of beer, but it was warm, a sign that I shouldn't get too hopeful yet.

"I'm helping her," I finally said.

Tammy shook her head. "That's not what Annie says."

"I don't even know if it's mine," I said.

Christ, why was everyone forgetting that part?

"Right," Tammy replied, sounding totally unconvinced.

I kept my eyes on the guys looking at the pictures on the wall until one dude gave me the finger.

"Believe her if you want," I mumbled.

Tammy looked me over like I was a frog about to be dissected in a lab. "What did she see in you, anyway?"

"Pool. Summer."

Like that explained anything. I couldn't even speak in friggin' sentences anymore, but at least the feeling in my legs was back, so I stood up. So did Tammy, this look of sadness on her face. At least I could feel pretty confident that she wouldn't slap me. A little frown formed between her eyebrows, crowned by a piece of hair that had slipped from the barrette. It was like my lame words or the sight of me had given her this bad headache. I sort of knew how she felt, if that makes any sense. She crossed her arms, the rash and tattoo disappearing.

It was as good a moment as any to turn and run, but I stuck to walking. Running wouldn't look good for me, and besides, I had no friggin' clue where I was going. I walked towards the living room, praying that I'd find Julian and Anthony amid the strange faces, but all I could see was Tammy. I imagined her staring at my back, her sad rash getting smaller and smaller in the crowd, until it almost disappeared, but not quite.

Chapter 10

I spent Sunday on the computer looking for doctors to help Annie. After an hour of searching, I began wondering whether they went under an alias, like other folks who had something to hide. I kept seeing the phrase "family planning", so decided to try that, even though this all felt a lot more like family prevention, if you asked me. Still, I got a few results.

By about three o'clock that afternoon, I had collected a couple of numbers and spent forever just staring at them. Not that I could have called anyway—I figured these guys took weekends off too. But what would I say tomorrow? I pulled out a piece of paper and started writing.

Hello, my name is—

No, giving my name didn't sound right.

Hello. ~~I am calling about having an abortion.~~ Hello, I am calling for a friend who needs your services.

God, could I get any more cliché than this?

"Hey Kye."

I looked up to see Adam standing in the doorway, his hand on the knob of the door like he had every right to just walk in without knocking. Man, didn't he have something to do, like sit-ups or Rebecca?

I shoved the piece of paper I had been writing on between my legs. "What do you want?"

"Wanna play some football?"

I shook my head. I was crappy at sports, and besides, who wanted to indulge in friggin' Abercrombie and Fitch glory anyway?

Adam walked into the room, his eyes now on the paper, which felt kind of weird considering it was practically nestled in my crotch.

"What are you writing?" he asked.

"Nothing."

"Is it another one of your movies?"

"I only ever wrote one movie," I said. "And what do you care?"

"It was a good one," he said.

I was pretty sure he didn't have a friggin' clue what my movie had been about. Hell, I could barely remember myself—I had written it in grade six. The paper was still between my legs, and I suddenly was terrified that it would slip to the floor for Adam's slimy eyes to see.

"What do you want?" I asked.

"I haven't seen Anthony around this weekend."

Let the interrogation begin.

"I saw him last night."

"What about today?"

I sighed. "We have homework."

"When have you ever gone a Sunday without seeing him?"

The answer to that was never, even though I couldn't seem to remember anything these days. Except for standing with Claudia at the bus stop thirty-two hours ago.

Adam walked over to my desk and looked out my window. I could have sworn that I felt his breath on my shoulder. At this point my hands were sticking to the paper like glue, and I pictured all my stupid words running down my fingers.

"I'm going away," he finally said.

If only.

"Did you hear me?"

I curled up my shoulders as if to block any other words leaving his mouth. "Leave me alone."

"Australia," he continued.

I had done a project on Australia in grade seven geography. Their winter is our summer or something like that. And it's far. I couldn't see what it had to do with Adam. It was obvious he was disappointed that I wasn't making the connection.

"That exchange program," he said almost impatiently. "I got accepted."

The paper slipped from my hand and fell to the floor.

"Some dude had to back out, so I'm in," said Adam. "It's pretty last-minute."

"When do you go?"

Adam sighed. "Next week."

Then he said, "I don't have to, you know."

"What do you mean?"

He walked over and put his hands on my shoulders. "If you need me here, I won't go."

I shook him off. "I don't care one way or the other."

"You don't look happy for me."

"Who gives a shit?"

The only thing I cared about was locating my piece of paper. I bent over, pretending to scratch my foot, then quickly looked under my chair. Nothing. Screw it. If I couldn't see it, then neither could Adam.

I got up and crossed the room. "How long will you be gone for?"

"Until Christmas."

I stared down at my bedcover. "Can I have your room?"

When I was little, I always liked Adam's room. Not that there was anything special about it. Mine was definitely cooler, with all my movie posters above my bed. Especially the *Trainspotting* one that Anthony got me last year for my birthday. The more I thought of it, the more I knew that I wouldn't be moving into Adam's room, but it gave me something to say in this awkward conversation.

Adam looked confused. "You haven't wanted to sleep in my room in ages."

I shrugged and glanced under my desk again. The piece of paper was still there, but Adam was walking closer to the desk now. He glanced down at it while I almost passed out from nerves. I couldn't tell whether he was reading anything or just staring.

Adam's toe touched the corner of the paper like it was a stone he was getting ready to kick.

"What are you writing if it isn't a movie script?" he asked.

I took a deep breath. "An essay for English."

"On paper?"

"Just brainstorming."

Adam crouched down and touched the paper with his hand, but just skimmed it, like he was touching water or something. Then he stood up again. "Nothing like writing longhand."

My heart skipped a beat.

"Wanna watch a movie tonight?" I asked as Adam made his way to the door.

I didn't like watching movies with Adam. He was always asking me questions like a friggin' old lady. But then again, he *was* going to Australia.

Adam sort of smiled. "Sure."

"Cool. Any requests?"

He shrugged. "You pick. I trust you."

Chapter 11

"Oh my god," said Claudia as we took our seats in the caf by some vending machines. "My French teacher gave us these surprise orals today." She rolled her eyes as she took a gigantic bite out of her banana. It was hard not picturing something else rolling around the inside of her cheek.

"That sucks," I said.

What sucked more was Claudia wearing a barrette just like Tammy's. Who knew that some small metallic thing to pull back my semi-girlfriend's bangs could ruin our very first one-on-one lunch?

Especially since Annie had been nice enough to not call me all morning, giving me a tad more time to figure out my script for the family planners.

I had memorized all two of my lame bullet point items that morning on the bus, deciding that bringing anything written to school would seal my fate. The paper I had been scribbling on on Sunday was now in a trillion pieces sitting in three different trash cans around the house. My parents had better things to do than piece that shit together. I hoped.

"Are you ignoring me?" A couple of nails scratched the small of my back. I couldn't remember my back being scratched since I was a kid, when my mom would rub it sometimes to get me to sleep. It felt good.

"Sorry," I said.

Claudia smiled; she had this really terrific smile, even with poppy seeds jammed between her teeth from her bagel.

I smiled back, and some girls a few tables over started giggling. I grabbed my juice box and started drinking like my straw could suck up every iota of self-consciousness I was feeling. I knew they were Claudia's friends, because I had seen her with them, but I still wasn't sure whether I should feel like the coolest guy in school or friggin' Elmo.

Then, somewhere between the vending machine and a few empty tables at the other end of the caf, skinny shoulders and glasses appeared. And as everything got a little closer, I saw the barrette. Tammy.

She was busy chatting with some other girl while pulling at the sleeves of her sweater, probably to hide her rash. I was sure she hadn't seen me, but I almost went into cardiac arrest anyway. The last bit of my juice got lodged in my throat and I started hacking like crazy.

Claudia put her arm around my shoulder. "Oh my god, are you okay?"

I nodded, still coughing.

She looked down. "Is that your cell ringing?"

I could have sworn I had turned the ringer off, but there was Annie, singing through my jean pocket. Then again, I had just seen Tammy for chrissakes. Any surprise after that was liveable, so I decided to shrug my shoulders and look around, like anyone else would have had their cell tuned to the electro-lounge-crap ring tone I had picked.

"Do you want some water?" Claudia asked.

I glanced at her face to see if she was the least suspicious about the phone, but I couldn't tell.

I nodded. "Yeah."

She turned and walked off, hair bouncing off her shoulders and her ass looking good in those jeans. Annie faded to voice mail. I still couldn't figure out how the ringer had gone on, but there was a shitload more important things I needed to focus on at the moment. Like what Tammy was doing at Fincher High.

* * * *

"Who's this girl?" Julian asked as he leaned his history book against his locker and started writing.

"Why do you always take my notes?" I asked.

"Anthony's writing is shit." Julian shook his head like it was some tragedy.

"But he's in your class."

"Be nice," he said, pointing to his mouth. "I just got a root canal."

"A filling," I corrected him.

"Whatever."

I decided to back off. If I needed his help with anything, giving him grief wasn't exactly a wise first step, even though Anthony's writing was tons better than mine, and he knew it.

"So did you see her?" I asked.

"Who?" Julian asked, continuing to scribble away.

I sighed, and he looked up.

"There were like, a million girls at that party," he said. "Besides, I was busy."

"With what?" I asked.

He started laughing. "I wasn't playing Scrabble, if that's what you're wondering."

I grabbed back my sheets. It irritated me that Julian never told me anything, but now wasn't the time to bring that up either.

He closed up his notebook dramatically, like he was ready to do me the biggest favour. "So, what happened?"

I took a deep breath and looked around. It sucked that Julian's locker was in the crappiest hallway at Fincher. I mean, Lawrence Fitzgerald, Richard Tustin, and Mark Beatty were all within a few feet. Sure, none of those guys was Damian Schofield himself, but they were his friends, and that was close enough. This was why I hardly ever went to Julian's locker.

Neither did Anthony, which was the only reason I wanted to tell Julian about Tammy here. And the only reason I was even considering telling Julian about Tammy was because the last two periods since lunch had been pure torture, and I needed to tell someone. Dr. Jacobi always said to ask for help. Anthony would have just dropped his jaw to the ground in horror. Julian could help, or at least I hoped so.

"This girl comes up to me at the party," I started.

Julian rolled his eyes. "I hope this gets better."

"And she's going on about how I..."

I needed something to hang onto, so I dug my finger into the spiral of my notebook.

Julian crossed his arms. "You're killing me with the suspense, dude."

And with every second that I waited, my plan was decomposing.

"How I got Annie pregnant," I finally whispered.

Forget about decomposing, it was like my plan—my story—had never existed; the one that I had hatched up last period while Mr. Murdock went on about polynomials. *That* story was more along the lines of Tammy going ballistic on me for not wanting to go make out in one of the hundred bedrooms on the second floor of Brian's house.

But maybe it was the beyond-bored look on Julian's face that got me nervous about the quality of my story. The conflict, the plot, and all that crap, not to mention the fact that there was no way he would ever have believed that some older girl could get stalkerish on me. Hell, not even Julian had a stalker.

Julian turned his face away from me, but not before I could see that it had changed, and I was reminded why the truth was the worst idea possible. I had suspected all summer that he had a thing for Annie. He sure had swum hard that night at the pool, even if he did end up sneaking into the chalet with Melissa, another lifeguard that Annie had invited along.

"Are we talking about Annie Cooper?" he asked casually, burying his head deep in his locker.

"Yeah."

"And what did you tell this girl?"

"I told her to fuck off," I said with the best *fuck* that I could muster. It still didn't come out right.

The first bell rang, and Julian slammed his locker shut.

"I guess that's why Annie was here last week," he said as he arranged his books and pencil case in his hands.

A small current of nervous electricity started twitching in my kneecaps. Why did he have to keep bringing that up?

"All I know is this chick is fucking psycho," I said a little too quickly.

"Your swearing sounds lame," Julian mumbled.

He started walking down the hall, and I followed.

"What's her name again?" he asked.

I looked over my shoulder to see who could hear, but the crowds were starting to thin.

"Tammy."

"Tammy what?"

That would have been useful information, but the only way to find that out would be to call up Annie herself, and I would rather make out with Christy Trabinalli, the ugliest girl in our grade, than do that.

So I just shrugged.

"She's in our school?"

I nodded. "I think she's older, like in grade eleven or something. She's tall."

"Eleven?" He gave a low whistle. "I'm impressed."

Claudia crept back into my mind for the first time since lunch.

"I just danced with her," I said.

Julian started laughing, so I joined in, even though I knew it was the last thing either of us felt like doing. I should have just gone home and asked my parents to home-school me for the rest of my life or something. Telling Julian anything had been a big mistake.

"So, she's lying, right?" he asked, after our fake laughter had died down.

I nodded and stammered something that resembled a yes. He shook his head. "You sure aren't Annie's type."

"Uh-uh," I managed to spit out.

My notebook was starting to slide from my hands, and I couldn't seem to get a grip.

"So what do you wanna do with this Tammy bitch?"

"She's not a bitch," I mumbled, thinking about her rash.

Julian laughed for real. "Okay, then there isn't a problem."

"I just want her to stop," I said suddenly.

I wanted everyone to stop. Tammy to stop going to Fincher, Annie to stop thinking I was the father of her stupid baby, and Claudia to stop liking me.

"And what makes you think I can make her?" Julian asked.

Julian was bigger than me, and way cooler. I guess I was hoping that this combination could somehow work its magic and make Tammy disappear.

Not knowing an easy way to express this, I just mumbled, "I don't know."

He moved closer to the door of his class, which was now full. "OK, I'll try."

I glanced at the clock in the hall. I had one minute to get my ass to class, exactly one hour before making those calls to the family planning clinics for Annie, and an eternity to figure out what I had just done.

Chapter 12

The telephone booth at the gas station three streets away from the school was the size of one of those plastic cups you take cough medicine in when you're a kid. I had picked the spot for maximum privacy and because I didn't want to run up the minutes on my cell, but my knapsack hadn't stopped rubbing against something since I managed to get all my shit through those swinging doors fast enough.

Now that the dreaded phone call was over and I had the appointment scribbled on the last sheet of my history notebook, the claustrophobia was setting in. I still had to call Annie, though, and I figured I was already in there.

"Hello?"

"Hi, it's me."

I didn't know why I still started our conversations like she couldn't wait to hear my voice.

"So?" she asked, all bitchy.

"The appointment is Wednesday at one."

I leaned against the door to get a bit of air.

"Can you make it?" I asked, when she didn't answer.

"Where are you?"

"A spaceship, does it matter?" I rubbed my forehead. "Will you be there Wednesday?"

Silence.

"Annie?"

I couldn't remember ever saying her name before. Ever.

"That's in two days," she half-whispered.

"It's just for a consultation."

"What does that mean?"

I sighed and started tracing over the words *I'm Board* that were etched into one of the phone booth doors.

"I guess it means that they'll talk about the procedure and explain everything," I replied.

"Where is it?"

"I'll have to check, but I think it's downtown."

"How am I supposed to leave school without anyone noticing?"

"You've done it before."

Another silence.

I rammed my ass against the telephone. It hurt like hell.

"Where do we meet?" she asked.

"At the mall in front of stop 61," I said. "At twelve fifteen."

"Fine."

"Don't come to my school," I added.

Then I hung up.

Chapter 13

"I thought this was supposed to be a clinic," Annie muttered as we walked into the waiting room and found two chairs in the corner next to a stack of crusty-looking *People* magazines.

I pointed to the sign on the wall that said *Women's Health Clinic.*

Annie glared at me. "It's a hospital."

I shrugged. I had decided to leave that detail out. She was already paler than a ghost when we met at the terminal, and I would never have gotten her on the bus if she knew we were headed for St. Luke's.

She kept staring at this girl sitting across from us with a guy who had his hand buried deep in her lap.

I looked over at the receptionist typing away madly on her computer. Her hair was greased back into this tight ponytail and she didn't smile. I strained my neck to see if I could follow the beige hallway behind her. I was afraid of spotting a doctor with bloody hands or something, but all I saw was this stupid painting of flowers and mountains and crap. I sighed.

"What if they ask a bunch of questions?" asked Annie.

"We're under twenty weeks," I answered. "That's all they need to know."

That was the cut-off according to their website. Twenty weeks was a long time. Longer than summer vacation, longer than how long I had known Claudia.

"Kye Penton?"

A friendly woman appeared, dressed like some kind of nurse and scanning the chairs, smiling a polite, nurse-like smile.

I got up and smiled back, even though I could feel the couple in front of us staring at me. Without saying a word, the nurse-woman led us down a hall and into a small room with bright lighting and banana-coloured walls that made Annie's face look even whiter.

"We spoke on the phone," the lady said as she closed the door behind her.

The only thing I could hear during that whole call was my heart beating so loudly someone in China could have heard. But I nodded anyway.

The nurse looked over at Annie.

"I'm Annie," Annie said, a trace of attitude running through her voice.

"I'm Melissa," she answered, still smiling.

She probably got attitude all the time. Annie may have been a statistic, but for Melissa, she wasn't even a blip on the radar.

"I'm here to answer your questions, okay?"

She was good at this; making Annie and me feel like we were two adults talking about grown-up stuff like mortgages—my parents talked a lot about that—instead of some loser kids looking for an abortion. Even if she did nod her head a little too much, like we were retarded.

"We're here to uh…" I looked down at Annie's stomach, as if it was going to come to me.

"I'd prefer to talk to Annie only," Melissa replied. Her smile was gone, but she looked at me apologetically, like she knew I was only the poor bastard trying to be nice.

"OK," I said, trying to hide my utter confusion.

"It's very important for me to be sure that she is making the right choice for *herself*," she added.

So now she thought I was just a bastard.

Her eyes drifted across the room to the door. "Normally we ask accompanying friends to wait outside during this part."

Accompanying friend, that was a good one. If I was good enough to get the appointment, I was sure as hell going to stay. This must have all been somehow written on my face because I could have sworn Melissa drew her clipboard a little closer to herself.

"I see you care very much for her," she said.

She sat back in her chair. The room got very quiet except for the buzz coming from the lights above us. I slowly walked over to the door and left the room.

Chapter 14

By the time we got on the bus to go back to school, it was almost two o'clock. I couldn't figure out what the hell Annie and Melissa had been talking about for so long. All I knew was that when Melissa opened the door again, she was patting Annie's back and telling her to take the time she needed. Easy for her to say; all she had was a friggin' clipboard to worry about.

I glanced at Annie's reflection off the seat window for clues, but I was stumped, and it wasn't like I could talk about it with her, because I had been kicked out of the friggin' room.

"Why didn't you at least make a follow-up appointment?" I asked.

But Annie just laid her head against the seat in front of her.

I started picturing my dad's signature; the way the *D* in David curled up a bit near the top. That was the hard part, the *D*. If I had to forge a name on an absent note for the teacher, I was going to go with the one with fewer syllables. My mom's name is Helena, making my dad the clear winner. I had never forged a signature before, but I could look at this as a practice run. If Julian would ever want me to skip with him. And if Annie got rid of the baby.

I looked over at her again, but she now had her arms folded across her chest. She still wasn't looking at me. A few minutes later, the bus pulled into the mall.

"You going to call me tonight?" I asked as we got off.

What I really wanted to ask was whether she'd go through with it, but then I pictured Melissa and her stupid smile, asking me and everyone else to be patient.

The wind was blowing like crazy around me. It suddenly felt cold, way too cold for the end of September. Soon it would be Halloween, and after that me and Claudia would have our first Christmas.

Annie looked at me with a frown. She put her hair behind her ears, like I had intruded on some awesome daydream she was having or something. I realized in that moment that I was probably just as much a source of shittiness for her as she was for me.

I could see the white line down the middle of her hair as she dropped her head. I tried shaking off the nagging thought that this wasn't going to exactly go as I had hoped, even though the weight that seemed to be hanging from her head felt like it was pulling down on my friggin' heart.

She kicked at the pavement with the toe of her sneaker, like she was hoping to dig a hole for herself. "I wanna keep it."

I felt my own feet sinking, and there was a sharp pang in my gut.

"Melissa said to take some time," I replied.

Annie covered her ears, like one more word from me would be too painful.

"I can make the appointment." I couldn't feel my tongue or the words.

"No."

Her voice was stronger now, and even, like all the drama of the last few days had been filed away into a previous century and she was focusing now on birth, diapers and burping.

"I read that it's just mild discomfort," I added.

Annie didn't say anything, and I sat down on the sidewalk. I blinked a hundred times to get rid of the blur that everything around me was folding into. Even the million crows flying overhead were barely making a sound. All I saw was my bus pulling into the terminal, but I couldn't even picture myself getting on it and going back to wherever it would take me.

"I can make the appointment," I said again. "Screw Melissa and her rules."

Annie started shaking her head as though even she couldn't stand how pathetic I was sounding. She looked straight at me now, pushing her hair out of her face, like it was getting in the way of what she wanted to say next.

"This baby is staying," she said, poking her finger into her stomach so hard that I wondered whether we'd even need Melissa.

"Well, I'm not," I mumbled.

Just to make my point, I stood up, and Annie turned and faced me. She did this slowly, like she instinctively knew, as I did, that this was a turning point, but wasn't sure if she was ready for a fight. I couldn't have been more ready for anything, and it felt good to be on my feet. The current of adrenaline had slowed, and once I shook some dirt off my pants, I knew where I stood. This was my life, and there was no way that I was going to let anyone mess it up, especially someone the size of a friggin' kidney bean.

"It's yours," Annie said.

"Show me a paternity test," I shot back.

"Don't be like that."

Her voice and chin were starting to shake. I just had to scare her a little more, and we'd be back in Melissa's office in no time.

"You mean annoying?" I approached her, and she crossed her arms. "A pain in the ass, perhaps?"

She backed up, but I stayed in her face.

"That's your job, Annie, but guess what?" I grabbed her shoulders. "It's over."

She yanked on my T-shirt, her feet buckling on her. She felt really light, considering she had a baby inside her and everything. She may have even been lighter than Claudia, but I wasn't sure. My hands slipped under her arms, and I just kept her up like that for all of five seconds, until I felt my biceps burn.

"There's a bench over there," I mumbled.

"Kye, please." Her voice sounded desperate, and her eyes looked dead.

I swallowed hard, as my shaking hands somehow managed to pry her fingers open to release my T-shirt from her grip. My own hands were shaking like mad.

When I stepped back, her mouth opened slightly but nothing came out, as though she was finally realizing what being alone meant and the thought was crappy beyond words.

"But I'm having it," she managed to sputter out as her whole body started shaking.

"Not if we go back to Melissa."

"I *have* to have it," she finally said. "Don't you get it?"

Her eyes shifted to the ground, which was why she didn't see me when I went to push her. I don't know how hard the shove was; I can't even remember feeling her weight against my palms or anything, to tell you the truth.

All I know was that two seconds later she was sitting on the grass patch behind the bus stop sign, dirt and dust sprayed on the front of her shirt. Two old ladies nearby looked from Annie to me, then to Annie again, horrified. I stood back, my hands shaking. I tried stuffing them into my pockets, but they felt too big, like they weren't even mine.

Annie just sat there confused, and I could see every little vein in her bloodshot eyes, and the tears that were still hanging on to her lashes for dear life.

I wondered whether she could see anything in me. I felt as numb as if I were a friggin' corpse that would never feel anything ever again, especially not regret for pushing Annie. Hell, I couldn't even bring up any tears. I tried imagining what it would feel like to cry again. The stinging in the nose, the tears welling up, the salty taste on my cheeks.

I checked to see if anyone had seen what I'd done. The old ladies had moved on to wherever the hell they were going, and the bus terminal was pretty abandoned. I could hear someone talking from somewhere nearby, but no cops were coming after me. At least not yet.

I turned around and started walking. Everything felt so far in that moment, especially my house, but I walked right by the bus that would have taken me to it. I didn't look back to see if Annie had gotten up, not even when I got to the street and knew that she wouldn't have seen me if I had. I didn't really care if she wanted to stay on the ground for the rest of her friggin' life; I just wanted to make sure she was okay. But I didn't turn my head once.

Chapter 15

I spent my weekend cooped up on the couch in the basement, just staring at the blank television. My mom came down every five minutes, with offers of a cup of chamomile tea or a movie or both. But nothing sounded interesting enough to watch; and chamomile tea is just gross, even if it was good for a stomach virus, which is what I was pretending to have.

I had decided on a stomach virus after spending all day Saturday thinking about which sickness could keep me home for a few days past the weekend. There were a ton of real reasons why I couldn't go to school anymore, but not a single one that would have looked good on a note for my teachers.

There was the fact that I hadn't slept a wink since Friday night, that I had this killer headache that felt like it would stick around forever. Oh yeah, and Annie was having the baby. It didn't matter anymore whether it was mine or not—that thing was going to have its chance to grow legs and arms and fingers and lips, and have a go at this shitty thing called life.

I also happened to royally suck at lying to my parents. I used to try and fake illness in grade school all the time, especially on gym days and stupid field trips, both of which gave Damian and his friends more chances to mess with me.

Sometimes I managed to stay home, but usually my mom would just figure I was lazy or shy or a bit of both and push me out the door. I hadn't really done too much faking since high school started, but this situation was definitely critical.

So, I had decided that a stomach virus was my best option. My logic was that I couldn't imagine ever being hungry again, so starving myself for effect wouldn't be hard. This would mean I would lose weight, which would freak out my parents, and hopefully they'd want me to stay in bed for even longer, maybe a week.

I looked at myself in the bathroom mirror to see how much weight I'd have to lose for it to start looking scary. I was pretty skinny to begin with, so it wouldn't take long for my ribs to start showing. How I was going to make sure that my folks saw this, I had no clue, since I didn't exactly walk around topless. Then again, weren't parents supposed to feel what their kids go through, as though it was happening to them?

I couldn't feel anything for Annie's baby. Not the warm water that it was swimming in that I had read about last night after everyone had gone to sleep, nothing. What more proof did I need that it wasn't mine?

Perhaps my parents would let me sleep on this couch forever, and if I was lucky, Annie would forget I was alive, and I could just die inside.

I heard the doorbell ring, and seconds later, my mom hollered down a little too enthusiastically, "Kye, some people are here to see you." This was followed by Anthony storming down the stairs, Julian right behind him. I didn't bother sitting up. A chill came over me, and I wondered whether that whole psychosomatic thing was kicking in, and I was sick for real. Or maybe that was just the stress of picturing Adam's face when he saw how happy and worry-free Anthony looked when he was supposedly dealing with a baby. But then I remembered that Adam was at work until past supper.

"Your mom said you were sick," said Anthony, looking me over as though wondering whether it was dangerous to get too close.

"Stomach virus," I answered.

"How many times have you barfed?" asked Julian.

I shook my head. "None."

"So how do you know it's a stomach virus?" Anthony asked.

Julian sighed loudly. "It's called diarrhea, you idiot."

It was nice to see that some things hadn't changed.

Anthony's face turned greenish as I suddenly realized that frequent trips to the bathroom would help my case, not to mention that if I was facing days cooped up with my parents, I would need the breaks.

I excused myself, and when I got back, Anthony and Julian were sitting on the floor, chocolate bars, licorice, and the movie *Scream* lying between them.

I leaned over and grabbed a Kit Kat. Even though it wasn't exactly the ideal diet for gastro, I hadn't eaten much in the last twenty-four hours, and it tasted delicious. I tossed the wrapper onto the coffee table.

"In case my dad asks you guys whether you brought my homework from Friday, just say yes."

Anthony looked confused. "But we're not in any of your classes."

"Can't you just lie for chrissakes?"

He looked down at the carpet, and I immediately felt like shit. It was no way to treat a friend, especially one that *I* had practically betrayed already. Hell, if Anthony were in my situation, he'd probably be out there right now buying toys and diapers for the baby, not hiding out in his basement.

"That girl you like came to see us at lunch yesterday," Julian said while Anthony put the movie into the DVD player.

Claudia. The one person I had been doing everything to avoid thinking about, even if I was sitting on the couch where she had been practically naked a few weeks ago.

"We gave her your number," added Anthony.

I realized I had never given her my number, and had no idea what I would say to her if and when she called. I figured my parents could take messages for a couple of days, and after that we'd see.

"Oh my god, you'll never guess what," said Anthony as he grabbed at a bunch of licorice like it was the last food on earth.

I hated when he acted all excited like that, especially in front of Julian. I probably shouldn't have cared that much at that point, since my whole social life was pretty much in the toilet, but it still bugged the hell out of me. Especially since the most exciting news from Anthony usually involved stuff like finding out that a teacher lived close to his house, or that a really cool kid's mom drove a shitty car.

Like last year Anthony had run into Matthew with his mom at McDonald's. Matthew was an alright kid, not as bad as Damian but not exactly an angel either. Anyways, Anthony found out that his mom drove this old Ford from the eighties or something, and me and him laughed about it for weeks.

From the way Anthony was grinning, I expected this to be at least as good.

"Someone at our school has AIDS," Anthony said.

My jaw dropped. "What?"

"HIV," corrected Julian.

Anthony shook his head. "It's really sad."

Julian rolled his eyes. "It's just a rumour."

I sat up, almost excited that some people in the world had crappier news than me. "In our grade?"

Anthony's eyes were fixated on the FBI warning on the screen as he mumbled, "Older."

"I think her name is Tammy Dalton," said Julian, grabbing the last chocolate bar as mine slipped from my hands and onto the floor. I didn't make a move to pick it up. I couldn't remember anymore what chocolate tasted like. Not even Kit Kat, my favourite kind.

Julian tapped Anthony's shoulder and pointed at me. "Look at his face."

Anthony shifted further away from the couch. "Are you going to throw up?"

"Yeah, you're looking kind of sick," said Julian.

I sat back on the couch and brought my legs up to my chest. The opening scene of *Scream* started, but all I could see was Tammy, even though she looked nothing like Drew Barrymore.

I think I finally mumbled, "Getting HIV really sucks," but at that point, no one seemed to hear.

* * * *

After the movie, Anthony took off, and Julian stayed behind, leaning against the railing of my porch, his arms crossed like he was offended or something.

"Didn't you want me to help you?" he asked.

"Yeah."

"Then start looking grateful."

I collapsed on the front steps, mainly because I didn't feel like standing, and also to add some dramatic effect in case my parents were standing behind the living room curtains or something. They hadn't sounded convinced that I should even be going outside, but I told them I wanted to see my friends off, and put on my jacket to reassure them.

I now pulled it off, suddenly feeling really warm. "I thought we were going to do it together."

Julian shrugged. "I didn't think that was your thing. Besides, you practically disappeared after Monday."

"How did you..." My voice drifted off.

"Plant anything with Peter Hayes and you're good."

Peter was in our grade and the most twisted fuck I knew. He didn't care about making a single person's life hell, like Damian, but preferred to sort of spread the wealth equally among everyone. To top it off he had this nasty acne all over his face, which made him look even meaner. Surprisingly, I had never been on the receiving end of his insults, but I had seen plenty of other victims. Hairy girls and fat people were his favourites. And now Tammy, who wasn't either; just someone at the wrong place at the wrong time. An innocent in every sense of the friggin' word.

"Peter doesn't even know Tammy."

Julian shrugged. "Peter knows people."

I stared down at the pavement, without a clue what to say next.

Julian took off his glasses and wiped them on his shirt. "Dude, who cares?"

Maybe he was right. It wasn't like I had any plans of going back to school anyway.

"What did you tell him?"

Julian shook his head. "What you should be asking is whether Tammy will be bugging you ever again."

He put his glasses back on, looking almost proud of himself. I couldn't blame him, since I sure as hell would never have had the guts to talk to Peter. Maybe I should have been thankful, but for some reason it wasn't the thought that came to mind.

"You look different," I said.

"What are you talking about?"

I pulled my jacket on again, suddenly feeling cold.

"Don't know," I replied. "You just do."

Chapter 16

Sunday morning I woke up and nibbled on a bit of toast even though I could have eaten the friggin' fridge. That I was so hungry despite all the stress about Annie and Tammy surprised even me, and I began wondering whether I was just as heartless as Peter Hayes. Or Julian.

I had gotten tired of hanging in the basement, so I went upstairs after my sorry excuse for a breakfast and hid in my bedroom. Adam came in a while later without knocking and stood over my bed, where I was lying in a fetal position, just in case anyone thought that my change in location was a sign of some kind of improvement.

"Mom just said that Anthony was over yesterday."

I gave Adam my best glare. "So?"

He shot me one right back. "So, how's he doing?"

"Can't you see I'm sick?"

"Why are you sick?"

"I don't know, ask my friggin' germs."

"Because it *is* Anthony with the problem, right?"

I sighed. "If you must know, we were talking about his problem."

"With Julian?"

"Yes, with Julian, OK?"

Adam smiled a smile reserved for older brothers who trap their younger ones in their own lies. He knew as well as I did that Anthony would never even confide to Julian his favourite colour, for god's sake.

My room had gotten quiet. All I could hear was my parents running around the house in this excited buzz that only happened when we were going on a big trip. I suddenly tried to pretend we were off on a vacation; maybe Wildwood or something. Like what we used to do when I was younger. I could almost taste the ocean and hotdogs.

Then the doorbell rang, and seconds later I could hear the faint sound of Rebecca's voice as she chatted with my mom.

Adam looked through my bedroom door, as though suddenly reminded why she was here; the reason for all the fuss.

He looked down at me again. "I can still back out."

"Why? I can't wait for you to go."

As long as I didn't think about the fact that we were talking about him leaving in a few minutes for Australia, and not just leaving my bedroom.

Adam flinched, like I had hit him hard. The last time he had looked like that was when our grandfather died last year. I could still remember Adam's face as they lowered the coffin into the ground. I had never seen my brother look so sad, and would never have thought I'd see him sadder.

He cleared his throat. "Fine."

Then my dad knocked on the door. He always knocked once, but hard. It was his little thing, I guess.

He poked his head in. "Kye, are you coming to the airport?"

"He's sick, can't you tell?" Adam asked sarcastically.

"Fuck off," I muttered under my breath.

My dad walked in and stood between us. "Hey, hey, hey." That was the toughest my dad ever got, like those three syllables were supposed to spell out every possible threat of violence and destruction.

Then he put on his classic love-your-brother look and wiped his forehead impatiently, like he does when he starts ranting about the Middle East.

"We're just messing around," Adam finally said.

I ignored him, and my dad stuffed his hands in his pockets grudgingly, like he knew somehow he was being conned but had no clue how to prove it. I kind of felt bad for him, but at least it looked like I was safe. Just as long as Adam stuck to his plan of making himself scarce below the equator.

As if on cue, my dad rummaged through his pockets for the car keys. "You sure you don't want to come, Kye?"

I shook my head.

Adam leaned down and tried giving me a hug. I flinched and brought the blanket as close to my chin as possible, even though I wanted to just pull it over my friggin' head. Anything to not have to see his face.

"Take care," Adam said as he walked out. "Remember what I said."

My dad looked over at me questioningly, but I just shrugged my shoulders as though my brother had spoken in Chinese or something.

My dad asked me another hundred times whether I wanted to come to the airport, until my mom hollered upstairs, "He isn't well, David."

Then, a few minutes later, the front door finally slammed and I heard the car start. I jumped out of bed and stood by the window, opening a single slat from my blinds to see the car pull out of the driveway. I suddenly remembered the summer that Adam had gone away to camp about five years ago. I had stood behind the same blind, my eyes glued to Adam in the back seat, as he was whisked off to three weeks of canoeing and roasted marshmallows.

Three weeks was nothing compared to eight, and I craned my neck until Adam disappeared behind the big tree on our front lawn. I just stood there for a moment, my eyes back on the driveway where the car had stood just a minute earlier.

Then I jumped on the computer. I had wanted to do a search on the stomach flu since Friday, and now I finally had my chance. I skimmed some sites really quickly. Apparently anything lasting over three days should be seen by a doctor, which meant that as of tomorrow morning, I was screwed.

Lying to my parents was one thing, but lying to a doctor was impossible. I had tried once before when I didn't want to go to school in grade six on Halloween because Damian always made fun of my costumes. But the doctor's white coat and stethoscope made me nervous.

The phone rang. Even though she hadn't called me on the home line in ages, it could have still been Annie. Then again, why would she call now? For a ton of reasons, I realized, reaching for the phone.

"Hey Kye."

It was Claudia.

"Hey," I answered. "How are you?"

"I don't have the stomach flu at least."

I tried my best to laugh. "Right."

"I guess seeing you isn't a good idea, huh?"

"I'm getting better," I said.

I was going to have to feel better someday, and according to Google, it had to be real soon. Besides, I wanted to see Claudia more than I had realized.

Her voice changed from shy and uncertain to almost peppy. "I could come over for a bit."

"Sure," I said.

My parents would be gone for at least two hours.

"Be there in 30." She hung up.

I stood up and tried shaking myself awake. I paced my room a few times, making sure my legs still worked. I smelled my armpits. I didn't stink, but I hadn't showered in a few days. I stripped down to my underwear and looked at myself in the mirror. I didn't exactly look Holocaust-skinny, but anyone lost weight after not eating for a few days. Then again, it wasn't like I was actually going to get naked with Claudia any time soon.

* * * *

Claudia got to my house quicker than I had expected, and I led her to the basement, only because the living room felt too formal and my bedroom was too weird. I caught her blushing as she sat down on the couch. I knew what she was thinking, and to tell you the truth, I would have been thinking the same thing if I hadn't been so focused on this starvation mission and the fact that my life was over.

Claudia got serious all of a sudden and looked at me with the kind of concern that made me feel like a six-year-old. I didn't mind so much feeling little, it actually felt kind of good.

"You look awful," she said.

I guess that killed off any chances of us doing it that afternoon.

"I would have called earlier," she continued, running her hands down her arms as though the silence was making her itchy. "But I wasn't sure…"

I knew what she wanted to say next. That she wasn't sure of us or of what we were doing. She was practically handing me my moment, my time to set the record straight once and for all so that she could stop wasting her time and find a guy who could take her to the friggin' prom in a couple of years. But the words that made up the truth wouldn't come out. What was the truth, anyway? That I didn't feel like going to school anymore? That Annie was having a baby? That's when she leaned over and kissed me. It was the third time we had kissed, and the best, except for me wishing I had swallowed five bottles of Listerine instead of just quickly brushing my teeth.

Claudia didn't seem to mind, though, even leaning in and rubbing herself against my chest. I got paranoid that she would be able to feel my ribs, so I pushed her back against the couch. From there, it was perfect. I did everything right. I cupped her face in my hands and leaned in far enough to make her open her legs a little. Suddenly everything that had gone to shit in the last few days was lifting, along with my dick.

Her breathing got faster, and she started whispering stuff that I couldn't make out. I caught my name a couple of times, which was amazing. I could have just listened to her calling my name like that forever. It was hot. And then she said, "Do you want to?"

I pulled away. Her face was rosy, and her chest was heaving up and down. I wanted more than anything to smoothe down the hairs falling into her eyes, but Claudia caught my hand before I had a chance, and curled her fingers up against mine. We stayed like that a moment, our hands tied in a warm knot.

Then I pulled mine away, and her expression changed.

"Don't you like me?" Her voice shook, like not even she could believe she had dared to ask the question.

"It's not that," I answered, sinking back into the couch, my eyes fixed on the black television screen.

"Could have fooled me," she mumbled.

She shifted further in the opposite direction, creating a space big enough for Annie, the baby, and everything else that stood between us. The smell of mothballs from my dad's old books was suddenly overpowering.

"It's complicated," I said.

It's complicated? Oh my god, shoot me now. What happened to all the cool lines I had memorized from movies? Hell, even "Here's looking at you kid" would have done. I still don't get what the hell Bogart was talking about when he said that, and me and Anthony have sat through *Casablanca* twice already.

Still, it sounds good—definitely a hell of a lot better than *It's complicated.* And it wasn't even true. Complicated meant that there was hope. Screwed was a better word to describe this situation.

Claudia obviously agreed, because she stood up and smoothed out her jeans, as though wanting to rub out any impurities gathered in the fabric from my touching them.

"Fuck you," she said and walked upstairs.

I didn't have the strength to follow her, and besides, from the way she was walking, it looked like she'd have no problem finding her way out.

Chapter 17

"What are you doing?"

"Nothing."

That was the answer I always gave Anthony whenever he asked me what I was doing. I've always hated that question, to tell you the truth. I mean, what if I was masturbating or something? The only person who'd get a straight answer most of the time to that question was Julian, which seemed cruel even to me, since I'm pretty sure Anthony cared a hell of a lot more about what I did than Julian ever would.

Still, this was not a moment to break old habits. I had somehow survived the third Monday back at school since my "illness", but I wasn't feeling any better than when I was curled up on the couch. On top of that, I had had to deal with two big tests in math and in English (Oertner decided to quiz us on Gatsby after all, the bastard).

"You aren't doing anything?" Anthony asked annoyingly.

I *had* been writing up a list of the pros and cons of having a baby, but I wasn't exactly ready to tell this to anyone, at least not until I came up with one pro. I didn't have enough room on my paper for all the cons, like not going to college, being grounded forever, and getting dumped by Claudia (if that hadn't already happened). At the bottom of the sheet I wrote out the word *LIFE* in big letters and put an *X* right through it.

"So what about *Juno?*" Anthony asked. "Julian will hate it, but he hates everything."

"Not everything," I answered.

"Give me one thing he likes," Anthony challenged me.

"Girls."

"Who doesn't like girls?" Anthony asked. "Anyway, about *Juno.*"

I started filling in the "o" in *grounded* on my list. "What about it?"

"Oh my god, we were talking about this at lunch."

I stopped doodling, like Anthony had caught me on camera or something. "Sorry."

He got silent for a minute. "Where's your head at?"

On Annie's dirty T-shirt, on this image of little fingers opening and closing and toes curling. That stuff happened in week twelve.

I curled my own toes. "Nothing."

Anthony sighed. "You suck."

This was the maddest I had ever heard Anthony, and considering I had known him since kindergarten, that was saying a lot. I pictured him suddenly yelling at me or hanging up the phone.

"Remind me what it's about again?" I asked.

This was a good question, since I knew that Anthony loved movies too much to not answer, even if he was pissed with me.

"This girl gets knocked up," he started.

"Don't say that," I replied without thinking.

"What?"

I gulped. "Knocked up."

"Why?"

"I don't know; it's disrespectful."

"Fine, so she gets pregnant," he started again. "You're so weird these days."

"It's been a while since we did a *Lord of the Rings* marathon," I suddenly said.

Hobbits were as far from real life as I could get.

"*Juno's* a funny movie," Anthony continued, ignoring me. "We should have checked it out earlier."

Timing was definitely everything.

"What's so funny about getting pregnant at sixteen?" I asked.

"I don't know how old she is."

"Even if she's eighteen."

Anthony sighed for the zillionth time since we had gotten on the phone. "Since you care so much, the kid gets adopted."

"Adopted?"

"Yeah," Anthony answered, annoyed. "Like my Aunt Cindy did."

Anthony's aunt adopted a couple of Chinese girls. She and her husband are both doctors, and they dragged these kids from halfway around the world to stick them in their stupid mansion. Annie's kid was within a ten-kilometer radius, for chrissakes. Why hadn't I thought of this before? Maybe it wasn't over after all. Annie might be having the baby, but who said she had to keep it?

I got up from my desk and started pacing the room, but it was a good kind of nervousness going through my body.

Almost excitement. I hadn't felt this good since I had gone for ice cream with Claudia.

"Let's watch the movie," I said almost eagerly.

"Forget it," said Anthony, sounding totally pissed off. "We'll do *Lord of the Rings*."

Chapter 18

Wednesday evening, I decided to call Annie. Not that working on the English essay that was due next week was even a remote possibility. I couldn't have written a decent thesis if it meant getting Claudia to like me again.

I hadn't used my cellphone in forever, and I knew before digging it out of the bottom of my school bag that the battery would be beyond dead. Looked like I would have to call Annie from the home line.

I picked up the phone on my desk and took a deep breath. As I dialed her number, all I could hope for was that her mother was at a yoga class or something.

"Hello?"

I gulped hard. "It's me."

Not a word, but she didn't hang up. I could hear breathing and something in the background that sounded like a vacuum cleaner. So far, the conversation was going as planned. Now all I had to do was talk.

"How are you?" I asked.

"Guess."

When I didn't, she sighed. "Have you told your parents?"

"No."

I could hear her snort on the other end. "Call me after you do."

"Wait a—"

"Until you've told them, everything you say is bullshit."

"Have you told your mom?"

"I'm the one getting fat, remember?"

"And?"

"She was fucking ecstatic, what do you think?"

I had thought a lot about what my parents would say if they knew. My guess was it wouldn't be too different from Annie's mom's reaction, which was why I had no plans of telling them. Not that Annie had to know that part.

"Why did you call, anyway?" she asked.

"I never said that I wouldn't help."

Okay, so it wasn't quite the same as saying that I would, but considering there was still a part of me that couldn't believe I had even made the call, I decided to cut myself some slack.

Annie was clearly in no mood to do the same.

"No, you pushed me to the ground instead."

My head started hurting.

"Why would I even let your abusive ass anywhere near my baby?" she continued. "It's a good thing we aren't together."

I stood up and started pacing in front of my bed. "You don't have to worry about that, I promise you."

That night at the pool and for that matter, the whole summer, seemed to belong in another century.

Annie burst into tears, and I just let her cry for a few seconds. I didn't know what else to do, and hanging up was definitely not an option.

"It's all over," she finally said. Her voice was library quiet.

"I can barely hear you."

She mumbled something else.

"What?"

"I'm in the closet," she whispered.

"Why?"

"If my mom knows I'm talking to you, she'll kill me." Her voice kind of changed, like she was trying to spare my feelings or something.

My fingers tightened around the phone. I was used to having people hate me; hell, I was a friggin' pro. But my parents' friends were always calling me mature and stuff. It felt weird having a grown-up hate my guts like I was sure Annie's mom only could.

"There's a rumour going around that this girl down my street has HIV," Annie suddenly said.

My heart skipped a beat.

"She goes to your school," Annie added.

"So?"

"Do you know anything about it?"

"Why would I?" I asked, fighting hard to breathe.

She didn't say anything for a minute, and I started imagining all the follow-up questions she could fire off at me.

But all she asked was, "What will they say about *me* when I start showing?"

I knew who she meant by *they*. Everyone else on the planet, all the Peters looking out for their next victim. I looked over at my curtains and suddenly pictured them around my neck.

That's when a bunch of noise came over the phone.

"Hello?" I said.

"Have you told your parents?"

This wasn't Annie anymore. This was someone older; someone who was obviously on Annie's side. In other words, someone who was supremely pissed at me.

"This is Annie's mother."

Of course.

"I'm speaking with Kye, I presume?"

My heart sped up. She knew my name. My mind jumped to everything else she could know about me. Where I lived, what my parents looked like.

"Yes," I stammered.

"It's nice of you to call."

She sounded pretty nice herself, but there was this sarcastic streak in her voice that adults always pull off. Like if you're late for a class and the teacher says, "Glad you could join us."

"Thank you," I blurted out.

"My name's Patricia," she said.

So I knew her name now too, but it still didn't exactly feel like a level playing field.

"I gather you'll be telling your parents soon," she said.

I didn't bother telling her my idea of skipping over that whole part and just helping Annie hand over the baby to some nice couple dying for a kid. Even though the sarcasm was kind of gone and her voice was going towards the sweet side, it was all a trap. You saw it in movies all the time. Pure psycho-ness was ready to explode on the other end of the line, I just knew it. Granted, most moms aren't the psycho type but any mom with a pregnant kid couldn't be trusted. "Yes."

I didn't even know anymore what I was saying yes to, but it sounded like the right answer.

"It's a good move, Kye."

I hated her using my name.

"Don't you think?"

She didn't give a crap what I really thought.

"Yes."

There was suddenly more shuffling, and then Annie was back on. I was almost happy to hear her voice again. I sat down and tried doodling on the piece of paper with my list, but my hand was shaking too much.

"Hey," she said.

"Hey."

"Sorry about that."

"It's okay."

It felt weird hearing her apologize for anything, since I still hadn't said sorry for pushing her.

I cleared my throat and took a deep breath, but my heart was still going nuts. "What do we do?"

Annie sighed. "Just tell your parents first."

And then there was a click, and I was out of Annie's closet and back in my room, where the only light I saw was from under the door.

Chapter 19

During morning break that Friday, I headed towards Claudia's locker for the first time ever. I knew it was on the second floor by the chemistry lab, but I had never dropped by or leaned against it while holding her, the way other guys do with their girlfriends.

I had to remind myself, of course, that Claudia was definitely not my girlfriend, and she sure as hell was not going to melt into my arms as I told her what I was planning on telling her. The best I could hope for was a quiet stare like girls use in the movies. It's never outright rejection; the guy always has a chance.

I wasn't counting on us breaking out into dance like Sandy and Danny in *Grease*, but I just didn't want her yelling at me or something. And not just because I didn't want other kids to hear her giving me shit, although I didn't. I just wasn't sure whether I could stand her being pissed at me. So to prepare myself, I ditched all of Jacobi's crap on positive visualization and started picturing Claudia yelling at me as I approached the row of lockers.

The bell rang, and the hallway by the chemistry lab filled up in no time. I wasn't sure how long it would take Claudia to get to her locker, so I stood around the lab door for a bit to kill time. I hated standing alone like a loser. I brushed the shoulder of some redhead with braces who was laughing about something with her friends. Probably about me, though I couldn't tell you why.

I couldn't see Claudia anywhere, so I turned and poked my head through the little glass window of the lab door. How many teen dads made it to grade eleven to pick chemistry as their option class, I wondered. That certainly wouldn't be me, and not just because I'd rather watch all the *Twilight* movies like, a million times before handling a Bunsen burner. As if to prove my point, the door opened suddenly, and the teacher just stared at me like I didn't belong.

I nonchalantly inched my way down the hall, keeping my eyes more or less glued to the floor. It's a good thing my eyeballs are really flexible, so I can stare at the ground and still not run into people. Lots of practice.

I saw her hair before I saw her face. It was loose and brushing the ground as she bent over to grab something at the bottom of the locker. She hadn't heard me approaching, and when she slammed her locker and turned to leave, I couldn't help but notice how fast the blood that had rushed to her face from bending down was draining. Her tightly closed mouth made this straight line across her face that I couldn't read, and she started playing with her hair.

I wondered whether this was something she did when she got nervous, and I realized I hadn't really been all that nervous until that point. Have some royal crap happen to you, and everything else is little. Maybe Jacobi should put *that* in her next book.

The first bell rang and Claudia's eyes drifted up to the ceiling for a second before settling on me again. The hallways suddenly felt narrower, and I knew that time was running out.

It was like that Valentine's Day back in grade six. I stared down at my shoes and could practically see it on the floor, the card I had made for Melanie Dobson. It was lying next to the toe of my shoe, not because Melanie had thrown it there but because I had dropped it, after pulling it out of her hand. I could still see that look on her face, that surprise and confusion, since, I realized later, she had simply wanted to ask where it was from, all the stuff I had written inside.

Claudia took out her phone and looked down at it. "I'm going to be late for math."

"Her name is Annie."

It was hard to tell whether she was shocked or whether the name was somehow already familiar to her, sort of like the way parents look at you as you fess up to something you're pretty sure they already knew about.

For a split second, I actually asked myself whether Julian had told her. Considering all the shit that had gone down with Tammy in the last couple of days it wouldn't have surprised me.

But I couldn't think about that now. I was here with Claudia, and I was losing her. She started walking away, and I followed, past the chem lab and then left towards the window. She suddenly stopped there and sat down on the ledge carefully, and looked down at her lap. I felt weird standing there, so I kind of leaned against the wall.

"So what about Annie?"

She wasn't as pissed with me as she looked, and this should have made things easier, but it didn't. It was now or never. I took in the biggest breath of my life, bigger than any breath before a race or shot at a basket in gym class with Damian and his friends snickering behind me.

"It's like this," I began.

But what was it like? What the hell could I pick out of this existence, these classrooms, Alexandra Stork's annoying laugh as she ran by us, Kevin Paradis picking up a pack of cigarettes that had fallen out of his pocket, that could resemble what I had to say?

"You like her, huh?" Claudia asked.

I shook my head.

"Then what, already?"

Her eyes were filled with tears, and she looked more scared than I think I've ever seen anyone, even Annie.

"She's pregnant."

I hadn't been prepared to say it like that, under the glaring sun coming in from the window that was making me half-blind. Claudia's books fell to the floor. I picked them up and put them on the ledge beside her.

I could see out of the corner of my eye that her mouth was open wide enough for the words I had just said to pour back out a million times over. I prayed that they wouldn't, even though most people had filed into their classrooms by now. A teacher ready to close her door glanced over at us as if to say, *Don't you guys have class?* I grabbed my books and tried my best to smile. Claudia didn't do the same. She looked like she had completely forgotten about math class.

"We're going to get into trouble," I finally said, as though now that I had made the announcement, we could just pick up and head over to period-four class. As though nothing had ever been said, nothing even close to the p-word.

Claudia stood up and slipped into the girls' bathroom, which was just a few feet away. Without thinking, I followed her. Thank god there was no one else there. I thought she'd lock herself into a stall like they always do in the movies, but she just leaned against the ugly blue-tiled wall and stared up at the ceiling, which was fine with me. I wasn't ready to sit in a girl's stall.

"What did you say?" she finally asked. Her voice echoed off the concrete walls, which freaked me out because I didn't want a teacher coming in and finding us; finding me.

"She's pregnant."

If I'm making this look like I answered her right away, it wasn't like that. It felt like eons, to tell you the truth, before I repeated the words that I knew she had already heard the first time.

I had never before seen tears like the kind that had started running down Claudia's cheeks. They were like friggin' mini-waterfalls, like someone had taken a transparent marker and marked big lines between her eyes and her lips where all the tears were gathering like pools.

"How— could—," she started, but she was breathing like you do when you're five years old and your mom won't take you to McDonald's, and you've cried every tear out of you.

I wanted to remind her that I didn't even know she friggin' existed when all this happened. But I had been doing everything I could to forget about that pool, that night.

"It's already got a heart," I said. "And fingerprints."

Claudia looked ready to kill me. "Why the hell are you telling me this?"

"It takes *three months* to get fingerprints," I said.

She turned her back to me and squeezed her face into the tiled wall. "I don't wanna hear any more."

"I didn't cheat on you," I added quickly, desperately.

After a couple of minutes, she turned around again slowly, her eyes closed. "How could you do this to me?"

"I didn't," I said to the floor.

But Claudia was already storming out of the bathroom.

I turned around and opened the faucet, throwing water on my face like guys do in the movies after they've killed someone. I shut off the water and quickly turned around, not wanting to catch my reflection in the mirror.

I leaned against the wall that she had leaned on, my body imprinting on hers. Slowly, I lowered myself to the ground, my wet hands digging into my lap. I had always heard that girls' bathrooms are way dirtier than the guys', and I could have been sitting in remains of shit or whatever. But I didn't care. All I cared about was Claudia and the fact that maybe she had liked me more than I could have known.

* * * *

Later that night, I should have been working on my speech for my parents when/if I ever broke the news, but I got carried away practising holding a baby instead. The last baby I held was probably some relative's that I can't even remember, and I'm sure I was forced to sit down surrounded by a ton of cushions so that even if the baby fell out of my arms it wouldn't die.

I checked out pictures on the Internet of people holding babies, but those made me sick after a while. Everyone looked so friggin' happy that I was ready to bust up my screen. I wasn't happy about this baby; I just didn't want to drop it. Then again, what did they know? They probably weren't even the real parents in these pictures, just stupid models who picked up the baby for a couple of seconds and then walked back to their real lives. Fuck them.

I kicked my bed but only lightly, because I didn't want to hurt my foot. That was the kind of loser I was. I collapsed on the mattress and closed my eyes, trying to imagine what I'd look like with this baby. But all I saw were what my parents' faces would look like after I told them.

I curled up into a tighter ball.

Chapter 20

I decided to tell my parents that Sunday, exactly forty-eight hours after telling Claudia. Long enough for me to semi-recover and get ready for the next round, but not long enough that I'd start considering alternatives like throwing myself off the roof of my house.

I had watched a movie with Anthony on the Saturday, only because I wasn't sure whether I'd see him again on the other side of this moment, two o'clock on Sunday afternoon; rain slapping against the living room window; my mom's hands tightly bound together, white and small; and my dad cleaning his glasses against his shirt for the millionth time since we had sat down.

The colour drained from my mom's face until she looked like the grey of the couch she was sitting on.

"What did you say?" she asked.

The word hadn't sounded any better the second time around: *pregnant*. Knocked up. Life over. Thanks for playing. And though I had somehow managed to repeat myself for Claudia, there was no way I could do that to my mom. The headache that had set in walking down the stairs twenty minutes ago felt like it was spreading throughout my whole body.

"What did you say?" my mom repeated.

At least she wasn't calling me all the words I had been calling myself for a week: *loser, idiot, jerk.* Some kind of friggin' motherly generosity thing kicked in.

"She's pregnant." I tried catching my breath but my heart had stopped beating.

She bent over and put her head in her lap, like she was praying for this all to be a dream, like she was praying harder than she had ever prayed in her life. My dad's face tightened, and he took off his glasses again for a clean.

I stared down at the smallest Kool-Aid stain on the carpet, the one I had made when I was ten or something. I was half hoping that someone would yell, to tell you the truth. But the only sound was the clock over the fireplace, ticking away.

"This is the girl who came over last week?"

My mom asked this almost formally, like I was going for a job interview or something.

"No, that was Claudia," I mumbled.

"Oh, so that was *Claudia,*" she repeated sarcastically.

"Does the mother go to your school?" my dad asked.

So that was how he was going to call her. I didn't want to think about Annie in any kind of a motherly context, but if I had to, "mother" wouldn't come to mind. Mom maybe, but "mother" made me think of some old lady with a tight bun and an apron.

"No," I replied.

He sat back a bit, like he does when he gets all hopeful about something. Did he think there was a way out just because she didn't go to my school, even though she knew exactly where it was? But my dad was way too technical for dreams.

"How far along is she?"

My mom covered her face like she was embarrassed. "David!"

"Helena, we need to know what we're dealing with," he replied in this even tone, like we were assessing a leaky kitchen faucet or something.

My mom shook her head so hard that her hair was whipping around her face. "This can't be happening."

"About three and a half months," I replied.

This shut the both of them up, like I knew it would. They were expecting to hear two months max, I could tell from how they just stared at me, their devastated faces sort of paralyzed. After a moment, they both started talking at the same time like they always do.

"*Months?*"

That was my mom.

"It's not too late," my dad said.

"Not too late for what?" my mom asked.

My dad just tapped his fingers together like he does when he's counting on someone to fill in the blanks.

"She doesn't want an abortion," I mumbled.

My dad's face didn't even change. "So, we're looking at adoption?"

"I was thinking about that," I answered eagerly, like I wanted a friggin' cookie for being so insightful.

My mom gave me a stare coated in ice. "You thought *I* was going to be raising this baby?"

"No, Mom—"

"Don't be ridiculous, Helena," my dad interrupted, his eyes still on the floor.

"She has her own mother," I said without even thinking.

My dad looked at me like he didn't even know me. "Are you being stupid, Kye Daniel?"

I gulped. The last time the middle name had come out was in the sixth grade when Damian had tricked me into sitting on a pencil, and I got this lead embedded in my ass, and I couldn't sit properly for a week. I had only told my parents five months later, and by accident on top of that. They were pissed.

"N-n-o," I stammered.

My dad shook his head in disbelief. "You sure are acting like it."

My mom suddenly looked like she was melting into the couch, and everything around her got blurry. I put my head down and rubbed my eyes, like there was something other than tears in them.

"This child needs a home," my dad continued.

"Baby," my mom corrected him, like it made this big difference. Then, she turned to me. "I don't even want to ask you how this happened, Kye."

They both pulled their legs further in, as if to protect their privates from the very idea of sex, that word that was hanging from the chandelier above the coffee table, and that was laced into the blanket that my mom's fingernail was playing with.

My heart skipped a beat. Now that the whole announcement was out of the way, this was what I was dreading the most, and I couldn't even take comfort in the pretty safe assumption that no parent wants a play-by-play of that kind of stuff. I looked at my mom, her eyes darting between me and my dad, like when a really hot girl has a low-cut shirt, and you want to look but don't at the same time.

"We taught you better," my dad said coldly.

Like we had practised putting on condoms together or something. Jesus Christ.

"You're so young," my mom added.

I sighed.

My dad held up his hand like I had already revealed too much. "Anyway, it's pointless now."

My mom looked at me pleadingly. "Just tell me it didn't happen in this house."

The word *house* came out in a whisper, like we were in a church or something.

My dad covered his ears and closed his eyes. I didn't know which answer to give them. Did they want to be disgusted to think I had dropped my jizzy all over their bed sheets, or did they want to be tortured with the big riddle of where their son planted his seed?

"No," I finally said.

My dad's eyes closed tighter. I could practically see the little lines on his eyelids.

My mom's, on the other hand, totally widened. She was into the riddle. Not that she was going to get any more answers. There was still some information I had a right to keep to myself.

My dad took a deep breath. "From this point forward, you are grounded indefinitely."

My mom looked over at him. They hadn't talked about this, I could tell.

"And we need to meet the mother," he continued. "Soon."

I was too numb to really process the grounding. But bringing Annie over to the house was something I hadn't bargained for. As long as it was just the two of us, things seemed somehow manageable, but throwing other people into the mix—especially my parents—seemed beyond dangerous.

My dad nodded towards the phone on the coffee table. "No time like the present."

"Hello?"

Why the hell did Patricia have to answer?

"Hi, is Annie there?"

A slight pause. "Is this Kye?"

"Yes."

Then her muffled voice calling, "Annie."

So she had decided not to start up another awesome conversation. I couldn't have been happier.

"Hello?"

I looked over at my parents, their eyes glued on me. They wanted to know how we got along, if this girl on the other end of the line was going to make things easy or hard. It was all a big test, and it was up to me to pass.

"Hey Annie," I said as clearly as I could. Mumbling would have been a bad way to start.

"Did you tell them?"

"Yeah."

"How do I know you're not lying?"

I glanced at my mom, who was looking like crap, made worse by that paisley sweater that made her look old and lumpy.

"They wanna meet you," I answered.

I could almost hear Annie gasp.

"Soon," my dad called out.

"Is that your dad?" asked Annie.

"So how about next Sunday at four?" I asked.

My dad rolled his eyes as my mom touched his arm the way she does when she's trying to relax him.

Annie paused for a minute. "I don't know about this."

"We'll be able to talk about the adoption and stuff," I added, looking to my parents for approval, but my mom just brought her hands to her mouth.

Annie gasped again. "Excuse me?"

I didn't mind riding out whatever vent was coming. I could take Annie being pissed at me; she had been nothing but for the last six weeks. But the looks on my parents' faces were just killing me.

"Don't fucking mess with me, Kye. You told me you'd help. You promised."

I guessed at one point I'd have to get all of my own anger out of my system. Jacobi said it wasn't healthy to keep things inside. Then again, Annie had someone to vent to. All I had to give shit to was my sperm.

I pushed the phone into my shoulder and nodded to my parents. "She's asking her mom."

My dad sighed impatiently and moved closer to me, like that was going to change anything. I wanted to kill him. Christ, he might as well have just been at the pool that night, giving me pointers by the diving board.

"Are you there?" Annie asked when I put the phone to my ear again.

"Yeah."

Her voice immediately turned bitchy again. "You can't just expect me to give this baby up."

"I understand," I said like I did.

"I'm carrying this baby inside of me, inside of my body."

Christ, she made it sound so idyllic.

Then I heard some talking in the background.

"We'll be there next Sunday," Annie said in a voice that told me she was as excited about the whole thing as I was.

Then again, at least Annie's mom wouldn't be chasing me down with a baseball bat at my own house. It was a territory thing, just like when I was in grade three and I was being bullied by this kid, Toby. He and his parents came over for a friggin' meeting to make us get along. Me and Toby munched on Oreos while my parents tried figuring out what the problem was. I could have told them that Toby was the friggin' problem, but he looked as pure as the middle he was licking off his cookies.

I didn't think I could pull off half as innocent a look. The worst Toby had done was call me names. I had given Annie a fetus.

"What kind of parents would get my baby?" Annie's voice was a near-whisper.

"We'll talk about that next week."

I hung up before she could say anything else.

"So next week?" my mom asked, like we were having them over for Christmas dinner or something.

I nodded.

"We'll be making a list of goals for our discussion," my dad said. "In the meantime, you're grounded."

At least that was one less thing I'd have to fake.

Chapter 21

Gym was never my favourite class. No matter what sport we did, I always ended up looking like a loser, to the point where by grade seven I was praying to have knee problems or something so I could just sit it out all year, like Tristan Thomas. Then again, Tristan was like this soccer pro, which was how he messed up his knees to begin with.

The only sport that made me a little hopeful about my comatose athleticism was badminton, but who knew hitting a friggin' birdie could be so difficult? I ended up hating badminton almost as much as any other sport, which was why when I saw them setting up the nets in the gym at lunch that Monday, I got nervous.

"Why are we here again?" I asked Anthony. That was just my way of letting him know that I could have killed him for dragging me to free gym. He had missed a few gym classes and needed to make them up before the first report cards went out.

Anthony was too friggin' stressed to answer. He loved gym as much as I did.

I walked over to the racquets, glancing when I could at the other kids that were there. Most of them looked harmless, with the exception of one really built dude; the kind that went to free gym just because he loved it so much. I counted only three girls, and they were ugly, thank god.

And then I saw Damian. I didn't understand why I hadn't spotted him first, since he was pretty tall for his age. Obviously, my jerk radar hadn't been put into practice in a while. I still saw Damian around when it was absolutely necessary, but I hadn't been in gym with him since grade seven, and I sure as hell had never played friggin' badminton with him.

I glared at Anthony, but he was all stooped over tying his shoelace at the pace of a toddler. He had seen him too.

I grabbed a racquet.

"What about me?" Anthony asked.

I felt like everyone was staring at us, especially Damian, but I was too chickenshit to look. I took another racquet and started off for the other side of the gym, as far from Damian as I could get without physically leaving the gym—which was nearly impossible with the gym teacher waving us in like we were some big happy family.

Anthony shot me a grin that made me want to bust out all his teeth. "We can play together." Our chances of looking like losers had just doubled.

Damian, who, of course, had somehow ended up just three people away from us, snickered. "Yeah, Kye, you can play with your boyfriend."

The guys between us laughed, like Damian was the funniest dude on the planet. I didn't know any of them.

Damian smiled widely, encouraged. "Are you going to teabag him afterwards?"

Anthony glanced at me like he wasn't sure whether the question was for him or me. I gave him my best shut-up stare, which was super important since I could tell he had no clue what teabagging was.

The teacher sure as hell knew though, and he was quick to yell, "Cut it out!" even though I don't think he gave two shits about anything except starting his stupid badminton game. Damian made his way to the net all dramatically, like he didn't just own the gym but the whole friggin' world.

By the time it was finally over, Anthony and I had lost miserably to two Asian dudes that looked like they should have been studying math or something. It made the defeat all the more mortifying, and I almost regretted not losing to Damian, whom we had by some miracle managed to avoid.

I tossed my racquet in the pile and headed for the doors.

"Aren't you going to wait for your boyfriend?"

That was Damian, who had somehow caught up with me, even though I could have sworn he had been chatting it up with the gym teacher, kissing ass and stuff. I suddenly wanted Anthony around, even if he was worth shit in these situations, but I didn't have the nerve to look around.

My heart started pounding, and I suddenly had this vision of Damian dragging me into the bathroom just across the hall and beating me to a pulp. I pictured my face all bloody. It was a pretty clear picture too. Not that Damian ever beat us up. He had never laid a hand on us, really. He sort of left other scars. Like that poster on emotional abuse hanging by the caf, with this kid looking all depressed and all these mean words scribbled around him. Calling Damian an abuser sounded lame, I admit, but he sure as hell was as close to one as I had ever met.

Take the last time he really made fun of me and Anthony. It was the summer between sixth and seventh grades, at 9:30 at night behind the store that we always go to. Anthony was freaking out because we were in a parking lot with two vandalized vans and his mom wanted him home for nine. I was down to my last bit of licorice and had my head down thinking of getting some more. We never even saw him coming.

Me and Anthony took off right away, like two girls, and he started following us, and not just for a couple of feet either. The bastard followed us for three friggin' blocks before disappearing. He had never said a word, but he had managed to almost make me and Anthony shit our pants.

I wasn't as scared this time, even though Damian was standing so close to me that I could smell his gross armpits.

"I'm surprised you guys are still together," he said, his garlicky breath brushing my nostrils.

"Get lost," I said.

"I mean, with the baby and all."

The gym suddenly started closing in on me, and the three feet between us and the doors leading me out of this hellhole suddenly felt like ten. The only thing that seemed within reach was the water fountain, which we just happened to be passing at that moment. I stopped and took a long gulp, feeling Damian behind me the whole time, the patient prick.

Anthony had caught up to us too, which was just friggin' wonderful, since I hadn't told the guys anything yet about the baby. Damian's smile got bigger, like he knew this.

"Fuck off."

You'd have thought that I had enough experience at this point to at least deny something convincingly. I had done nothing but deny with Damian. Deny I was gay, retarded, you name it. In grade six he even claimed that I had a swastika tattooed on my dick.

I took off, leaving Damian just standing there. That was what Julian had done the first time Damian had asked him what he was doing hanging with two losers like me and Anthony. It looked so cool, and me and Anthony were super impressed. I wondered what I looked like doing it now. Too bad Claudia wasn't there to see that I could handle the kind of pressure that went with getting a girl pregnant. How stupid did I just sound?

Chapter 22

Between walking away from Damian and hearing the last bell lay the longest afternoon anyone has ever lived. Every time I started wondering how Damian had found out about Annie, my stomach felt like it was being twisted into another knot.

Tammy couldn't have told him. She might have been Annie's friend, but she was also supposedly an inch away from offing herself. That's what they call it in the movies. If I sound like I didn't care, it's not true. The whole thing gave me goosebumps, to tell you the truth, which was why I couldn't think too much about Tammy.

I didn't want to think about Peter either, but he was the only other person that could have said anything to Damian. Or Julian. But Julian was my friend.

At least, that's what I kept telling myself as I made my way over to his locker after last period. That's where me, him and Anthony were meeting before heading over to my place. Grounded or not, I had to tell the guys about Annie before they found out some other way, and my run-in with Damian pretty much confirmed that there was a good chance of that happening any second—if they didn't know already.

My neck and shoulders were killing me. Probably from walking around with my head so low all afternoon. Not that I knew for sure that everyone was staring at me—that, Dr. Jacobi would tell me, was just my perception—but it almost felt worse; like Damian or whatever other back-stabbing traitor had announced it over the friggin' PA system.

Anthony was already at Julian's locker. Julian looked up and nodded at me and I nodded back. I couldn't read his face one bit. We started walking towards the doors, nobody saying a word. I was dying to talk about something stupid, like the crappy sandwich my mom had made me for lunch or the ugly combat boots that this kid Ashton was wearing, but I couldn't say anything for some reason. I just felt this huge cloud hanging over us as we made our way over to my house.

In my basement, Julian plopped down on the couch, his eyes glued to his cell. "So are we going to the dance?"

I curled up in the armchair, leaving Anthony to sit on the floor.

"Halloween dances sound lame," I said, thinking about Claudia all dressed up.

"They have them every year," said Anthony, fishing out a granola bar from his knapsack.

"I think I'm going with Angela," said Julian, looking up at us with a big smile. "Just waiting for the deets."

Anthony frowned. "The what?"

"Details," Julian answered like he was wasting his breath.

Anthony rolled his eyes, but not at me, which kind of hurt my feelings.

"Who's Angela?" I asked.

"That girl in my math class," Julian answered. "Anthony knows."

This was probably Anthony's only chance to feel like he was anything close to being Julian's friend, and he milked it for all it was worth, giving me this look full of attitude.

"Why haven't I heard of her?" I couldn't help asking.

Julian looked at me. "Probably because you haven't been around."

Was he trying to telepathically tell me he missed me or something?

But then he quickly dropped his head again.

"What are we doing here anyway?" he asked, like we were stuck in detention instead of in my house.

Anthony shrugged. "Kye has tons of movies."

"I don't wanna watch anything," I said.

Julian laughed. "Oh my god, there's hope for one of you after all."

"I thought you liked movies," Anthony said, taking a shot at the wastebasket by the TV with his granola bar wrapper. And missing.

"I'm bored," said Julian.

I took a deep breath and ran my hand down the arm of the chair.

"I need to tell you guys something."

"Do I finally have a gay friend?" Julian asked, jabbing at his phone.

"He's not gay," muttered Anthony.

Julian started tossing his cell up in the air and catching it.

"Do you have a crush on me?" he asked, throwing his cell up in the air and catching it. I pictured myself grabbing it out of his hand and tossing it out the friggin' window.

"I don't have a crush on anyone," I answered.

"What about Claudia?" asked Julian.

Christ, I wanted him to shut up.

"She gives me these dirty looks in math class," Anthony mumbled.

At least she was still looking at Anthony. In English class, Claudia had switched places with some Jennifer girl from the other side of the classroom. It only lasted about five seconds though, before Oertner asked her to go back to her regular place, behind me. Something about staying at our assigned desks for the year, like changing was dangerous or something.

"We aren't together anymore," I said.

"People break up all the time," said Julian.

"Not Kye," said Anthony.

It was the closest he had ever come to revealing anything about the real me to Julian, but Julian didn't look all that interested.

I had actually managed to forget about Claudia hating my guts for a minute last night, and started thinking about that baby growing inside of Annie; all nine centimetres of it.

Without thinking, I put up two fingers, trying to remember the spacing I had measured out on the ruler last night.

"That's a small dick," said Julian, laughing.

I put my hand down and folded my arms.

Julian put his cell in his pocket and crossed his arms, getting serious. "So is it true?"

I sat up straighter. "Is what true?"

"Oh my god, stop with the James Bond crap."

Anthony looked at me, all confused. "What's he talking about?"

But I could barely see him next to Julian and his friggin' crossed arms, towering over everything. Holy shit, he really was serious.

"Damian told me," Julian said.

My heart stopped. "Damian?"

Julian rolled his eyes. "That guy that was shitty to you in grade seven."

"Since birth," mumbled Anthony.

Unfortunately, he was too far to kick. Julian had no idea about our history with Damian. Me and Anthony had summed it up for him one day about three weeks after meeting him, with a couple of stupid name-calling stories. We figured anything more and we would have burned any chances of him wanting to even go to the same school as us.

Julian sighed. "Your arch enemy, then; happy?"

"What the hell did he tell you?" asked Anthony.

Julian looked down at him like he felt downright sorry for him in that moment. Then he looked over at me. "Are you going to put him out of his misery?"

Anthony and his feelings were the last things on my mind.

"Are you and Damian friends now?" I asked.

Julian didn't even blink. "He told me in history class."

Bullshit. I wanted to kick myself for ever telling Julian anything, not so much because it was clear that sooner or later word would make its way around the planet, but because I hadn't even been able to surprise him with this. No, shock him, the way I was about to shock Anthony.

I looked over at Anthony, who was ready to rip his eyebrows right off his friggin' face, like he did whenever he was stressed.

"Tell him," said Julian.

Telling Julian to fuck off would have been easier.

I took a deep breath. "She's pregnant, okay?"

"*You* got her pregnant," Julian added.

I stared down at this strand of hair caught on my jeans. I wondered for a second if it was Claudia's, but it was too short.

Julian's face turned to stone as he looked around the room, like he was finding the perfect thing to smash into bits. He then looked at Anthony.

"You should have at least told him first," he said finally.

"Like you care," Anthony mumbled.

"Fuck you," Julian shot back.

I got up from the chair.

Julian looked ready to laugh. "You have bigger things to worry about than hitting me."

He seemed surer I was going to do it than I was. I had never hit anyone in my life except Josh something-or-other from grade four, and that doesn't even really count. It was barely a punch. It hurt a lot, though. They made things look so easy in movies.

"You think you're so cool because you fucked Annie," Julian said, saliva practically drooling down his chin. He took out his cell and started playing with it again.

Anthony's face changed, like it was only dawning on him then what this all meant. "Annie? From the pool?"

"That's right," said Julian.

"When did this happen?" asked Anthony.

I knew he wanted me to answer, even if he was staring at the coffee table, but Julian was on a roll.

"One night at the pool." Julian looked up from his phone wearing a smirk. "And then after it was over, Annie told me how lousy you were and how she wished she had picked me."

"I don't see how that's even possible, because you were in the chalet with what's-her-name," I replied, anger filling my chest.

Even though I knew he was bluffing, everything Julian was saying sounded true. Why wouldn't Annie have picked him over me? He definitely looked better in swim trunks.

"Where was I?" asked Anthony.

I thought Julian would be brutally honest about that too; that he hadn't wanted Anthony along, and I had done nothing to convince him otherwise. But he just kept his eyes on his phone.

Anthony turned to me, his face now red with betrayal. "I thought we were going to tell each other when we..."

His voice trailed off. I'm not sure I would have stopped him if he had kept going. Then again, Anthony revealing to Julian our I'll-tell-you-everything-about-my-first-time pact didn't exactly make me feel all fuzzy inside.

"I have a math test tomorrow," Anthony mumbled, standing up.

For the first time in a while, Julian looked right at me. "I'm guessing she's getting an abortion?"

I shook my head. "She doesn't want one."

Julian practically laughed. "Nobody wants one, you idiot."

"She wants to give it up for adoption."

Julian sighed. "You watch way too many movies."

"Not anymore," muttered Anthony, his eyes glued to the carpet.

Within a minute, he got up and went upstairs. When we heard the front door slam shut Julian turned to me. "He's pissed."

He said it like *passed*, which is how he pronounced the word when someone was *beyond* pissed.

"He'll come around," I said.

"How do you know?"

I swallowed. "It's called friendship."

Julian snorted. "Funny word coming from you."

"You know what else is funny?" I asked. "How Damian even found out."

"So Peter's a bit of a big mouth," Julian replied.

My heart started pounding. "How did Peter even know?"

Finally, the question I had wanted to ask since lunch. I thought I had gotten him too, but Julian was ready with his answer.

"I had to tell him something."

I could barely breathe. "Why couldn't you just keep it to Tammy being crazy?"

Julian shook his head like I was too young to understand. I wondered if he also thought I was too stupid to be his friend anymore.

"I get it," I finally said.

"You get what?"

I considered bullshitting my way through some story of all the rumours I had spread in my lifetime, but that just seemed sad.

Instead, I shrugged my shoulders. "That you had to tell him something."

We didn't say anything for a while. I glanced at the clock by the television. Crap, it was almost four thirty.

"I feel bad for you," Julian finally said.

"She's going to put it up for adoption," I replied in a shaky voice.

"You're so screwed," he added like he hadn't heard me.

Did this mean it was over? Was Julian moving to the other side to join Damian and all those other guys? I had been wondering when this would happen from the first day we met Julian. I just never thought it would happen because I had messed around with a girl that he liked.

And that's how it was feeling, like a friggin' loss, even before he went upstairs and slammed the front door harder than Anthony had, leaving the words *I'm sorry* stuck in my throat.

Chapter 23

The first thing I noticed about Annie's mom, on Sunday afternoon when I opened the door, was her hair. It went all the way down to her waist and was jet black, but not in a fake, dyed way. Every strand looked real, and it didn't make her look like a witch or one of those crazy vegetarian hippies. She looked kind of good, actually, especially for a mom. She didn't look particularly excited to see me though, but no surprise there.

My parents had emerged from their silent treatment to pose now by the entranceway with these looks on their faces like they had discovered a new appreciation of this whole ordeal: that life was precious, even with an unborn one about to mess up their own.

I realize that I haven't spoken about my parents much, and how they were adapting to this trailer park reality they had been sucked into. There wasn't much to say, mainly because we were avoiding each other like the plague. Especially my mom, who was standing in the doorway, staring at the shoe rack where Patricia and Annie were placing their sneakers, all the while pulling at the sleeves of this blouse she only wears to funerals.

I was sure she'd begin crying within fifteen minutes. My mom's pretty emotional, but not in a dignified, saintly way. Just in a way that weirds me out. I mean, she sobbed through the movie *Titanic*, for god's sake, along with all the other losers who thought that was the most touching film they would ever see.

My dad looked like he was heading to the office, with this blazer over his pants. All official and stuff, like he had to remind us this wasn't a party. I caught his hand slipping into my mom's as Annie and her mom stepped in the house.

Next to these misfits, Annie's mother looked like a seasoned pro, standing all relaxed with her hands in the back pockets of her jeans. If it hadn't been for this fake mean-old-lady smile on her face, I would have almost believed she had been through this before.

"Nice to meet you," my mom said, trying to smile back.

Patricia said something polite in return, like "likewise" or "same here" or whatever bullshit grown-ups tell each other.

"This is Annie," I said in a shaky voice, pointing in Annie's direction, even though she was standing right beside me. I hadn't looked at her much since she walked in; just long enough to notice that she didn't seem any fatter.

When she smiled I could see her chin trembling, and my mom pulled her into this long, weird hug.

"Let's go into the living room," my dad finally said, ending this stupid girl-bonding crap.

He pointed Annie and her mom to the smaller couch, and we took the larger one, my dad making sure he was sitting across from Patricia and me next to my mom. I'm sure my parents had had these seating arrangements prepared ahead of time, along with the cookies sitting on the coffee table between us. They were placed in all sorts of fancy patterns, and my mom stuck the plate under Annie's nose.

"I remember the cravings I used to get," she said with a forced giggle, and her face immediately reddened. I was ready to just die, and my dad shot her the disappointed look he gives when you try bothering him during the news or something.

"Now, we're all here for a purpose," he started, staring at the cookies whose circle was now broken by the one that Annie had taken.

"Yes," my mom added, throwing a glance at my dad to show that she was back on track.

Patricia was doing this perpetual nod. I wasn't sure whether she was already in on the plan or whether she was just tuning in to this universal understanding that separates adults from the kids who don't use condoms. As if to make my point, Annie looked over at me with these pleading eyes. I grabbed a cookie and bit into it.

"Now, I think we can all agree that we want what's best," my dad said, looking over at Patricia, and then at Annie, who sort of nodded. He was doing a terrific job of ignoring me.

"The question is, what is best?"

And with that, my dad put his hands up in the air and sat back looking almost satisfied with his grand contribution to the discussion. He looked over at Patricia like he was passing her the puck, but Annie spoke up instead.

"We don't want an abortion," she said in a voice just barely a notch above a whisper. She looked over at me as if asking me to back her up on this lie. The bitch.

I could hear Patricia gasp. "What?"

So she was on my side, in a strange way.

Annie shrugged a million times and stared at her hands. I was waiting for her passionate speech about how it was growing inside her and all that crap. But it didn't come. Hell, she couldn't even tell them that it had a heart.

Patricia rolled her eyes.

"Don't be mad at me." Annie's voice was still really quiet. She wanted to be polite in front of my parents; wanted them to believe in her victim charade a little longer. I suddenly wanted to throw the cookie platter against the wall and watch the crumbs just explode in the air like the hand grenades in *Saving Private Ryan* or something.

Patricia's eyes scanned the room like it was the worst place on earth. "Give me a reason not to be mad, Annette."

The cookie was slipping from Annie's hand, and Patricia took it from her and put it back on the plate.

I thought I heard my mom sniffle beside me, but I didn't look at her. My dad took a deep breath and leaned forward again.

"We need to find a solution," he said, like he just realized that moving Annie and Patricia to another continent wasn't an option. Then he looked over at me, for the first time since they had walked through the door.

Patricia and Annie's eyes followed, and suddenly I was the friggin' centre of attention, like it was my fault we were all there in the first place.

"What about adoption?" I asked to no one in particular.

"What other choice is there?" asked Patricia.

Annie sat back on the couch, her arms folded.

"Stop acting like a baby," Patricia snapped. "You're an adult now."

"No, I'm not," Annie replied, pouting.

Patricia pointed to me. "You should have told him that a few months ago."

"I didn't force anything," I mumbled.

Patricia held up her hand. "I don't need details, Kye."

My parents flinched. They didn't need details either.

Annie started crying, and my mom passed her a tissue she had dug up from her skirt pocket. Then, to really make the rest of us look like heartless assholes, she leaned over and started talking to Annie like she was a friggin' psych ward patient.

"I can only imagine how hard it would be for you," she said as more tears rolled down Annie's cheeks.

My mom had started crying herself but, left with no tissue, was wiping her cheeks with the back of her hand. Even then, I knew that she was only thinking about Annie at that moment, and not about her own life being shit on by an annoying grandkid in the neighborhood that she'd have to explain to her yoga friends.

"It won't be easy," said Patricia, her voice a tad nicer. "But it's the best thing for everyone."

"But especially for *you*," my dad added quickly when Annie disintegrated into a blubbering mess.

He stopped here, I guess to let Annie reflect on all the friggin' potential she would be wasting by playing mommy. Then he took another deep breath. Christ, was he ever going to shut up?

"We all want what's right for our children."

I guess his cheesy way of letting Annie know that he was including her in that special parent circle.

"I think in the meantime Kye should take up his responsibility in this," he rambled on, and he and Patricia both looked over at me.

I nodded, although I didn't have a clue what I could do, besides be there for Annie.

"We have our first appointment with the doctor on Wednesday," Patricia said.

So they were a "we" now. I guess that's what motherhood was all about, taking on everything, even a pregnancy.

"Kye will come along," my dad said quickly, with a smile that said *See how easy this is?*

"What about school?" I asked.

My dad and mom both shot me a look like they were wondering whether *I* was adopted.

Patricia just said, "I think this is more important," but her forced laugh at the end told me she would have preferred telling me to fuck off.

"Absolutely," my dad chimed in a little too eagerly.

As if on cue, my mom pulled out a piece of paper from the same pocket that had carried the tissue now balled up in Annie's hand. The paper was folded just once, clean down the middle, a sign of its part in the plan.

"Patricia, we're giving you our number," she said all dramatically as she passed over the paper.

Even though Annie could have found my home number on the Internet, my mom's gesture still felt like the last nail in the coffin. The last thing Annie needed to make me all hers.

Patricia took the number and nodded in my direction. "He can give you ours. And I already have an adoption agency in mind. I'll let you know when the appointment is."

Both my parents raised their eyebrows in this fake anticipation, like they just couldn't wait to go to a friggin' adoption agency.

Patricia was the first to exit the living room, with Annie wiping her eyes and following right behind. Within seconds, we were all standing by the front door, five people forced into this narrow hallway by nothing more than a sense of stupid obligation.

After I had said enough goodbyes to prove to Patricia that I was not a complete dick, I slipped back into the living room where I could breathe. I was still close enough to overhear my mom making some pathetic and awkward remark to Patricia about how strong she was or something like that.

"I was a single mother at twenty-two," Patricia retorted. "It has nothing to do with strength. It's experience."

Chapter 24

Lunch period was still the only thing left in my life resembling any kind of normal, but even that was going to shit in a handbasket. I mean, take the following Tuesday. Sure, we were all still under the tree freezing our asses off, but Anthony was studying for some "exam" that probably didn't even exist, seemingly unaware that our time with Julian was running out. And I needed Julian now more than ever, especially since having Patricia and Annie sitting in my living room forty-eight hours earlier.

Not that I was able to transmit this desperation to Julian himself, who hadn't said a word since sitting down, too busy playing some game on his phone.

I was barely touching my lunch. but I didn't want Julian, or Anthony for that matter, to see, so when I was sure that I couldn't stuff another morsel of tuna sandwich and crackers down my throat, I wrapped everything up in my bag again and nonchalantly slid it over to the garbage can.

That's when out of nowhere, Julian pulled out some chips and plopped them down on the ground. It was a big bag too, not one of these crappy microscopic things they sell at the dollar store.

"Dig in," he said to no one in particular.

Salt and vinegar weren't my favourite, but were they the peace offering that I hoped they were? My heart almost skipped a beat as I grabbed a few, suddenly feeling hungry for the first time since the lunch bell had rung. Anthony, though, just held onto his apple like he was feeling up Miss Universe's tit.

Julian looked back down at his phone.

"This game is friggin' addictive," he said, shaking his head. "My parents are nuts about it too."

He laughed, something I hadn't heard in a while.

"I don't think they even have sex anymore." He looked up at me. "Pretty fucked up, right?"

I saw Julian's mom once, for like five minutes. She looked like a pin-up for Costco. I couldn't imagine anyone willingly having sex with her, but I shook my head and forced a laugh anyway, almost choking on the vinegar that was burning my tongue.

"What are you doing on Halloween?" Julian asked.

Anthony kept looking at his textbook, as if he knew the question was only for me.

"Why?" I mumbled. "You wanna beat me up?"

Julian laughed. "Don't be an idiot."

My gut told me that this was the surest sign I'd ever get from Julian that my chlorinated fling with Annie was forgotten. Or so I hoped. I just wished I could say the same about Julian opening his big mouth to Peter.

"I'm grounded," I said.

"For what?" Julian asked.

I didn't say anything, and things got quiet for a minute as we all sort of stared at the big red lettering on the chip bag between us.

I leaned over and took a few more. "I think I should find a job."

Julian looked confused. "But the baby is going."

"I think they'll like me being responsible and stuff," I explained, chip crumbs flying out of my mouth.

Julian pulled up his sleeves. "That's bullshit."

He started tossing his phone around from hand to hand and was silent for a moment. I started getting nervous.

"Wanna stock shelves at the drugstore?" he finally asked.

"What do you mean?"

"My neighbour Liam works at the drugstore on Langdon Boulevard, and he was telling me about this job opening."

I hadn't thought much about what it would be like working, but Julian was offering me a job. This was even better than the chips.

I forced a smile. "Sounds cool."

"Do you have a resume or something?" he asked, his eyes scanning the ground like I'd just have copies stashed behind the tree or something.

"I can make one," I said. "What should I put in it?"

Julian shrugged. "Your name, schooling, anything amazing you've done, like horseback riding and shit. Except getting a girl pregnant."

The first bell rang. Julian laughed, and I tried to join him, but the vinegar had completely numbed my mouth by then. Anthony looked like he was ready to kill me, but I didn't care. Hell, I almost didn't care that Julian had told Peter everything. I didn't even care if they were friends. Okay, so that was pushing it. The thing was, *we* were still friends, and the chances of Julian abandoning us to hang with cooler guys at Fincher had just gone down to a more controllable level that I could live with.

Chapter 25

Patricia reached behind to unlock the back door so I could get in.

"She's always late," she mumbled as she fastened her seat belt.

It was Wednesday, and "she" was the lady doctor we had just gone to visit. Well, Annie and Patricia had gone in. I just sat in the waiting room with my head buried in a *Ladies' Home Journal* from last Christmas. Still, reading true confessions from cat lovers sure beat standing around while Dr. Whatever-her-name-was felt Annie up.

I looked at the crumbs all over the back seat of the car, and at the million unopened newspapers strewn across the floor. I would never have thought Patricia was such a slob. The car was from 1998 or something like that, and I was still kicking myself for having let her pick me up from school that afternoon. I didn't even let my parents pick me up at school, and they had a decent car. Not Patricia's piece of crap that was on the assembly line before I was friggin' born.

By some miracle, the car started, and we made our way out of the parking lot. Annie had her hands folded and her eyes on the ground, looking like she had been raped or something. Who could blame her? I wanted to comfort her, but I wasn't so sure what to say, since I wasn't even sure why I had come along. I guessed from the self-satisfied look on Patricia's face that it was for whatever moral support me and my guilty dick could transmit through those beige doctor-office walls separating me from the exam rooms.

"How are you?" I finally mustered up.

"Fine," Annie mumbled.

"At least it was a lady doctor," I offered.

"Absolutely," said Patricia sarcastically, all the while her head turning everywhere as she changed lanes.

Her tone kind of made me nervous. "Is there something wrong with the baby?"

"We can only hope not," Patricia answered. "We just have to go back every month."

"Every month?" I asked.

I'd have to remember to bring a Sudoku book along or something.

"There'll also be an ultrasound," she added.

"That's when you see the baby?" I asked.

"That's right," she replied. "You can finally see your beautiful baby."

Man, she really was bitchy. Annie probably would have been more than happy to move into my house with my mom and her tissues.

We got to a red light, and the Nissan came to a screeching halt.

"So, Kye," Patricia started in the kind of sing-song voice that always leads to some of the shittiest moments possible. "Have you found a job yet?"

"I'm going to apply this weekend."

"Really?" she looked at me through the rear-view in mock surprise. "What kind of a job did you have in mind?"

And the shitty moment sets in.

"I was thinking of working at the drugstore," I said.

Patricia started tapping on the steering wheel. I didn't know what the hell that meant.

"Or McDonald's," I added. "I'm flexible."

I'm flexible. Jesus Christ.

"Those are both excellent sources of income for a baby."

"But we're giving it up for adoption," I said. "Right?"

I strained to catch a glimpse of Annie through the rear-view mirror but kept making eye contact with Patricia instead. "You better make sure Annie here's on the same track," Patricia answered, nodding in Annie's direction like I didn't know who she was.

I started panicking a little, and then a lot when Annie sank lower into the seat.

"Because if Annie doesn't want to give this baby up," Patricia continued in a tone that was quickly becoming angrier, "fries and apple pie won't cut it."

We got to another red light, and Patricia turned to look at me. Her face was really red, and she looked like she hated me more than Damian and all those other guys thrown together.

I rolled down the window a little to get some air, but all the wind from the North Pole wouldn't have been enough.

"Can you drop me off here?" I asked, my hands now clutched firmly around my stomach.

"But your house is further up."

It was the most Annie had spoken since they had picked me up after school.

"It's okay," I replied weakly.

Patricia pulled up to the curb like she couldn't wait to get me out of her precious Nissan. I stepped out and slammed the door. The car had barely turned the next corner when I puked all over someone's hedge. No one saw me, but then again, for the first time in my life, I didn't care if the whole friggin' world had its eyes on me.

Chapter 26

Me and Anthony had only been to Julian's a handful of times. Four, if I count exactly. The first time was a couple of weeks after we first met him, I guess. All the snow had finally melted after this wicked snowstorm on like, April Fool's or something. I remember this because I was wearing my sneakers out for the first time since the previous November and it felt kind of good. Anthony was quizzing Julian on his movie trivia as we walked towards Julian's house. He couldn't answer half of Anthony's questions, but it didn't matter, because he was making all these funny jokes instead, and things felt a little normal.

We were stopping by so Julian could drop off his school bag before we headed to my house to hang. The farthest me and Anthony got was the entrance, where we stood on the mountain of shoes piled up at the door. Julian made some kind of joke about having more sisters and brothers than the Mormons, though the house was quieter than a library.

The second time we were at Julian's house was the last day of school of grade eight. It was friggin' boiling outside, and you'd think he would have had the decency to invite me and Anthony into his house. And I knew he had air conditioning too, because all his windows were closed. Instead, we hung out on his porch. It was very nice, I'll admit, but who gives a shit about a porch when it's fifty degrees Celsius outside?

The third time was later that summer. We were on our way to the pool, and Julian needed to get the swimming trunks he looked so friggin' good in. He invited us into the kitchen this time, where we munched on two ice-cream sandwiches each. Me and Anthony were in heaven because we both love those things, and Julian seemed to have, like, ten boxes in his freezer.

So, this was the fourth time me and Anthony were going to his house, and I'd probably remember this time too because it was Halloween. It was also my biggest ever attempt to pull a fast one on my parents. They had decided to go for dinner and a movie, something they do every Halloween, not because they're romantic but because they're too cheap to get candy to hand out. I had told them I wasn't too hungry. My parents exchanged a couple of glances, like I was this high-risk prisoner from San Quentin or wherever the hell the really bad guys go.

That was pretty much how they'd been treating me since I had broken the news, if they talked to me at all. My dad mostly kept to himself, and when he did speak to me, he sighed a lot, like it was this big physical effort or something. My mom acknowledged my existence a little more, but always with a tear in her eye, like any second she would have a meltdown of Olympian proportions.

Anyways, my parents finally decided it was safe, so they took off. I left about fifteen minutes later and through the back door in case anyone knocked on the front and asked where the candy was. It was still really early though, and all I saw were a couple of small kids with their parents. There was this mist in the air from the rain that had stopped minutes earlier, thank god. I hated umbrellas. They were always popping inside out, and I could never get them back in place without looking like a total idiot.

On this particular night, no rain meant I could stuff my face in my jacket and hide, even though I figured I easily had three hours before my parents would be pulling up the driveway. That had to be enough time for Julian to find Angela's house and ask her out to the dance tomorrow night.

That was the whole reason we were going, but I didn't care. The only part of this plan I didn't like was meeting up with Anthony half way so we could walk over to Julian's together. I hadn't spoken to him much at all in almost two weeks, and I had no clue what he would say to me.

"Where's your costume?" Anthony asked when I reached the corner he was waiting at.

"It's kind of hard to dress up when you're grounded," I answered. Still, deep down I was getting nervous. I hated costumes, but I hated being left out even more. How could I have forgotten this important detail?

"Where's yours?" I asked.

Anthony pulled out what looked like a bed sheet from inside his jacket and shook it a bit until another one fell out. He handed it to me without a word, and I didn't say thanks. I was pretty grateful, even if I was expected to stuff my head into a sheet that had been used for god knows what.

I was relieved that Anthony didn't put his on right away, so we walked the rest of the way with the sheets under our arms and in silence. I was pretty much following his lead, since I suck at directions. Anthony though seemed to know the route like the back of his hand. I started wondering whether he had been hanging with Julian without me, but I didn't want to know, so I didn't ask.

When we got to the house, Julian was standing on the front porch with his arms crossed.

"Where the fuck did you walk from, Siberia?"

I wanted to kind of smile at him or something, but he wasn't even looking at me.

"Is that your costume?" he asked pointing to our sad sheets.

"Where's yours?" asked Anthony.

Julian pulled out some sunglasses from his back pocket and put them on.

"I'm John Travolta."

"In what movie?" asked Anthony.

"*Grease*, what else?" Julian shook his head. "You disappoint me, dude."

He obviously wasn't talking to me, and I'd be lying if I said there wasn't this tiny pang of jealousy or whatever you want to call it. He hadn't looked at me once, and I was starting to wonder whether I had imagined him inviting me along earlier that day.

"Anyways, Angela can't see me this way," Julian said, walking down the porch steps.

I wasn't sure *he'd* be able to see anything, and I just pictured him cracking his head open if he missed a stair or something.

"I thought we were doing this so you could ask her to the dance," said Anthony.

Julian started down the street, and we followed. Some things never changed.

"I just wanna see her first," he mumbled.

"To guess your chances?" I asked.

"That's right," Julian said, still not looking at me.

I shut up and looked down at the street.

Anthony pulled on his sheet and had to turn it about a million times to get the stupid slits over his eyes. I glanced up and down the street. There were more kids out now, but none that looked older than eleven. It was as good a time as any, so I yanked the sheet over my head, and was happy to not have to struggle with it like Anthony. Still, Julian was amused.

"Did you forget the eyes or something?" he asked, starting to laugh.

I pulled it off and tossed it to Anthony.

"I'll go as myself," I said.

So much for being invisible.

We made our way down the street, me stuck between a ghost and friggin' John Travolta. It was my usual spot, but it felt different.

"Are we getting any candy?" asked Anthony after we had passed one block.

"Do you have any pubes at all?" asked Julian, adjusting his sunglasses.

"You're not going to go up to her door with those on, are you?" I asked.

He tore the glasses off his face suddenly, like I had personally offended them. He looked like he wanted to say something but then didn't. He did stuff the glasses in his jacket pocket though. I was kind of pleased in some strange way.

We walked in silence for another block and then stopped in front of this red brick bungalow with two gigantic trees in the front yard. It was dark, but you could see that the lawn was coated in leaves. The living room didn't leave anything to the imagination though. It was lit up like a friggin' helicopter was going to land or something, and I could see this girl with a long, brown ponytail sitting at the dining room table. It was a really long ponytail too, even longer than Claudia's. She was probably not as cute, but it was kind of hard to see. Her arms were moving a bit, and you could see she was talking to someone in another room, like the kitchen or something.

I scanned the porch for a pumpkin, but it was bare.

"I don't think they're giving out candy," I said, while Julian started getting all jittery and pulled his glasses out again.

"They're Jehovah's Witnesses," he answered.

"My neighbour is one of those," said Anthony. "They don't even do birthdays."

"Do they date?" I asked.

Julian looked at me a second before turning and walking up the driveway, leaving me and Anthony alone.

After a second, I turned to Anthony. "What time is it?" I asked.

He shrugged his shoulders and plopped down on the curb. I had forgotten that he didn't have a cell.

Julian was still standing in front of the door like he had a poker up his ass. I couldn't tell whether he had already rung the bell or not.

When he turned and looked in our direction, I waved, but he didn't wave back.

"I have to be back by nine," I mumbled to nobody in particular.

"How are you going to deal with this baby if you're grounded?" asked Anthony.

"I can see Annie," I answered. "I think."

"What about your friends?"

"I don't know," I said sadly.

Anthony looked like one of those dogs from the puppy mills that I did a project on last year.

This ray of light suddenly came across Angela's lawn as the door finally opened, and the girl that had been sitting at the table appeared.

"Take off that thing," I told Anthony.

It was just a matter of time before some high school senior came along and mortified us both. Anthony pulled off the sheet. Thank god he still listened to me.

And then I said something that surprised even me.

"I told you that night at the party."

Anthony looked up at me. "Which party?"

"The only one we've ever gone to."

He was really thinking about it, you could tell, going through our whole, miserable high-school existence until he hit on that night at Brian Chadwick's. His hand was holding up his chin like he does when he's super-concentrating. I felt friggin' awful.

"I don't remember you telling me anything," he mumbled, and picked up a little stone off the street.

"It's because the music was so loud," I said.

"It wasn't *that* loud," he replied, tossing the stone away again. "And we barely saw each other anyway."

I sighed. "You were the first to know, OK?"

But I knew it wasn't that simple. The thing was, I didn't know how to apologize for that, for this—for all of this.

Just then, Angela's door closed with a loud squeak, and Julian began making his way down the driveway. He was putting on his stupid glasses again.

I turned to Anthony. "You know in *Trainspotting* when Renton has to fish through that toilet for his drugs?"

"Yeah?"

Of course he knew, that was why we were best friends.

"That's how I feel."

Anthony didn't say anything. Julian had joined us again anyway.

"So?" I asked.

Julian shrugged. "She can't go to the dance because it's a Halloween one."

"Why?" asked Anthony.

"Because she's a Jehovah's Witness," I said.

Julian shrugged again and started walking. "I don't care, I'm still going."

"With who?" I asked, trying to keep pace alongside him.

"I don't know," Julian answered. Then he slapped Anthony's back. "Maybe with this guy."

Julian would go to the dance with a chick with Down's syndrome before going with Anthony, and me and Anthony both knew it. It sounded more like he had plans with other, cooler people.

"Is Peter going to the dance?" I asked as innocently as I could.

Julian froze in his tracks, but not because of my question. It was a pretty gutsy question, if you asked me, but nothing out of my mouth could have ever made him stop the way he did. He removed his glasses and put a hand over his eyes, like he would if it was really sunny, even though it was pitch dark except for the faintest light coming from the streetlamps.

"What's wrong?" I asked.

But he just started walking again, and me and Anthony followed; through the parents and kids moving between the houses, and the sounds of candy rustling within the trick or treat bags. We made our way through everything that was normal, until we reached what wasn't.

It looked like a typical enough house, but there was something at the foot of the driveway that I could tell made everything different. Something that was making parents yank their kids away, and teenagers either start laughing or shake their heads.

"What does that say?" asked Anthony as we got closer.

"I think it says *hi*," I answered.

Julian shook his head. "HIV," he whispered. "It says HIV."

It was then that I noticed the strip of toilet paper that was supposed to finish up where the other strip had left off. Except the wind had tugged one side of the *V* towards the driveway until it was barely recognizable. Barely.

"Why the hell would anyone do that?" asked Anthony.

"Because someone obviously has HIV," replied Julian.

We were now only a few feet from the house, but we had all stopped.

I took a deep breath, suddenly wishing I was still wearing Anthony's sheet. "Could that be—"

"Tammy Dalton's house," said Julian.

"Holy shit," I said.

"Holy shit indeed," replied Julian.

A look of disgust came over Anthony's face. "That's just cruel."

"But impressive," said Julian.

"Let's go," I said.

Julian held up his hand. "We need to fix it."

"Who cares that the *V* is crooked?" I asked.

"Not the *V*. The whole thing."

Anthony glanced at me to see if I had any better clue of what Julian was talking about. I would have given a shrug but my shoulders felt like two fifty pound dumbbells that Adam lifts at the gym.

I thought about him now, scooping me up from here and taking me home. The thought of my basement couch never seemed so good.

But Adam was in Australia, and Julian was giving me and Anthony his you-guys-are-such-retards look.

"We need to get rid of it," he insisted.

"Of the toilet paper?" asked Anthony.

Julian turned to me. "What do you think, dude?"

"Go for it." *While I try figuring out how to climb that big-ass tree across the street and fly home.*

Julian shook his head and slid his Travolta glasses over his eyes again. "*You* do it."

My heart stopped. "Why?"

"Don't you want to?" asked Julian.

"Not really."

"It'll make you feel better."

"How the hell do you figure that?"

"Just do it, Kye," Anthony begged, tugging madly at his eyebrows.

My eyes jumped between the lawn and the front door of the house. The wind had picked up and the toilet paper was slowly being morphed into a new, less threatening design.

Julian stepped forward and gave me a small push. "Do it before someone opens the door and thinks you were the one that put it there."

I squatted down and brushed the surface of the grass with my fingertips. When I touched a corner of the toilet paper I flinched.

"Nobody wiped their ass with it," said Julian.

"At least you hope not," said Anthony.

Julian burst out laughing.

I quickly grabbed all the toilet paper I saw and turned around, glaring at Anthony.

"Since when the hell are you the witty one of the bunch?" I asked.

"Leave the funny dude alone," said Julian.

My eyes shifted to Julian. He was probably looking all smug behind those friggin' sunglasses. I wanted to tear them off his face so badly my hands were twitching.

"And why did you want me to do that, anyway?" I asked.

Julian sighed, like the answer was obvious. "You like to do the right thing."

I stomped off. I should have at least dumped the toilet paper in Julian's hands, but I couldn't turn back now. I breathed a small sigh of relief when I spotted a garbage can up ahead. I could hear Julian and Anthony laughing again about whatever the hell was so funny. I quickened my pace and tossed the paper in as soon as I got close enough. For the first time ever, I didn't miss.

I didn't say another word all the way to Julian's house. I didn't even know what the hell I was doing walking him back in the first place. I decided to tell myself that Anthony wouldn't have wanted to be left alone, but he ignored me almost as much as I was ignoring him and Julian.

The conversation didn't get much better after we left Julian at the foot of his driveway. I was too busy noticing that every house we were passing on our way to our neighbourhood looked like *that* house. I tried picturing whether there were any kinds of houses like that on my street, but thinking suddenly felt damn near impossible.

"Are you really gonna work at the drugstore?" asked Anthony as we approached Langdon Boulevard.

I shrugged. "Don't know yet."

When we got to the corner where we parted ways, we kind of looked at each other for a second.

"Do you think that was Tammy's house?" I asked.

Anthony shrugged.

"I don't think so," I said.

"Why not?"

"Just because."

Anthony pulled off his glasses and started cleaning them with a corner of the sheet tucked under his arm. "So it's being adopted, right?"

"What?" I asked.

He looked at me like I was from another planet. "*You* know."

"Oh," I replied. "That's the plan."

I stared into the darkness ahead.

Anthony folded his arms across his chest and looked down at the sidewalk, all pensive. "What's going to happen to us?" he asked after a moment.

I'd like to say that I gave him some deep answer about how our friendship would survive anything, and all that crap.

But I'm pretty sure that the only thing that came out of my mouth was, "I still don't think that was Tammy's house."

Chapter 27

"Liam's got a birthmark across his face. Don't make fun of it."

That was Julian's big piece of advice as we walked towards the drugstore for my interview on Sunday. It was also practically the first thing he said to me since picking me up at home. We hadn't really spoken since Halloween and I had spent all morning preparing myself mentally for any snarky one-liners he had been working on that had to do with toilet paper or HIV. Thankfully, from the way he was walking, I could tell that Julian was way too focused on my pending stockroom career to think about anything else.

"So I just ignore his face?" I asked.

Julian shook his head. "It's a birthmark, you idiot, not a fucking coffee-table book."

I adjusted my tie for the millionth time, while making sure my resume didn't get squashed in my hand. It was a one-page piece of crap; the most amazing thing I could come up with was this science fair prize I had won in grade six, and that was only because my partner, Isaiah Blunk, didn't mind making the presentation.

"Don't mess this up, dude," Said Julian, as we reached the glass doors of the drugstore.

"Don't worry," I answered, grabbing at my tie one last time. "My parents are obsessing about this job like it's a friggin' Rhodes scholarship."

I had to wait about ten minutes in the front of the store, watching some cashier with blue hair pick her nails. Liam was somewhere in the back. I wondered if he stayed there all the time and was working up the courage to come out where people could see him and his birthmark. That's what I'd do. After the cashier called him the second time over the PA system, I considered offering to go to the back myself and put the bastard out of his misery.

About thirty seconds later, though, Liam showed up. He was maybe thirty or so and barely looked at me as we shook hands. I passed him my crummy resume. I wasn't even sure what Julian had told him about me, but he kept glancing at the paper like he was trying to remember what my name was or something. I was curious to get a look at the birthmark, but his face was too low. Probably not an accident, either.

"So it's Kye?" he asked as we sat in the white box with a drooping plant in the corner, which Liam called his office.

"Like kite except the 'y' replaces the 'i' and 't'," I answered. I had actually practised this the night before, in case he had problems with my name, and it still sounded confusing. Liam's eyes kind of fluttered back and forth, like I had just thrown the trickiest Mensa question at him.

"So this is your first job application?"

"Yes." I moved forward to show my seriousness, and the vinyl seat made a fart sound.

"Why do you want to work here?" He asked this like he wasn't even sure why *he* was working there.

"I've been going to this drugstore since I was a kid and thought it was a way to give back." The giving back part was my father's idea, and I knew it would sound lame, so I mumbled it.

Liam gave me one of those little appreciative smiles anyways.

"What are some of your best qualities?"

"I'm punctual, reliable, and honest," I repeated from memory.

"What would you say is a point for improvement?" He asked me this like he was satisfied with himself for thinking up this super-difficult question. Then again, he didn't know my dad.

"I'm a little too much of a perfectionist," I replied without any hesitation.

I had to do everything to keep from laughing out loud. Did people honestly say this shit?

Liam sort of raised his eyebrows, surprised, although I was pretty sure I had just been the most predictable interviewee on earth.

"How old are you?"

"I'll be sixteen in a few months."

He mumbled something and looked me up and down a second.

"Okay, you can start next Sunday," he said, lifting his hand from his cheek for the first time since we had sat down. Before I could get a good look at the birthmark, though, he was grabbing some papers off the desk and shuffling them, my resume somewhere in the pile.

* * * *

When I got home from the interview, I called Annie. Patricia picked up.

"Hello?"

"Hey, it's Kye," I replied, kicking myself for not saying hello instead to sound more polite. Then again, why did she always have to answer the phone?

"Nice to hear from you, Kye."

"I got a job," I announced, before she could bitch me out for not calling since they had dropped me off after the doctor's appointment on Wednesday. I had wanted to tell Annie first for whatever reason, but it didn't sound like I'd ever get to her unless I said something to make Patricia start to like me a little.

"Will you be asking me if I want fries with that?"

Man, was this woman ever speechless?

"I'm working at the drugstore."

"Doing what?"

"The stock room," I answered. "Like, supervising and stuff."

I probably wouldn't be supervising anything until I was eighty, but it sounded good. Or so I thought before this torturous silence settled over us. I looked over at my curtains and suddenly imagined wrapping them around my neck.

"Can I speak to Annie?" I finally asked when I couldn't stand it any longer.

"She can't come to the phone," Patricia answered.

"What's wrong?"

"She's not feeling well today."

"Why not?"

"Perhaps you can ask her tomorrow."

"Why not today?" My heart sped up a little.

"Hold on."

After a minute or so and me thinking Patricia had hung up, she came back on the line.

"Annie's getting teased in school."

I could tell Patricia had moved to another room, because her voice sounded, I don't know, more natural.

"How bad is it?"

I figured Annie had been getting teased for a while already, so it must have hit another level if Patricia was telling me about it.

"She doesn't want to go to school anymore." Her voice broke. "It doesn't sound like she has any friends."

I suddenly felt really sad. Lonely people get me very depressed.

"I'll come over," I said, though I wasn't sure what exactly I would do once I got there.

"Not today," Patricia responded, almost panicked. "It'll look too obvious."

Her voice was shaky, and I felt kind of sorry for her, even if she had been a bitch lately.

"I start the job next weekend," I suddenly said, as though my entry into the world of minimum wage was supposed to make up for Annie being a social outcast.

"Goodbye, Kye."

I suddenly thought about what Patricia might say if I asked her whether she hated me. Perhaps I could give her three options. Hate me, tolerate me, or like me. Not a boy-girl like, but the way an adult likes a kid if that kid plays the violin really well or whatever.

I knew this was the kind of crazy idea that you never go through with, but you think of anyway. Like, when I was in grade three or four, I used to fantasize about tying Damian up to a tree in the forest behind our school. Sometimes, on days that he really pissed me off, I'd make it January and freezing outside, and I'd picture his balls just turning to icicles.

I never told Anthony about this dream though, because it sounded more than just a little messed up. Then again, it's not like I'm actually crazy or anything. Not like that dude in *Reservoir Dogs* who chops that dude's ear off. The guy doing the chopping came up with that whole scene on his own. All improvised and stuff. I mean, coming up with *that* shit is a tad more twisted than my tree fantasy. At least, as far as I'm concerned.

Chapter 28

I was eager to see if the guys would react to my job news a little bit better than Patricia had, so I told them during Monday morning break. Just to prove how shitty my life had become at that point, I couldn't even wait a whole 24 hours to announce the thing that was going to rob me of my weekends as of next Sunday.

Julian just kind of nodded but Anthony stared at me as I rummaged through my locker for my English books. "You never told me about no job."

I pointed at Julian. "He set it up for me."

"Liam didn't like you much," said Julian. "But I convinced him you were a good guy."

I shut my locker and looked at him.

He slapped my back. "Kidding."

I took a deep breath.

"I can't talk to that guy," said Julian. "His birthmark messes me up."

"Yo, Julian."

Oh Christ, no. That couldn't be Peter's voice. But it was. The same voice that I had been hearing in my head nonstop the last three weeks. Hearing it tell everyone about Tammy. And about me.

"But he can talk to *that* guy," muttered Anthony, as Peter got closer to us.

"You're telling me," I said under my breath.

"How's it going, man?" asked Julian.

Julian had never called me man. It was always dude. And Anthony was always idiot.

"I'm still hung over from Friday night."

Julian laughed. I laughed too, but only for a second, and then I freaked out that maybe Peter would actually notice me.

"What happened Friday?" asked Anthony, in a tone that made it sound like he actually cared, which I knew he didn't. I personally had been dying to know whether Julian had ended up going to the Halloween dance or not. I also wanted to know whether Claudia had been there.

Since telling her about the baby, I had only seen her at distances too far to make any kind of run-in a pipe dream. Even in English, when I knew that all I had to do was turn around and look at her eyes, and the little freckles on her nose; even then, she might as well have been in China.

If Peter hadn't been standing there with his ugly, pimply face, I might have even asked Julian what she wore, and who she was with. Or maybe not.

Julian shook his head. "That dance was insane."

"They served alcohol at the Halloween dance?" asked Anthony.

Oh my god, why couldn't he just be a deaf-mute sometimes?

Peter looked at Anthony like he was noticing him for the first time, which he probably was. He sort of looked him up and down, taking it all in. The messed up hair, the big pimple in the middle of his forehead that never seemed to go away. And the glasses.

"Yeah," Peter replied with a straight face. "They had a whole fucking bar set up."

Anthony looked at me, confused, but I ignored him. Peter was looking at Julian again with a smile so big it made all the pimples on his cheeks squish together until I thought they would all pop.

"Just saw Tammy come out of the counsellor's office," Peter said.

"Oh my god, when?" asked Julian.

"Just now."

I tried glancing at Anthony's watch to see whether the first bell would finally ring and save me from another word about Tammy, but I couldn't make out any of the numbers. How the hell could I at least beg him to make another asinine comment about the dance to get Peter off the topic of Tammy? Anthony was my best friend, but we weren't connected telepathically.

Not only that, but he looked ready to join in the friggin' conversation.

"That stupid toilet paper," he said.

Peter looked at Anthony. "Toilet paper?"

"There was this toilet paper on her lawn on Halloween," Anthony said stuffing his hands in his pocket. "It said HIV."

I wanted to say that we didn't know for sure it had been Tammy's house, but I couldn't speak.

Peter slapped Julian's back for the millionth time. "In a couple of weeks they'll be giving her shock treatments."

Allison Greary from our grade who was passing us by at that moment, glared.

"You're such an asshole, Peter."

Peter didn't even blink. "Go shave your moustache, Allison."

He and Julian started laughing, and I joined in, mustering up the guts to even mumble, "Don't forget the hairs on your chin too."

Julian and Peter laughed louder, and I felt this little surge of courage to close my locker and start walking away.

Anthony was saying something to me, but I didn't turn around, focusing on the water fountains and bathroom up ahead, beside the staircase I was going to take to get to English class.

"Hey, thanks for waiting," Julian said, catching up with me.

I didn't say anything, not even a sorry, which I normally would have done.

He shook his head as we got to the second floor. "Don't be like that."

If I hadn't been so pissed off, I would have been flattered that he at least had noticed that I wasn't exactly bursting with fruit flavour at the moment.

"Counselling?" I whispered.

Julian rolled his eyes. "So she went to see Mrs. Combes."

Mrs. Combes was the career counsellor and had her office right by the gym. I had gone to see her once in grade eight to take a few of those aptitude tests so they can figure out whether you're going to be a fireman or a doctor when you grow up. She had those little beige dots on her hands that old people get, and she always wore a red flower in her hair.

She was pretty harmless, and Julian looked at me as if to say *See?*

He tapped my back, the way he had Peter a few minutes earlier, and took off down the next hall.

I looked at people filing into their classrooms, the books under their arms being the biggest weight they had to carry. I never hated so many people at once.

Chapter 29

When I walked out of the drugstore after my first shift the next Sunday afternoon, Julian and Anthony were waiting for me by the bus stop.

"How's our stockroom stud?" shouted Julian.

I quickly scanned the sidewalk, but there were only old ladies, and old ladies didn't scare me.

Sometimes, like just then, I wondered whether it had been a mistake to never tell Julian about Damian and all that crap, but then I'm always glad I didn't. I still didn't know what I thought of Julian, to tell you the truth, or how much I did or didn't trust him. Either way, he was hanging with us on a Sunday afternoon when he could have been doing something else.

Anthony looked at the drugstore like he was Harry Potter looking at the wizard school for the first time.

"What's it like in there?" he asked.

"Lots of cold medicine and tampons," replied Julian.

"It's not that bad," I mumbled. Then again, I had only handled paper towels and laundry detergent that day.

Julian started walking, and we followed.

"My mom says I'm going to have to get a job next summer," Anthony said.

"I'm going to bartend," said Julian. "My cousin Zack makes tons of money on tips. And, of course," he added, slapping my back, "let's not forget the girls."

"But we aren't eighteen yet," I pointed out, like the genius that I was.

"It's called fake ID," he answered.

Anthony stared at Julian. "You have fake ID?"

"Not yet. But soon. And you'll get one too."

He and Julian looked out into the street ahead of us like they were distracted for a moment by the great future of bar-hopping and whatever else lay ahead of them.

Anthony glanced at me and giggled the way you see kids giggling at amusement parks. I personally thought he'd need another decade before he could get into clubs, but I just smiled back.

"You'll get one too," Julian said to me.

"Sure," I said, even though getting my hands on some fake ID wasn't exactly on the top of my to-do list.

I looked down at the sidewalk and started following this little trail of broken glass from a beer bottle that had been smashed.

"It won't be around forever," Anthony said.

He had been nicer to me since Halloween.

"You're still giving it away, right?" asked Julian, as we crossed the street.

Why did they have to make the baby sound like an old VHS tape, for chrissakes?

"Stop asking me that," I said.

"Sorry for giving a shit," replied Julian.

"We're giving him up for adoption, alright?" I said.

"It's a boy?" asked Anthony.

"No, it's just not an 'it'."

Julian and Anthony glanced at each other. They had gotten the message, and we were all quiet for about a block or so.

"So why are we going to her house again?" asked Anthony.

I shrugged. "Because she needs some company."

"Is she depressed or something?" asked Julian.

"Something like that."

I supposed sitting in your room and not going to school for a week was pretty depressing. Then again, you could go to school every day and feel like killing yourself.

"I saw this show last week where a girl was so depressed she was, like, cutting herself up and stuff," said Anthony, his eyebrows all scrunched up at the memory.

Julian shook his head. "That's fucked up."

"And she was doing it to her privates," Anthony added while tripping on a crack in the sidewalk.

"*Privates?*" Julian mocked, throwing his head back and laughing.

We stopped at a red light.

"I'm serious," said Anthony.

"What are you, like six?" asked Julian.

I started laughing too. After everything that had happened, I didn't want to laugh at Anthony, but it *was* funny.

Anthony sighed. "Fine, a cunt then. Happy?"

Julian howled. "Cunt? Oh my god."

By now two women were standing with us at the corner, and they gave us dirty looks. I stopped laughing while the blood crept up to my skull, but Julian was pissing his pants. Thank god the light turned green, or else I would have had the job of shutting Julian up. I think I've managed to do that, like, never since I've known him.

Julian coughed and cleared his throat. "Just call it a vagina."

"Can we move the hell on?" I asked.

Annie's house was only three blocks away now, and the last thing I wanted on my mind was friggin' vaginas.

"Her mom's name is Patricia," I said.

"What mom wants her pregnant daughter meeting up with three guys?" Julian asked as he pulled out his cellphone from his jacket pocket and started studying the screen.

"Yeah," agreed Anthony. "Won't she think we're there to gangbang her or something?"

Julian burst out laughing again. "Gangbang? You can't be serious."

His phone rang while Anthony was blabbing away about the accuracy of the term *gangbang*.

"I have to go home," said Julian, stuffing his phone back in his jacket.

"Why?" I asked.

I can't say I was totally disappointed. Having Julian and Annie in the same room was a weird thought, even though Julian hadn't seemed bothered by the idea when I asked him yesterday on the phone. But what if he was ditching me and Anthony for something better?

"My mom," Julian explained. "She's such a bitch sometimes."

"You didn't even talk to her," said Anthony.

"It's called texting," said Julian.

"Your mom texts you?"

Julian glanced over at me and rolled his eyes. "I'll see you guys around."

"Tomorrow," I said. "At school."

Julian nodded and turned around, calling over his shoulder, "Say hey to Annie for me."

Even though I had no idea whether he could hear me, I added, "It sucks that you can't come."

But not as bad as if it had been Peter or someone else calling him; someone better than us.

When Patricia opened the door, the first thing I said was, "Annie knows we're coming." She still shot Anthony a suspicious look.

"This is Anthony," I said.

He mumbled a shy hello and extended his hand awkwardly. Patricia looked unsure but impressed. Even *I* had never shaken Patricia's hand before, and I wondered whether she was secretly wondering why Anthony hadn't gotten Annie pregnant instead.

She motioned towards the hall. "She's downstairs."

Me and Anthony took off, finding a door that looked like it could lead to a basement. As we walked down the stairs, Anthony leaned over and whispered, "Is she huge?"

I ignored him and wiped his spit from my ear.

Annie was sitting on the couch, dressed, thank god. I was a little worried she'd be wearing a nightgown or something, all stained with food and stuff, but I think she had even washed and fixed her hair. It fell around her shoulders in a way that made her face look thinner. She must have also had some kind of lip gloss on, because when I got closer, her lips were all shiny. It sort of brought me back to the summer in a weird way.

She stood up but kept her eyes on me, as though afraid to look at Anthony. I saw that the TV and DVD player were already on, and a bowl of chips sat a little too perfectly in the middle of the coffee table. She was nervous.

"Julian couldn't make it," was the first thing I said. "It's just us."

I glanced at Anthony.

"Hi," he said. He didn't shake her hand.

Annie raised hers in this little wave, and then they both looked at me as though waiting to get cues about what happened next.

I decided to take a seat on the couch, and Annie sat down at the other end. Anthony plopped himself on the floor and took off his jacket. It all felt a little weird, and I was praying that things would quickly get more normal.

"What movie are we watching?" asked Anthony, leaning over to grab some chips.

"*Erin Brokovich?*" replied Annie.

Oh man, she was *not* going to talk in questions.

Anthony nodded, even though I knew he hated the film. "After that we can watch *Transformers*," I added, pulling the DVD out of my jacket.

I thought this would cheer Anthony up, but he shot me a look that I recognized. Putting on a film with Megan Fox and not being allowed to make comments about her amazing body in front of a pregnant girl was about as torturous as watching *Erin Brokovich.*

When the movie was over, Patricia came down with some pizza. She had probably been dying to check on us since we had arrived. I was just grateful for food. The chip bowl was completely empty, and my stomach was still in knots. All I had had for lunch was a bag of M&Ms that I had bought at the drugstore. I got a 10% employee discount. Big friggin' deal.

"You guys having fun?" Patricia asked, like we were four years old.

At least she sounded nicer. I guess Anthony had passed the rapist test.

We all muttered some form of yes. I glanced at Annie, and she was actually kind of smiling, even after seeing Julia Roberts in little skirts for two hours.

Patricia plopped the pizza on the table along with some napkins and went back upstairs.

"How's it going?"

That was Anthony asking Annie. My heart almost stopped. It was weird, because as much as we were there to keep her company, I was half hoping he wouldn't talk to her. Anthony wasn't exactly a genius at saying the right thing.

"I'm fine," Annie replied, while glancing at me in that way that I knew meant she wanted me to change the subject.

"It's a good pizza," I said, grabbing my second slice of the most disgusting frozen pepperoni and mushroom I had ever had. Anthony nodded in agreement, and we just kept munching. Annie on the other hand was barely nibbling, and I worried that she was starving herself or something. I wanted to ask her about it but didn't want to embarrass her in front of Anthony.

As if on cue, Anthony stood up and wiped his hands on his pants. "Where's the bathroom?"

Annie pointed upstairs, and Anthony disappeared.

"I guess my mom asked you to come?" Annie asked, looking down at her lap.

"No."

"Bullshit."

She was sitting up taller now, but I still noticed her stomach was starting to look like this mini hill down the street from my house that I used to go tobogganing on in the winter. Low enough to climb but high enough to give you butterflies.

I noticed a couple of textbooks sitting on the floor by the couch.

"You're doing homework?" I asked.

She frowned like she suddenly had this really bad headache.

"I'm not a dropout," she said. "No matter what she told you."

I shook my head like crazy, not sure whether to duck. "How are you feeling?"

She shrugged and fell back onto the couch. "Whatever."

"How is school these days?"

Annie laughed a really sad laugh. "Oh my god, back to that already? You're worse at this stuff than a grandmother."

I cleared my throat. "Are you still going?"

Annie started pulling at a thread on the couch. "Whatever."

"You can't stop going to school."

Annie looked down at her belly. "Soon, I won't be able to get out the fucking door."

"Don't exaggerate."

Annie grabbed at her shirt. "My clothes don't fit me anymore."

"Do you need some new ones?" I asked as though I had all these connections to the maternity wardrobe underworld.

"My mom bought some," Annie replied, her eyes shifting to a department-store bag sitting by the stairs.

Without thinking, I walked over to the bag and started hauling out sweaters, pants, and tents that I couldn't figure out the back from the front.

"This is nice," I said, holding up something massive and red that looked like a top.

Annie turned her back to me as much as she could.

"You're pregnant." I said.

"More than sixteen *weeks* pregnant." She turned to me, peeling back the strands of hair stuck to her cheek. I could see she was crying. "Can you imagine me at twenty weeks? Or seven months?"

"Be quiet, Anthony will be back," I said looking up at the stairs.

"My mom's talking to him in the kitchen, don't you hear?"

I sat back down.

Annie covered her eyes. "I wish I could just be invisible for the next few months, you know?"

I leaned back on the couch. "Do I ever."

She pulled out a tissue from her pant pocket. It looked so worn down that I almost wondered whether it was still the tissue my mom had offered her two weeks back.

"It's not even about my fucking body," she said, wiping down her cheeks.

She blew her nose, and it made this sound like a foghorn. Adam used those words to describe a terrific fart I had made last Christmas Eve during dinner, and I liked how it sounded— the word *foghorn*. I had never heard one myself.

Annie tossed the tissue on the coffee table, and it landed on the pizza. I moved it away.

"Is there someone in particular giving you a hard time?" I asked.

She looked at me and laughed. "Why, are you going to beat them up for me?"

I shrugged. "I don't know."

She stared up at the ceiling.

"You have to go back to school, Annie."

She nodded.

"If you don't, they'll think they got you," I continued, feeling my whole body tense up. "They'll think they've won."

She looked at me a moment and then asked, "Why do you care?"

I didn't know what to say, so she sank back into the couch, her hands cupping her chin.

"I got a job," I said.

"Doing what?"

"Stuff at the drugstore."

I decided to leave out the whole bullcrap about being a supervisor.

Annie's eyes shifted away from mine and settled on something behind my shoulder. I saw her hand come down on her belly like she was going to hit it, but she kind of held it instead.

"My mom made an appointment at this family planning centre," she said.

That friggin' term again.

"What do we do there?"

Annie sighed and started pulling her hair back like she was going to put it in a ponytail or something. "Some social worker or agent or whatever they're called will help us find someone to adopt the baby."

Then her hair fell out of her hands, and she turned away completely.

"How do I do it, Kye?" she asked after a moment, her voice trembling.

"Do what?" I asked.

"Have this baby and not care?"

Annie leaned over and grabbed her pizza again and started munching, like she already knew I wouldn't have an answer.

I stared down at a tiny drop of pizza sauce on my thumb. In that moment grabbing a napkin felt like too much work, so I just decided to lick it off, except when I went to bring my hand to my mouth, Annie grabbed hold of it.

It was a tight grip, and when I turned to her, I noticed her pizza slice was sitting on the couch next to her overturned plate. With her other hand she was clutching her stomach, and her cheeks were pinker than I even thought possible.

"Oh my god," she said.

My thoughts suddenly went from Annie's cheek colour to her delivering a preemie right there on the carpet, all bloody and helpless.

A semi-smile appeared on her face. "Oh my fucking god."

Okay, so I could forget about the preemie on the carpet. I swallowed hard with relief, but I was still confused.

"What the hell's going on?" I asked.

"It— it—"

Anthony was coming back down the stairs and stopped when he saw Annie.

"Should we get your mom?" he asked, frozen on the last stair.

"I think it moved," said Annie, looking at me with these huge eyes, like the ones you get when you're in super shock about something but you aren't sure if it's a really bad thing.

"The baby?" I asked staring at the pink sweatshirt stretched over her stomach.

Annie nodded and her hand touched her belly again, only in a different spot. "Kind of like a muscle twitch, but that's what it's supposed to feel like at first."

"Holy shit," said Anthony, his arms flailing like a girl's.

I put my hand over Annie's stomach, even though she hadn't exactly given me permission, and she placed it on the spot. I had never felt her stomach before. It was a bit hard, like a soccer ball, only one that needed a little more air.

"Do you feel it?" she asked.

I nodded, even though I couldn't feel a thing. The big tree in my front yard shakes when it's really windy. I wondered whether the baby sort of looked like that tree.

Annie started laughing, but almost guiltily, like she wasn't sure whether she deserved to.

"I can't believe it," she whispered. "I mean, I knew it was going to happen but..."

Anthony was standing beside us now, and I could feel his excitement.

"Can I touch?" he asked.

"Wipe your friggin' hands first," I said.

But he ignored me as Annie put his hand where mine had been.

A smile slowly came over his face. "Holy crap, that's so weird."

"Did you feel anything?" I asked.

The idea of Anthony feeling the baby when I couldn't seemed beyond unfair.

"No," he admitted.

"It's so cool," Annie said to no one in particular. She looked the happiest I had seen her in a while. Her cheeks were still red, but in a healthy, outdoorsy kind of way, and her eyes shone. Sadness was still creeping into the lower part of her face though, and her jaw looked all tight, like she wasn't sure whether this was a good moment or not.

I gave her my best smile, and she smiled back, and Anthony went to get Patricia.

We never did watch *Transformers* that day.

Chapter 30

I got home just before seven that evening. My mom was practically standing in the door, like she had been peering down the street every two seconds from suppertime onwards. When I walked in, she was looking at me suspiciously, as though instead of spending a few hours with Annie like I had promised her I'd be doing, I had been busy making babies with all the girls at Fincher.

"How was it?" she asked. She was watching me take off my shoes and hang up my jacket like she was learning how to do those things for the first time.

"It was cool," I replied.

"Did you have fun?"

"The baby moved."

Suddenly, all the muscles that had been keeping her face tight and expressionless just collapsed.

"Really?" The word broke as it escaped her throat.

I nodded. "I didn't feel anything."

"It's hard so early."

I shrugged.

"How does all this make you feel?" she asked.

"I don't know," I mumbled.

Truth was, I knew deep down I was kind of excited, but admitting that would have sent my mom over the edge, and I knew she'd be up that night with my dad devising some plan to get me feeling shitty again about the whole thing.

My mom folded her hands tightly in front of her. "Your friend passed by tonight."

"Who?"

"That girl..." she began snapping her fingers like she was struggling to come up with a name. I wasn't.

"Claudia?"

I hadn't said her name out loud in forever. It felt weird, but thinking about her didn't. Within ten seconds I had made myself a sketch about what she would have looked like at that moment. Probably her hair down and some soft, pink slippers on her feet. I had no clue why I thought of the slippers, but I pictured Claudia being the type of girl that would like that sort of thing, but not in a dumb way.

"Oh, right," my mom said casually, heading towards the kitchen.

Missing Claudia's call royally sucked, no question, but I wouldn't have had anything prepared to say, and my head was still kind of fixated on what had happened just an hour ago. I wouldn't have wanted Claudia to think that I was going all gaga over the baby, which I wasn't. A couple of kicks didn't change anything, especially since I hadn't felt any of them.

Still, as I went up the stairs, I found myself trying to imagine what the vibration of a little foot or arm against a stomach felt like. But when I got to my room, I lay down and closed my eyes, and all I could think about was Claudia; my hands around her waist and her hair blowing everywhere.

* * * *

"So it moved."

"Really?"

"Yeah. What time is it there again?"

"Lunchtime."

"That's crazy."

"Why aren't you on Skype?"

"I don't know, Mom gave me this phone card."

"So it really moved."

"That's what Annie says."

"Now *that's* crazy."

"Yeah."

"Did you feel it?"

"No."

"Maybe next time."

"When are you coming home again?"

"Christmas."

"That's far."

"Don't worry, time goes by faster than you think."

Chapter 31

Julian pointed to a cluster of girls standing outside the DVD store. "Man, she looks hot."

"Which one?" asked Anthony.

"The one with the white jacket. Who else?"

Anthony and I both searched for the white jacket until we found her between two other girls that didn't look bad themselves. The white jacket one was the cutest, if you liked the fake-looking kind, like Julian did.

"Girls in white jackets always look hot," mumbled Anthony, glancing back at the copy of *The Sound of Music.*

"What do you mean?" Julian was still staring at the chick.

"Have you ever seen an ugly girl in a white jacket?" Anthony asked.

Julian looked at me and started laughing. "I don't know where he comes up with this shit."

"Name me one ugly girl in a white jacket," demanded Anthony.

"My mother has a white jacket," I offered.

Julian laughed harder.

"Old people don't count," said Anthony.

"Oh crap," Julian mumbled, "she's going."

Sure enough, Miss White Jacket and her friends were taking off down the mall.

"I bet you that fur around the hood is coyote or something," I said, turning back to the movies.

"Coyotes are ugly," Julian answered. "She so isn't."

He turned and playfully slapped Anthony's head.

"Seriously, dude, he's not getting his mom *The Sound of Music*, so just put it away."

When Anthony didn't do anything, Julian grabbed the DVD out of his hands and put it back.

"What are you supposed to get your mom anyway?" asked Anthony, shooting Julian a dirty look.

That was a hard question to answer, primarily because I wasn't shopping for my mom. Anthony had totally forgotten that her birthday was in May, not November, as I knew he would, making it the perfect set-up to shop for Claudia and not face questions from the guys. Not that Claudia's birthday had been on my radar since that first afternoon in the basement. I had Matt Miles to thank for the reminder, which was the only thing I probably would ever owe him anything for.

He had gotten these roses for his girlfriend Mandy's birthday yesterday, and she was dragging them all over school like a friggin' beauty queen, and I stood there looking at her thinking how Claudia was just not like that. She wouldn't be the type to run all over the school showing off some flowers I had gotten her, and not just because she kind of hated my guts at the moment. She just wasn't the type to think she was shit hot just because of some flowers. And that's when it clicked. November twelfth. Tomorrow.

"Why don't you get her a jewelry box or something?" asked Anthony as we walked out of the DVD store.

"Too expensive," I said, digging my hand in my pocket to feel the twenty that I had pulled out of my piggy bank. My first pay cheque wasn't coming through until next week.

"I never get my mom presents," said Julian.

Anthony frowned. "She's your mom."

Julian snorted. "So?"

"So, you should be thankful," replied Anthony.

Julian laughed. "For what? For sleeping with an asshole and making me?"

A few weeks ago, this tiny bit of personal information on Julian would have been cool. But now, after everything that had happened, I didn't know what to do with it.

Julian looked uncomfortable too and quickly changed the subject. "How are you even allowed at the mall?"

"I told my mom I had a chemistry tutorial after school," I replied.

Julian glanced at me admiringly. "He lies."

My chest kind of lightened up, and I felt a teeny less guilty about dragging him out to the mall. He was still eating lunch with us and stuff, but something had changed. I just couldn't figure out what. Then again, I had more important things to figure out, like getting the perfect gift for Claudia.

"Where the hell are we going now?" Julian asked.

"I want something to eat," said Anthony.

"I need to take a piss," I said. "I'll meet you guys in front of the drugstore."

On the way to the bathroom, I stopped in front of some store that was selling lavender and *pot pourri* and all sorts of other crap I would never get Claudia.

I kept going and was within inches of the guy's bathroom when I ran smack into someone.

The feel of the hard belly against me was the only sign I needed. It was the only thing I seemed to see these days. Not Claudia, not everyone at school that probably knew, not anything. Just that belly.

But I didn't look down at it as she pulled away from me with a "Sorry."

I was suddenly focusing on all the other things about Annie that had become familiar. I knew just the width of her shoulders and hips. I probably could have even guessed how high her head stood off from her neck, if it hadn't been for the coat collar pulled up to her ears. In some strange way, I knew her body more than I knew Claudia's.

When I met her eyes, I was half expecting her to give me one of her hesitant waves, but her hands were now behind her back, hiding something.

"What are you doing here?" she asked.

"It's a friggin' mall," I answered, then worried that I probably sounded mean, which I wasn't trying to be. "I'm shopping for a birthday present."

Her eyes narrowed. "For that girl?"

I had never talked to Annie about Claudia, and I wasn't about to tell her about the present. The subject of Claudia always seemed pointless, birthday or no birthday.

"For my mom," I replied.

Annie's face relaxed.

I looked around, half expecting Patricia to come out of the bathroom or something. Or my mom, wondering why I wasn't hanging with Mr. Nash in the chemistry lab.

"What are you doing here?" I asked.

She shrugged. "Just hanging out."

"Alone?"

"Is that a crime?"

I suddenly caught a whiff of fried food that had settled around us, and I glanced at the hand still behind her back.

"Is that McDonald's?"

She held up a bag, grease spots forming this little line right below the yellow M. I suddenly realized how hungry I was, but going to the food court would have meant less money and time for Claudia's gift.

"Can I have one?"

She passed the bag over to me, and I caught sight of her peeling nail polish.

"Is this shit even good for the baby?" I asked.

Annie pulled the bag back, but not before I managed to pull out a fry. "It's fast food, not crack."

I shoved the fry in my mouth. "I'm just asking."

She tossed the bag in the garbage can that stood a few inches from us. My stomach gurgled in protest.

"It's not like we're keeping it, anyway."

"Yeah, but we don't wanna hand over a junk-food baby."

Annie put a hand against her neck like she was sweating or something, then unzipped her jacket to show an enormous black sweatshirt that seemed to be swallowing her whole, lifeguard shoulders and all. "Why are you so mean?"

"I'm just a bit worried," I admitted.

"Why?"

I shrugged. "Nothing."

Annie stuffed her hands in her pockets self-consciously, only to nervously pull them out again, along with a bunch of crumbs that scattered to the floor.

"What do you have in there?" I asked.

"Nothing," she mumbled.

I stepped forward, and Annie looked amused.

"So you're going to go through my jacket now?"

I just pushed her hand away and dug into her pocket. She didn't fight me either, just stood patiently until I pulled out something soft and cake-ish

"Why do you have a muffin stuffed in your pocket?" I asked.

She grabbed it out of my hand and shoved it back into her jacket.

"It was my breakfast, okay?"

It suddenly dawned on me. The food, the lingering at the mall alone.

"You aren't going to school, are you?"

She turned slightly to show me her knapsack.

"What's in there, broccoli and cereal to finish up the four friggin' food groups?"

She glared. "Don't forget fish."

"Whatever."

"And dairy."

"What do you have for homework today?"

She shrugged.

"What do you have for homework?" I repeated.

"What does it matter?"

"It matters."

"If you have a future it does."

"You *have* a future, OK?"

Annie snorted. "Easy for you to say. Must be nice to walk around school without anyone knowing."

I thought about Peter and Damian.

"People know," I mumbled.

She shook her head. "Not the way they know about me."

"It's not like it's gonna last forever."

"It sure as hell is starting to feel that way."

"Don't you have any friends?" I asked, praying she would mention anyone other than Tammy.

Annie just stared at me with empty eyes.

"Everyone's a loser," she mumbled.

"You're not alone," I said sort of awkwardly.

"No, I have this to keep me company," Annie shot back, grabbing her belly only to let go after a few seconds, like it was suddenly too big and heavy.

She also started to cry. Slowly at first, as though trying to see if she could release all her pain in just a couple of tears before patting her cheeks dry and moving on. But the sobs only got louder, until she covered her face completely. A couple of ladies walked by and shot me dirty looks. To make it look like I wasn't this abusive boyfriend or whatever the hell they thought I was, I put a hand on Annie's shaking shoulder. It looked like it did the trick, and they moved on, but my hand stayed where it was.

"It's going to be alright," I mumbled.

Her fingers opened up a bit so I could see the dried lips of her mouth.

"It's not," she replied. "And what do you care, anyway?"

"I care a lot."

I don't know why I had to quantify how much I cared. Maybe it was her miserable jacket pulled so desperately over her stomach, or the fact that she was hanging around the mall. I guess I felt more sorry for her than I'd realized.

Which is why I didn't react when she suddenly threw herself forward. Her arms came up over my neck and she drew me into the tightest hug ever. Her stomach crushed mine, and I could feel her heart pound through her jacket. I hugged her back, trying not to take in the smell of her hair or her breath. Both were slowly creeping up my neck, like the way a feather tickles the skin, until the breath was hitting my nostrils, and her mouth was on mine.

I pushed my hands against her shoulders. "What the fuck?"

She kissed me again, and I moved my face away so quickly I felt a shot of pain go through my back.

"Get the hell off!"

When she didn't budge, I shoved her, and her back hit the wall with a thud that looked ten times more violent than when I had pushed her to the ground at the bus terminal. I got scared for a second that the impact would hurt the baby, especially when her hand clutched her belly. But I realized that this was just her maternal instinct kicking in. It seemed like the only thing that was real in that moment. Not Annie's body splayed against the wall, nor her look of embarrassment as she covered her eyes again. Just that motion towards her stomach; protective and strong.

Annie's eyes shifted over to something or someone else. Maybe more old ladies that were glaring at me.

"Jesus Christ, did you have the crap of the century or something?"

Julian. He was still too far to see Annie; and he definitely couldn't, I was sure of that, because his eyes were on the phone. But any second, he would look up and see her, and his face would change, and whatever peace I had managed to maintain with him would evaporate into thin air, along with whatever reputation I had left.

I turned back to Annie, without a plan of where I would hide her, but she was already running back to the bathroom, her jacket flying behind her like a cape.

Chapter 32

When I got home from the mall, I stood in the shower for what felt like hours, hot water running down my face and body. Like really hot. The kind of hot that would have gotten my dad pissed about the bill.

He was always worried about bills. I guess these are big problems when you're an adult, but I was pretty sure that what I was going through was worse, especially dealing with that whole image of Annie in those green sweatpants. The smell of her hair against my nostrils, the feel of that hours-old muffin in her pocket. I almost wanted the water to wash away the fact that I had been shopping for a gift for Claudia when I didn't even have a clue when Annie's birthday was.

I ended up buying Claudia's gift at the drugstore on my way home from the mall. The gift itself was okay; at least I thought so. An Eminem CD. I had no clue what music she liked, but I figured Eminem was cool enough. Friggin' Damian himself probably listened to him, all reflective on what the songs mean, thinking they were written for him or something.

I didn't even know that they sold CDs, but Liam told me something about diversifying and competition or something like that. He looked all proud, like it had all been his idea, this diversifying shit, even though nobody even listens to CDs anymore. I don't know why I thought Claudia did, but I didn't care all that much at that point, deciding to just hope that her parents still had a CD player lying around somewhere in the garage.

Still, there was no way I was going to return the gift. The thought of having to explain everything to Megan the cashier made me almost as nervous as the thought of giving the CD to Claudia.

I thought of calling up Annie and telling her that I ended up buying something at a drugstore. A friggin' drugstore. *Does that make you feel better, Annie?*

The CD looked even worse when I put it on my nightstand. I tried ripping off the yellow neon sticker that said $9.99 followed by like, five exclamation points, but after a few minutes I had only managed to remove a sliver of the dollar sign. Those muffin crumbs in Annie's pocket had been bigger.

I stuffed Eminem in the drawer and lay back on my bed, my head pounding. I felt like shit, and not just because of my run-in with Annie. I *was* thinking of Annie, but I was mostly thinking of the time in grade five when I was invited to this guy Justin's birthday party and Anthony wasn't.

I was half-convinced it was all a mistake anyway, because I barely knew Justin. I had to hide that present from Anthony a whole friggin' week, and even though he would have never figured it out, it killed me. I even avoided playing with him, saying that my mom had sprained her ankle or something, and I had to take care of her. He never asked me about it, but I felt guilty for weeks after that.

Claudia was different, since I didn't have another girlfriend or anything like that. Not that Claudia was my girlfriend. And even if in some twisted way Annie found out (which she wouldn't), it's not like I owed her a present.

I still wanted Eminem as far from my eyes or anyone else's as possible, so right before going to bed, I moved him from my nightstand to my dresser. The middle drawer, where I kept all the fleece pajamas that I never wore.

At around three in the morning though, I got all freaked out and stashed the CD behind this crappy soccer trophy from when I was eleven. It was the only summer I had ever taken soccer, so I guess that's why my parents wanted me to take those stupid pictures. I looked so lame in my uniform and balancing a ball on my knee like I was this badass player on the way to the World Cup or something.

When I headed off to school later that morning, my stress level was through the friggin' roof as I tried to figure out where I was going to leave this present for Claudia. I couldn't exactly hang it on her locker, unless I taped it or something, but I didn't want her thinking I had put tons of thought into this either. It was nothing but a CD pulled from a stand containing gum and *National Enquirer*, for chrissakes.

By morning recess, I had it all figured out. I'd put it on her desk in English. Of course. Why the hell hadn't I thought of this before? I just had to be the first one in class, which wasn't a problem because I had had a quiz in French just before, and I got out early, even beating Oertner to class. My seat was still warm from whoever had been there just before. Gross.

The problem, I realized soon after pulling out the CD, was that I couldn't just dump it like that on Claudia's desk. People would see it, and I didn't want to embarrass her. Or myself, for that matter. I panicked. Only five minutes to go before class started. Oertner had now shown up and was already writing some crap on the board, and other people were slowly coming in. Still no Claudia though, so I refocused.

I opened my notebook and pulled out the first blank sheet I saw. I had never made an envelope before, but how hard could it be? Sure, I didn't have one of those mini pink or yellow staplers that girls always have, but there was no time to dwell on that.

I started folding the paper up while trying to remember what the hell a proper envelope looked like. What I *did* remember was opening one that had been left on my desk in grade seven morals and ethics class, and pulling out a note with Damian's handwriting that said *you suck cock*. The fuck had been in my morals and ethics class. Don't even get me started on the irony.

My envelope for Claudia was crap; it was all crooked and the flap was way too short, but with barely a couple of minutes to go, it didn't matter. I stuffed the CD in and put it on her desk. Would she know it was for her and open it? I thought about taking it back and writing her name on it, but the class was filling up now, and I could just see someone yelling across the class, "Hey Claudia, you got a package," or something stupid like that. I didn't have Damian in any of my classes this year, but jerks in general weren't exactly a dying species.

I took a deep breath, wondering how the heck I could be excused from class and somehow drop back into reality a couple of hours from now; in the hall or somewhere where Claudia would be holding the CD to her chest and bouncing towards me, all excited.

There she was. Her hair was up in this messy ponytail, and she looked friggin' amazing. Her cheeks were kind of pink, like she had just come in from the cold, and she had this low-cut top that pushed her tits up just enough for the world to know that they were awesome.

I even convinced myself for a second that she had worn that top for me. This was, after all, the first English class since she had passed by my house. Or maybe my mom was wrong, and she had never been by. Maybe it had been Tammy or something. And now friggin' Eminem was sitting on her desk, and...Ryan Pacetti was walking in with Claudia. No, talking to her was more like it. And she was smiling, her head bowed down all shyly, like the way she used to smile at me.

To say this sucked doesn't even begin to describe how much this sucked. Ryan was one of those guys that every guy would want to be like if guys worried about that kind of stuff. I bet his parents were banking on him being Prime Minister or something.

I stared straight ahead, my eyes glued to all the white on the board that Oertner had just written out. The words might as well have been written in Chinese, since I was listening to Claudia behind me drop her books on the desk and slide into her chair, all the while saying something or other to crusty Ryan.

I would normally have been interested in listening in, except I was too busy staying focused on whether she had seen my sad envelope. She was probably ignoring it, like I was scared she would. I threw my head on my desk and closed my eyes. I should have just called her back yesterday. The gift was such a bad idea. A shitty idea. A crappy-shit-diarrhea idea. And I still had fifty minutes of class to go through before I could find a hole to die in.

"Do you have a pen?"

Claudia. Or was it? When I dared to turn around, sure enough, she was looking at me. Almost smiling, if I really wanted to get specific. I rummaged through my pencil case.

If her showing up at my house was any proof that I still had a chance with her, the blue-ink Bic that I was passing over sealed the deal.

Her eyes kind of stayed glued to mine for a second, and then she smiled for real. I smiled back, all the while very aware of my envelope still sitting on the desk. I didn't know whether to keep the conversation going or just turn around and crawl into my notebook at the agony that Eminem was causing me. I had about a minute to decide before Mr. Oertner and his noisy keys turned around and started the class.

"Hey," I said.

"Hey," she answered, opening up her books.

I turned slightly in my seat to keep the conversation going. "My mom told me you came by on Sunday."

She kind of frowned, and I wasn't sure if she'd just deny it. Perhaps that hadn't been the best opening. To make matters worse, Oertner decided to interrupt this hopeful conversation with "OK class, let's get going."

But Oertner had it all wrong. I wanted to slow down, at least long enough for Claudia to open the envelope. But Oertner was already scribbling like mad on the blackboard, so I gave her a small smile and turned back around, praying that she probably wanted a little privacy to see what my envelope was all about.

Lunch was right after English, so I decided to wait for Claudia to come out of class. I wasn't sure whether she'd want to talk to me, but after that pen loan, I was willing to take my chances.

Standing outside the door, I poked my head around, trying to spot her, sort of like people do at airports. There was no way I was going to call out her name, since I never yelled, not even if I was on the scariest roller coaster. Not that I'd ever go on a roller coaster. When Claudia walked out, our eyes met. Even better, Ryan was nowhere in sight.

"Your mom said you were at Annie's," Claudia said as we started down the hall together.

Christ, leave it to my mom to mess up the one good thing that I seemed to have going for myself.

"Yeah," I answered, since there was no point in denying it, then quickly adding, "She's depressed," Girls just loved that melodrama stuff.

Claudia moved in closer. "Is she okay?"

"I think so," I answered. I couldn't get away from the subject of Annie too soon.

She pulled the Bic out of her pocket. "Thanks a ton."

I wished she had been thanking me for the CD instead, but it just stayed tucked between two pages of her notebook. At least she hadn't left it on the desk.

We were at my locker within minutes. I decided to fool myself into thinking that it was the natural meeting point for us right before lunch, rather than the more obvious fact that my locker was the closest to English class.

"Are you and Ryan eating lunch together or something?" I blurted out.

For some reason that only losers would understand, I wanted to know for sure.

She looked at me weirdly. "Don't think Rachel would like that."

Rachel was this super popular girl in our grade. I had also forgotten that she was Ryan's girlfriend. She had a cute body, I had to admit, but Claudia was way prettier.

"Right." I could only pray that my smile didn't look too relieved.

Claudia suddenly looked sad.

"What's happening with us?" she whispered as she looked down.

Us. This nice feeling came over me, and I almost giggled.

Claudia, on the other hand, looked like something had been ripped out of her gut to give me the nice feeling that was in mine.

I began playing with the locker door, wondering what the hell I could say that would resemble what she wanted to hear.

"Wanna have lunch together?"

"What's up with you and Annie?"

As a stupid attempt to get us back on the subject of our potential lunch, I pulled my lunch bag out of the locker and closed the door.

"Nothing," I answered. "We're just..." my voice trailed off and Claudia looked annoyed.

"Having a baby," she said.

I quickly looked around to see who could have heard her.

"Everyone knows, you know," she said.

"Not everyone," I replied after catching my breath.

"People just don't wanna hurt your feelings."

"I wouldn't be so sure," I repeated, thinking about Damian and everyone else that didn't give a shit about my feelings.

Claudia shrugged, like she was exhausted.

"Anyways, if you have other plans for lunch, I understand," I mumbled.

She stood there for a moment, staring at me, before she headed for the doors and went outside. I had a gut feeling that she wanted me to follow her, so I did. When I got closer, Claudia lifted her head, her eyes watery. "Can I see you sometime?"

I gulped hard. "When?"

"I don't know," she answered, now crying. "Like, Saturday maybe?"

"I don't think my parents—"

"It's not like it'll be around forever," she interrupted, wiping her cheeks. "The baby, I mean."

I couldn't stand watching her cry, so looked over her shoulder at a group of kids walking across the football field.

"It's gonna be adopted, right?"

"That's the plan," I answered.

Claudia suddenly shoved me. "What other choice is there?" She started talking faster, like people who have meltdowns do. I almost got scared. "Pay for diapers with your fucking allowance?"

As I desperately tried to think of something to say that showed that I gave a shit, she took off for the school, like she was feeling the cold around us for the first time.

Chapter 33

Friday couldn't have been a crappier day to visit an adoption agency. Don't ask me what would have been a perfect day to do it; all I know is that Friday sure as hell wasn't it. A weekend cooped up with my parents after this event only meant a ton of discussions that I didn't feel like having.

It was already bad enough that my mom had gone behind my back and set up this appointment "in collaboration" with Patricia—those are my dad's words, but it still felt like betrayal to me, and I wanted to scream the whole friggin' drive to Open Arms.

Could anyone come up with a tackier name for an adoption agency? Besides, it wasn't like it was open arms all around. The only people with open arms were the ones *getting* the baby. The real parents had more like empty ones.

Sheila was the name of our counsellor, or agent, or whatever it was that she called herself when we arrived. She seemed nice enough as she invited us all to sit in these leather-looking chairs. Annie and I sat next to each other. Since our run-in at the mall, she had fixed herself up. Her hair was put up in this kind of bun, and she had aimed for a fashion level above sweats with some actual jeans.

Sheila sat behind her desk and folded her hands. I couldn't help but notice her nails; they were long and purple. Kind of trashy for an adoption agency if you asked me.

"So," she said, a big smile opening across her face. "Shall we begin?"

That's how we all got started, with Sheila waving her arms around a lot as she walked me and Annie through the whole process, what we had to do, complete medical and social histories, blah blah blah. And then she said something about open adoption, and Annie spoke up for the first time.

"Is that where the birth parents have some kind of contact with the child?"

Sheila's smile got bigger, if that was even possible. "That's right."

Annie shook her head so hard, I thought the whole bun would come undone. "We don't want that."

I sat up. "Why not?"

Annie looked at me. "Because we would be in this baby's life forever."

She dragged out the word *forever* to make it sound like it was ten syllables or something.

I looked over at the clock on the wall. We had already been in that office for half an hour. *That* sure as hell felt like forever.

"We need to talk about that," I said, more to Sheila than to Annie.

"I don't need to know when it learns how to walk and talk," Annie said.

"Well, maybe I do," I replied, even though I had no idea whether I actually did or not.

I didn't know what my parents were thinking at this point, and I didn't look over at them to find out.

Annie sank in her chair. "I just want this whole nightmare to be over."

Sheila's smile was still there, like it was holding on to whatever morsel of positivity was still left in the room. "It's important that the birth parents are aligned in all the decisions made."

I glanced at my dad, who had this look on his face that meant *Don't be a retard.*

Patricia gave a similar look to Annie.

"Can you send us some profiles of parents?" Patricia asked Sheila.

Sheila nodded. "We have some wonderful waiting couples."

I couldn't wait to meet all these friggin' wonderful waiting people.

* * * *

About thirty minutes later, we were all standing around outside Open Arms, the information forms that Sheila had given to me and Annie flapping in the wind. Annie handed hers to Patricia, and I folded mine a million times so it would fit in my jacket pocket. I didn't feel like giving it to anyone.

It was friggin' cold, and Patricia and my parents looked at each other like the way me and Claudia had looked at each other after that ice cream at Safari's. Like they were trying to figure out what to do next. Meanwhile, me and Annie just kind of stood around freezing our asses off.

Finally, my mom suggested that we all "relax" at the coffee shop across the street. Annie glanced at me like I had this virus or something. I wanted to give her a glare that said that

I was just as anxious to share a friggin' coffee with her, but I got paranoid that Patricia was watching, waiting to catch me fucking up yet again.

We all slowly made out way across the parking lot, me staying behind my parents, who were talking to Patricia about getting their winter tires put on or some crap like that. Their fake chumminess annoyed the shit out of me.

My parents and Patricia pointed me and Annie towards a table for two by the window, and they chose something all the way at the other end. Hell, you would have thought we were on some kind of date or something.

Annie plopped herself down on a chair like she didn't care either way, but I could tell she couldn't have hated my guts more. Patricia passed this brown envelope to her before following my parents across the restaurant.

Annie's eyes were glued to the table, and she didn't take her jacket off—like she was keeping it on in case she had to bolt suddenly. I decided to keep mine on too, even though it was kind of uncomfortable.

"What do you feel like having?" I asked.

Annie shrugged. "Nothing."

I went over to the front counter and ordered a hot chocolate even though I didn't feel like having anything either.

When I got back to the table Annie was staring out the window, the envelope sort of leaning against what looked like a dessert menu.

"What's that?" I asked, nodding towards the envelope.

Annie grabbed it and put it right in front of her. "Nothing."

"Fine." I sat down and blew a bit on my cup.

We didn't say anything for a couple of minutes. I looked over at my parents, who couldn't have made it more obvious that they were more than interested in what me and Annie were discussing, which wasn't much at the moment.

I glanced out the window. "It's getting cold outside."

"So?"

"You should wear a hat or something."

She almost laughed. "I guess I should get a ski jacket for the baby too?"

I sighed. "I'm just trying to help."

"Awesome." Annie rolled her eyes.

I glanced over at my dad who gave me a lousy thumbs-up.

I turned back to Annie. "Look, I'm sorry about the other day at the mall."

Annie suddenly grabbed the mysterious envelope and tossed it across the table. It missed landing in my hot chocolate by a hair.

"Easy," I said.

"I bet that's what you like calling me to your friends."

"What?"

She shook her head and pointed to the envelope.

I picked it up. It felt too light to contain a bomb.

If Annie moved any more in her seat, she would fall right off.

"Open it," she said, irritated.

I was afraid to. Had Tammy taken pictures of me and Claudia? I suddenly had a worse thought. Had Annie lost the baby and taken a picture of it for a souvenir or something twisted like that? Of course, it couldn't be that. Why would anyone sit through all that crap with Sheila unless they had to? Besides, Annie didn't look devastated enough, except for her eyes, which were sort of tired-looking. I wondered if I looked that old too.

"Will you just look at it?"

I opened the envelope. My hands were shaking, and it took a bit of fumbling before I pulled it out. I wasn't sure what it was at first. It looked like one of those shots of a tornado that you see on television, before things get really crazy and roofs are yanked from houses and stuff. A lot of black with white streaky patches.

What the hell was this? I moved the picture further away, the way my dad does when he has to read something and doesn't have his glasses. That's when I saw the head. It looked huge, and really bony. And then the little puffs of white, which I knew from Internet research were its hands.

"Where did you get this?" I asked.

Annie rolled her eyes. "Walmart."

"When did you go?"

"Yesterday."

I threw my hands up in the air. "What the fuck?"

Annie threw her hands up too, but in a mocking way. "Oh, Kye, you sound angry."

I looked over at Patricia, who was sipping whatever the hell she had ordered while listening to something my dad was saying. As though sensing that someone was watching her, she glanced in my direction, her eyes almost expressionless. Not at all like Adam's when my parents went for my ultrasound.

I've heard the story enough times. Adam oohed and aahed as they smoothed the jelly over my mom's stomach, and kept wanting to touch it. He was only four. It wasn't his kid on that screen, just a little brother that was going to steal all his toys.

Not his flesh and blood.

I felt my anger rise. "You didn't call me."

Annie crossed her arms. "I didn't think you'd be interested."

"Because I wouldn't shove my tongue down your throat?"

She turned her head away like I had slapped her, and I could see her body tensing up. With every second of silence that passed, I imagined her gathering more and more courage to tell me off. But what could she say? That I was an asshole for not making out with her? She had gone for a friggin' ultrasound without me. Which was worse?

For a fleeting second, I asked myself whether it was for the best that Annie had gone alone. Maybe it wasn't so bad looking at the picture under the soft light of this orange lamp hanging over the table, rather than in some little doctor's office, holding Annie's limp hand and thinking about the great future ahead with this black and white thing with a spine that looked like Lego blocks all stacked nicely together.

"She couldn't tell me if it was a boy or a girl."

I looked at the picture again. It was hard to believe that this was going to be anything other than an alien.

"Can I borrow this?" I asked.

Annie looked at me suspiciously. "Why?"

"You've had this since yesterday."

"My appointment was at four."

"Whatever." I was in no mood to argue. "Can I?"

She pulled the picture out of my hand and slid it back into the envelope before handing it to me.

"Be careful." She almost whispered this.

I glanced over at my parents. They had probably seen the envelope. I pulled the information form Sheila had given us from my pocket and started unfolding it.

"What are you doing?" asked Annie.

"I don't want them asking about the envelope," I replied. "Unless your mom feels like telling them."

Annie shook her head. "She would want you to tell them."

How friggin' thoughtful of her.

"And since I don't feel like telling them, let's talk about something else that I can report back."

"Okay," replied Annie, suddenly on my side. "Are you gonna fill out the form?"

"I think it's all stupid."

"Me too."

I shook the paper a bit. "I mean, what do they mean by social history?"

Annie shrugged. "I guess if you take drugs, that sort of stuff."

I couldn't help but laugh.

Annie almost smiled. "Are you gonna come over and look at parent profiles with me?"

I stopped laughing.

"Well?"

"Sure," I said with a lot of hesitation. "Let me know when Sheila sends you some."

Annie took a deep breath. "Hopefully today."

"Hopefully," I mumbled back, trying hard to ignore the excited look on Annie's face. Like she was going to friggin' Disney World or something.

I found myself secretly praying Annie wouldn't hear from Sheila again until Christmas.

Out of the corner of my eye, I saw my parents and Patricia getting up from their table.

I put the papers in the envelope and stuck it in my jacket.

"Are we good to go?" asked Patricia as she approached our table, my parents not far behind.

Annie looked at me. "Don't lose it." She got up and left before my parents got close enough to hear what she had said.

Chapter 34

On Saturday, I put the envelope in a grocery bag and carried it to work like it was my lunch. I didn't want to leave it at home, in case my parents found it. All they knew was that I had put the information form from Sheila in the envelope, not that it contained a picture of their future grandchild.

I decided to call him Joseph, after my dead grandfather. The name came to me that morning, staring at the photo as I got dressed for work. I knew that we didn't know whether it was a boy or a girl, but it looked like a Joseph either way. Don't ask me why. He looked pretty fragile, his little hand up against his head like he had a headache already. I could definitely relate.

I didn't know how well Joseph would do in the locker at work. They were pretty small, those lockers, and after stuffing in my jacket there wasn't much room. I never knew how Liam did it—he had a briefcase, a jacket, *and* his lunch.

I spent the morning stocking baby formula, of all things, and watching the people walking up and down the aisle picking stuff up. There was one mom with a little newborn stuffed in this knapsack thingy, tied to her chest. I tried to figure out whether she was happy or not, but I couldn't tell.

At lunch, I walked to the employee lounge—that's what Liam called it, even though it looked a helluva a lot more like an oversized prison cell. The place was still empty, so I pulled Joseph out of my locker and just looked at him a bit while I nibbled on my sandwich, like I was reading the paper or something. I imagined myself holding him; the head sort of nestled against my neck, the little hands grabbing and touching my face, just like that lady with her newborn.

I usually ate alone because there wasn't really anyone else to talk to except for ancient Darlene who had been working there since before the place opened. She collected crucifixes. All I had to do was look in her direction and she'd start telling me about them. Once, just after I had started, she had shown me some pictures of her living room, packed with crucifixes. I guess it was her way of breaking the ice.

I finished at three, and when I got out, Claudia was standing there. At first, I didn't see her, because the wind was blowing Joseph around like crazy, and I was getting all paranoid that the bag would just take off down the street.

"Hey!"

My head snapped up at the sound of her voice.

Claudia's head was bent a little, away from the wind, and she was wearing these baby blue rain boots that went all the way up to her knees.

"Hi," I said, my hand loosening its grip on the plastic bag for a second.

From the way she was standing in front of the drugstore, it almost looked like she had come to pick me up from work. Joseph kept blowing around, but now I saw it as him cheering me on or something. I come up with the weirdest shit sometimes.

I suddenly felt a few drops of rain on my head, so I unzipped my jacket and put Joseph in, hoping Claudia would be too busy worrying about the rain and her hair to notice. All girls seemed to worry about this.

But she was just kind of looking up at the sky.

And then it really started to pour. Claudia opened up an umbrella that I hadn't noticed until now. She pulled me under. I loved it when she touched me.

"Anthony told me where you worked," she said, our faces so close I could smell this sweet mint on her breath.

All I could do was nod, while trying to make sure Joseph's little body hadn't got caught in my jacket zipper.

"What's in the bag?"

"Just some photocopies for a project," I replied. I wasn't ready to show Joseph to anyone yet, not even to Claudia.

My cell rang, and I fished it out of my pocket.

"Can you come over?" Annie asked when I picked up.

"What's wrong?" I asked, glancing at Claudia, who had suddenly taken an intense interest in the umbrella handle.

"Sheila has sent some waiting people," she said and hung up.

I sighed and looked at Claudia.

"Who was that?" she asked. Her voice sounded tense, like she was trying not to show that she already hade a pretty good idea.

"I need to quickly go over."

I realized I hadn't even said her name. Annie was so present in our lives it didn't matter what me and Claudia did in a school hallway, or how closely we stood under this umbrella.

Claudia nodded understandingly, and I wondered whether she realized that she couldn't come along. That everything about Annie's house would tell her that she didn't belong.

But Claudia just handed me her umbrella. "I'll wait there." She pointed to the bus shelter at the corner. "Give me your photocopies."

Joseph. If he came along with me, Annie would want him back.

"Why do you look so weird?" Claudia asked.

I looked down at the plastic bag then up at Claudia. "You have to be careful," I said as I handed the bag over to her.

She giggled and held on to the bag all innocently, which was why I felt really shitty about having her stay in a dirty bus shelter. Who knew how long I'd be? But without another word, Claudia had slipped into the shelter and sat on the bench, cradling Joseph in her lap.

Annie pointed to the computer screen. "They look nice."

We were sitting in her living room, looking at pictures of rich, nice, childless people, or as Sheila had called them in her e-mail, "waiting families".

"Well, they aren't gonna look like pedophiles," I replied impatiently. "And when did you get these again?"

"Yesterday," Annie replied.

"Why didn't you send them to me?"

Annie glanced at me, annoyed.

"What about her?"

She was pointing to a lady leaning against a tree with a bucket of what looked like apples. I once went with my fifth grade class on a field trip, and whenever the teacher wasn't looking, Damian would try and push me off the ladder. I hated apple picking.

I shook my head. "I don't like her."

Annie sighed. "What's your problem?"

"Nothing, alright?"

"She's sweet."

"She's holding a basket of apples."

"So?"

"So..." My voice trailed off here as I figured out what to say next. "So, imagine the baby is there, somewhere, in the shade or something, right? And she's so busy picking those stupid apples that she forgets about him." I took a breath. "Or her."

Annie looked at me like I had just been dropped from Mars. "Besides, I didn't realize we had to make our choice in the next five minutes," I added.

A sad look crossed Annie's face, and she nodded towards the kitchen where Patricia was doing whatever she was doing. She hadn't said a word to me when I walked in, but I was pretty sure she was listening to everything we were saying. Every friggin' word.

So I had gone from being a sperm that didn't have a say in anything, to a puppet in this dumb-ass charade of good, responsible parenting.

"Can't you e-mail me this stuff?" I shifted in my seat. I was suddenly restless and wanted to get the hell out. Besides, there was Claudia.

Patricia appeared drying her hands with a tea towel that, for some reason, I was pretty sure she was imagining as my head.

"How about you take some time to discuss it now?" she asked.

I glanced at Annie, whose eyes were glued to the screen, but I could tell they weren't really looking at anything.

"Isn't she gonna want a say in this?" I muttered when Patricia had gone back to the kitchen.

"Yes I will," Patricia yelled. "And so will your parents."

"She wants to have a meeting next week." Annie's voice was so low I barely made out what she said. "So we have to pick someone before then."

I turned and stared at the faces covering the computer screen. Little thumbnails of smiles and nice hairdos. I suddenly felt overwhelmed.

Annie started reading Miss Applepicking's letter out loud.

"Don't," I interrupted.

"Why not?"

"Because it's crap. They want the baby, and they have more money than we do." I crossed my arms. "Tell us something we don't know."

"She's a single mom," Annie said.

"Nothing wrong with that," Patricia hollered. Man, could that woman's voice travel.

"Do you want a single mom for our baby?" I whispered.

Annie stared at me, her eyes getting big. Maybe talking about single moms with Annie wasn't such a good idea, since she had been raised by one, and I guess she hadn't turned out half-bad, although she *was* pregnant.

It was funny, because this was the first reaction I had seen from her in a while, so I didn't mind her looking at me like I was a freak. Except her face just stayed like that for what felt like forever, all eyes.

"What?" I finally asked.

She turned back to the computer. She looked shy all of a sudden, like she was deciding whether to tell me off or stuff her head under the blanket that lay on the arm of the couch right next to her. I wondered if that was how she looked that night at the pool, and I suddenly felt like shit for not being able to remember.

Then her hands brushed the surface of the keyboard. "You called it..."

"What?" I asked.

"Ours," she finally said. "You called it ours."

Annie turned and looked straight at me. She almost looked like she had been cast under some spell. Like she almost believed that this one word that had slipped out was going to change everything between us and that lump under her sweatshirt that I had started calling Joseph.

And then, just as quickly, she rolled her eyes and muttered something I didn't understand.

"Let's keep looking," I said, but Annie was already looking intently at the profiles, to ease her awkwardness or mine; I couldn't tell which.

"There's Kelly and David." She pointed to a picture of a couple hugging each other in front of a Christmas tree. What was it with trees, for chrissakes?

"Dear Birth Mother," Annie began to read.

"What about the father?" I asked. It felt weird saying that word out loud.

Annie ignored me and continued reading. "We can't imagine what you must be going through." Her voice started cracking and she stopped there.

I leaned over and pulled the computer onto my lap. "Forget them. They're blond."

"What's wrong with blonds?"

"They're just fake."

Claudia was a blond, but she didn't count, for some reason that was convenient in this stupid argument of mine.

I pointed to the screen. "The only thing missing from this picture is a kid dressed up in one of those tacky Christmas outfits."

Annie was half smiling.

"You want that to be your kid?" I asked.

And the smile was gone.

"Our kid," I mumbled, but it was too late. Annie's face kind of crumpled, and she buried it in her arm.

Patricia magically appeared at this moment and got comfortable, leaning against a bookcase.

"We'll e-mail you the profiles so you can take your time looking at them," she said. "Then I'll call your parents."

There was no way for that last part not to sound like a threat.

"I'll get going," I mumbled.

I headed towards the front door, not even waiting for anyone to show me out, which is why I was surprised when Annie suddenly stepped out with me, her white socks tiptoeing on the porch as if it was coated in ice.

"You can't change your mind now," she said, with her eyes on the driveway the whole time; it was black from the rain.

I didn't say anything, and Annie went inside again, which was fine by me, since I wasn't ready to find out what she meant, even though I had a pretty good idea.

Our baby. The words kept running through my head as I walked away from Annie's house.

My baby. I almost let go of Claudia's umbrella.

Holy shit, Claudia.

I dashed over to the drugstore, and was relieved to see her still there. In the bus shelter, everything exactly as I had left it. It was only when I got closer that I saw Claudia's face through the foggy glass pane. Joseph was still in her lap, but her eyes were wide, like something had changed. Something big. And I was suddenly reminded of how long I had been gone.

Chapter 35

"You're still not on Skype."

"I like the phone card."

"How's it going?"

"Annie wants to give the baby to some apple lady."

"What?"

"Nothing. Annie went for the ultrasound."

"Really?"

"I have the picture."

"Did you show Mom and Dad?"

"Are you nuts?"

"What does it look like?"

"I think he's a boy."

"Why?"

"Don't know. Just do. Is it hot down there?"

"Yeah, it's beautiful. One thousand times better than Wildwood."

"Lucky."

Chapter 36

"How much money does your mom make?" I asked Claudia the following Tuesday at school during break.

"Why do you wanna know?" she asked, looking at my fingers as they wound through hers.

"Like, twenty thousand or something?"

She shrugged. "Maybe forty?"

"Wow, that's a lot."

"What's a lot?"

Julian. I wasn't expecting to see him until lunch, so I was half-surprised and half-flattered when he poked his head between me and Claudia. That was until he moved slightly, and I saw Peter standing behind him.

"Forty thousand dollars," replied Claudia.

Julian made this snorting sound that he makes when you say something dumb. "That's nothing. My dad makes, like, five hundred grand a year."

Claudia's eyes widened. I was too busy trying to figure out how many breaks Julian and Peter had spent together recently to be impressed.

Peter laughed, and Claudia for some reason joined him. It was the last thing I felt like doing. If I worked at the drugstore full time, I could make about sixteen thousand a year or something like that. It hadn't looked so bad on the piece of paper I had scribbled on last night, but next to Julian's dad it looked friggin' hopeless.

Julian glanced at me. "Why?" he asked. "Looking for a raise at the drugstore?"

I didn't want to notice the way Julian poked Peter as he said this, but it was hard to miss. Thank god that Claudia was still holding my hand. The cold metal of her big clunky ring cooling my skin was the only thing remotely comforting at that moment.

"It's just a math project," I mumbled.

"Who the hell gets projects in math?" asked Peter.

He looked at Julian, and a good thing too, because I didn't know how I would manage under Peter's gaze. So far we had managed to steer clear of anything to do with Annie and the baby, and I wanted it to stay that way, especially in front of Claudia.

Julian was different. His reactions were one thing about him I could still predict with pretty decent accuracy. Like what was happening right now. The slightly raised eyebrows, the stiffened jaw.

"Who *does* get a math project?" he asked.

Claudia put her hair behind her ear. "I have to go."

She planted a small kiss on my cheek before taking off down the hall, Peter checking her out as I silently wished for that kiss to have lasted long enough to stuff my face in her hair and let everything around me disappear.

Once Claudia had turned the corner, Peter punched Julian's shoulder. "See you after school, man."

He walked off, but Julian didn't look like he was going anywhere. He just started playing with his phone the way people do to look busy.

"What are you doing with him after school?" I asked, turning to my locker.

I started going through my books, trying to remember which friggin' subject I had next, but nothing was coming to me. I finally pulled out about four notebooks and prayed that one of them was what I'd need. I slammed my locker door as the first bell rang.

Julian's hands were still all over his phone like he was getting texts from friggin' god himself.

"What are you doing?" he asked.

"Standing here," I answered, trying to smile.

Julian's eyes rolled. "What are you *doing*?"

"Nothing," I forced out.

He put his phone away. "Have you changed your mind or something?"

I hoped that he couldn't see how hard I was swallowing. "No."

"Well, if you ever do, just take one look at her." His chin nodded towards the space beside me where Claudia had stood just seconds earlier, "And ask yourself, 'Do I want my friend Julian fucking her?'"

He called himself my friend. This sounded so amazing that the colour only started draining from my face as the rest of what he said sank in.

Julian started laughing. "Relax, dude, I'm joking."

The second bell rang.

I suddenly felt majorly thirsty, but the fountain was way at the other end of the hall.

"Where's Anthony?" I asked, remembering him suddenly.

Julian shrugged. "I don't know, but you shouldn't forget about him either."

Chapter 37

A couple of days later, stepping out of the drugstore, it stank bad enough to make me think of being a kid again. The rain had been pouring down all day and had left a smell that could only be one thing. Worms.

Me and Anthony used to find the longest and ugliest worms and cut them in half. Then we'd grab each other's jackets and jump up and down in excitement and disgust at the worm still moving, before we both felt friggin' guilty. Then I'd be left to smash the worm out of its misery, while Anthony cried like a baby. Sometimes it took a bloody long time to kill that worm too.

It was pitch-black out, even though it was only 6:30. I was hungry and cold, so I decided to take a shortcut through the park.

Some guys were chilling on the bench facing the swings. My gut rose, and whatever hope I had that they were chess club geeks was smashed when they laughed. Only cold-hearted assholes laughed like that. Especially those like the dude sitting up on the bench. Two others were kind of standing around. I could handle two of anything, but three was bad news.

I looked over my shoulder. There was still time to go back to the street without looking like a loser. I could have forgotten something at the drugstore or decided at the last minute to take a bus. All these possible excuses were running through my mind when a voice called out, "Hey, is that him?"

I think it was the dude on the bench but I wasn't sure.

"Hey dude, how's it going?" he asked.

I gulped down whatever food was in my system and stuffed my hands in my pockets, just in case I had to use them for all the karate moves I didn't know. The path I was on would lead me right to that bench, and the only alternative was the grass, which gave off this glow like it was littered with diamonds or something. I didn't need to put my foot on it to know that it was soaked through. I froze in indecision before quickly bending over and yanking at my jacket zipper like it was broken.

When in doubt, make it look like you're super busy with something. That's my own advice, not Dr. Jacobi's, and it's gotten me out of a few potentially embarrassing situations. That's why I always carry a jacket along with me. Even in a heat wave in August, I'll be the guy with a jacket. It's a useful strategy, as long as you can live with the fact that you usually end up becoming aware of something else that's friggin' abnormal about yourself. Like just then, I suddenly realized I was still wearing my ugly work uniform.

"Hey," said a new voice. "Hold up."

My fingers, still on my zipper, began to shake.

"Where are you running to?"

I turned around. Beneath the streetlamp, I could see stringy hair, a tall build, and a dark jacket, probably red.

"No-nowhere," I replied.

"No-no-no-nowhere," he mimicked.

The other two broke into wild laughter, and I was able to locate them as standing somewhere behind me.

"Is your voice fucked up or something?" Red Jacket asked.

"No," I answered.

I felt a shove on my back, and it took me a second to realize I had been pushed. Not hard enough to fall, but it was close. I had to be prepared in case there was a follow-up. Like now. I turned around and gave my best glare, which must have had a lot of impact, considering how friggin' dark it was.

"You got that girl knocked up, right?" asked one of the two guys behind me.

Red Jacket shook his head. "You'll have to excuse my nosy friend."

I somehow managed to zip my jacket closed. Normally I hated being tickled by the zipper right underneath my chin, but now it made me feel safe in some strange way.

"Dude, you scared the boy," shouted Red Jacket over my shoulder.

Some more laughing. Then I felt their bodies come closer until I knew I was surrounded.

The pushing continued. First one person then the other; they were each having their turn while Red Jacket just watched. He was clearly the leader of this friggin' trio, but I couldn't figure out anything else, like whether he went to Fincher, like Tammy, or whether I had seen his jacket in an aisle at the drugstore.

"Do I know you?" I asked.

They all laughed, and Red Jacket responded with a push of his own; he made it a good one too, and when I fell back, there was no one to catch me. My ass hit the ground before I could do anything to break my fall. I didn't have to look up at Red Jacket to feel his pride as he watched me sitting on the wet pavement like a pathetic one-year-old.

Before I could even think of getting up, a wet shoe was on my shoulder. It belonged to one of the others, who just stood frozen in this one-legged stance.

"So is it really true about the girl ?" asked Red Jacket.

I shook my head, but this only made them laugh harder than ever.

"You shouldn't lie," said one of the others.

"Shut up," said Red Jacket. Then he turned to me. "You really shouldn't," he repeated.

My underwear felt pretty soaked through at this point, but I tried to just be grateful that my face wasn't hamburger meat.

"Yes," I said.

They all turned and gave each other high-fives. Then Boot put his foot down, and I slowly stood up. It felt like my underwear had pruned up and gotten lost somewhere deep in my asshole, but I resisted all temptation to put my hand anywhere in that vicinity.

"Nothing to be ashamed of," said Red Jacket. "Hell, I'd tell everyone."

"I'd whip my dick out and show the world," added Boot.

"Hey," said Red Jacket, "that's a great idea."

They wanted me to believe this *idea* had just come to them, but I could see it had been part of the plan all along; something thrown in and discussed for anywhere from a few minutes before spotting me to hours before, or even days.

Boot and the third dude started hopping up and down like kids getting Happy Meals. Red Jacket didn't budge, looking real confident that this idea would become a reality soon enough without having to force anything.

"No, what?" asked Red Jacket.

It was only then that I realized I was shaking my head.

"You do have a dick, don't you?" asked Boot.

The third laughed. "Maybe he doesn't."

My hands stopped shaking and everything felt numb.

Red Jacket sighed. "Well, now I'm curious."

"Me too," said the other two in quasi-unison.

"You have to show us this dick," said Red Jacket.

Boot and Number Three started falling over each other laughing. I wanted more than anything to sit down on the ground again.

"Let's go, dude," said Red Jacket. His voice had lost all the phony friendliness from a minute ago and was now just plain mean. "Need some help?"

"We'll give you a clue," said Boot, stepping forward.

There was no way Boot was a jock, because his slap wasn't even close to my crotch area. I couldn't take any chances, though, so I sort of doubled over like I was in friggin' agony, and this kept them amused for a few seconds until everything got quiet again. I couldn't hear cars pass on the street, or even a bark from a dog being walked. It was like everything had gone dead.

I straightened up and took a deep breath, my jaw muscles twitching like mad as I unzipped.

They all shut up, like they were in almost as much shock as I was. I stopped before the zipper was all the way down, but Red Jacket said, "I don't see it yet."

When he did, he shook his head. "Man, did she feel anything?"

Boot laughed. I didn't hear a peep out of Number Three.

I went to put it back inside, but Red Jacket grabbed my arm in time.

"Shit, Elliott, you almost touched it," said Boot.

Red Jacket turned away from me, and I could see Boot stepping back. "Sorry, man," he muttered.

My brain started running through all the guys I had ever met called Elliott, but the only one I kept hitting on was the kid from that movie *E.T.*

Red Jacket looked back down at me and shook his head. "Pretty fucking sad, dude."

"Pretty sad indeed," added Boot.

This made Number Three laugh. "Indeed?"

Red Jacket held up his hand, and the two others shut up. "Did you say something, dude?"

They all turned and looked at my face instead of my dick, so I took advantage of the moment to stuff the latter back inside my pants. No one seemed to notice, and I couldn't help but feel a little more confident.

"Do you know me?" I asked again.

Red Jacket glanced at his two sidekicks.

"Fuck he has balls," said Red Jacket.

"At least he has that," said Number Three, and they all started laughing.

"Hey," said Boot looking down again. "Where did it go?"

Red Jacket stepped forward until I could smell his stupid cologne.

"Where did it go?" he whispered.

Without thinking, I stepped out onto the grass, the water running through my socks almost instantly, but I continued, keeping my eyes on the street that opened up at the end of the park. The path would be clear of the three musketeers in a couple of feet or so, but I'd have to stick to the grass for now and die of pneumonia later.

I had to find a pace somewhere between walking coolly and running for my friggin' life, deciding finally to slow down just enough so that whatever little bit of dry sock I had left got completely soaked. My heart was beating in my ears so bad, but at least I couldn't hear them anymore, except for more laughing and a couple of *shits* and *fucks*. I could only pray they weren't saying, "Fuck, we'll get that little shit later."

When I got to the lamppost at the end of the park, my jelly legs almost caved on me, so that my foot made a crooked landing on the street. Holy shit, did that hurt.

I could still hear the guys behind me cracking up, and their voices felt closer than ever.

Chapter 38

When I got to Caster Street, I stopped under a streetlamp and hauled my cell out of my pocket. My hands were still shaking, so I kept pressing nine by mistake and had to start over.

When it finally rang, I had no clue what I was going to say. I was so busy looking behind my shoulder to see if they had followed me that I almost didn't hear when she picked up.

"Hey Claudia, it's me."

"Kye?"

"You already forgot my voice?" I added a small laugh, but she didn't laugh back.

"What do you want?"

"Nothing," I replied. "Just calling."

I sure as hell wasn't ready for that question.

I balanced myself on my good foot, a position that lasted about five seconds before I sat down on the wet and dirty curb.

When she didn't say anything, I continued.

"I just wanted to hang out a bit."

"Now?" she asked.

"It's not that late," I replied without checking the time, and conveniently forgetting that my parents at this point were probably going nuts with worry.

"I mean with everything that's happened," she replied, sounding kind of impatient.

"What's happened?" I asked, rubbing my ankle, like that did anything but make the pain worse.

Claudia let out a sigh, and I could almost picture her running her hands through her hair the way she does when she's irritated at something. I always liked the way her hair looked after those moments. Kind of tangled and messed up, but in a good way.

"I know what Julian told me," she replied, like she hadn't even heard my question.

"Which was?" I asked, throwing another glance down the street. No one.

"Everything."

"What are you talking about?" I asked.

"You tell me," she answered. "You're the one with all the news."

"Like what?"

The only way she could know what had happened was if Red Jacket himself was standing next to her. Could it be? Within a second my heart had sped up, like it had never quite slowed down from before.

"You wanna keep it," she said. "You wanna fucking keep it."

I paused to process what she was telling me, and then to try and process how Claudia would think that. Then somewhere in between those thoughts, I realized I had to answer her.

"Are you crazy?"

"That's what I should be asking you."

"I don't wanna keep it," I said quietly.

"That's why you asked about the money," she continued, like she hadn't heard me. "You don't have a stupid math project."

"I'm fifteen years old, for fuck's sake."

Claudia started crying. "I can't do it anymore. I'm sorry."

My heart dropped into my stomach. "Can't do what?"

"Figure it out."

The line went dead. I thought I had it all figured out already. Now, nothing made sense, least of all Julian. Since when was he so chummy with Claudia anyway? Why would he tell her something like that? I tried picturing myself asking him these questions at school tomorrow. It wasn't working, so I fixed my eyes on the lamppost, only Julian wasn't nearly as tall, so it felt weird. Besides, only crazy people spoke to lampposts. Sure, my head was friggin' killing me, and my foot needed some ice, but I wasn't mental yet.

Then I remembered Red Jacket's cologne and wondered whether Julian ever wore the same kind, and my hands started shaking so bad again that the phone dropped onto the street with a bang that seemed loud enough to be heard by the whole friggin' neighbourhood.

Chapter 39

Miss Apple Picking wore a lot of bracelets. They slid up and down her arm as she shook hands with me, Annie, Patricia, and my parents. They brushed against my shoulder when she patted my arm and asked me, "Did you hurt yourself?"

My sprained ankle had been my excuse to stay home from school that day and watch *Simpsons* reruns while trying to decide how I could ever see Julian again without being haunted by the question of whether he knew Red Jacket.

Even though my parents looked sympathetic enough about my injury, any extra drama would have helped, so I should have replied to Miss Apple Picking's question with a big yes instead of my semi shrug. Then again, me and Annie were once again stuck in Charlene's office, about to inspect this lady who wanted Joseph, and she was already pukingly nicer than she had looked in those stupid pictures. There was enough drama already.

"I'm Marla," she announced to everyone in this confident tone, as she took a seat to the farthest left of Charlene. One of her bracelets got stuck further up her arm, but she didn't yank it down, smiling at everyone instead, especially at Annie. It seemed like she was practically staring at her, as if she was going to whip out a Swiss Army knife and deliver Joseph right then and there and run off with him. I inched my chair a little closer to Annie's.

When we were all seated, Charlene began her boring little intro, like one of those orals in English class that you're convinced will go on well past the day you die. I tuned out after the first word, only catching words like *confidential* and *no obligation*.

When she finally stopped, everyone shifted in their seats. After all, we weren't there for Charlene. We were there for Marla, to see if she'd be a good "fit". Charlene used that word a lot, and I hated it. It was too friggin' polite and was meant to make us forget that Annie was the real mom, and everyone else—including Marla—was a fraud.

I could feel myself tensing up, and I had to be careful not to glare at Marla. Patricia and my parents seemed to love her, especially my dad. Marla's education was practically giving him a hard-on.

"Yale?" he repeated with a look that adults use to kiss ass. "My, my."

He glanced at me as if to say, *You'll be lucky if you do some one-year mechanic program.*

Marla looked at me and Annie. "I'm excited to find out more about you guys." She sounded easy-going, like one of those distant relatives asking for an update on where we were at in our stupid lives.

Annie looked at me. I sighed.

Well, my name is Kye, and I got this girl next to me pregnant last summer. At least, that's what she has me convinced of somehow, although I still don't know for sure. She looks pretty cute when she isn't pregnant, and the baby will be adorable. I think. Not that you'll ever know.

"My name's Kye," I mumbled.

I could see my mom's geeky smile out of the corner of my eye, like I was four years old and reciting the alphabet for the first time.

Marla—big surprise here—smiled too. "Cool."

Annie held her hand up in one of those waves. "I'm Annie."

"Why don't you tell them more about yourself?"

That was Charlene, looking kind of pissed that this was going nowhere; like we were messing up her little show.

I suddenly pictured myself saying, "I like movies, swimming, and—" with a big ceremonial wave to Annie's stomach— "fucking."

It took everything to not burst out laughing, but my dad gave me a strange look anyway.

"I'm a lawyer by trade," Marla jumped in. "Corporate law."

Me and Annie nodded, like we knew exactly what that was.

"I also sit on the board of a charity feeding hungry kids breakfast, and I have a cottage in the country."

That must have been where those apple trees were. I studied her face. She didn't look like she was trying to make us feel like shit. I guess it was just happening naturally.

Marla started playing with her bracelets for a second. "I have a very fulfilling life."

My mom leaned forward so she could see past my dad at Marla. "But you'd like a child."

I suddenly pictured me and Annie holding my mom down while someone else punched her face in. But I didn't know who we'd recruit. Everyone in that crummy beige office was on any side but ours. This helpless expression came over Annie's face, while Marla looked at my mom almost gratefully. Bloody hell.

"I've always wanted a child," she replied in this whisper that almost shook.

Her eyes beamed into Annie's like she was channelling some power right to her uterus. Annie covered her stomach and looked away. I forced a cough to remind Marla that I was there too. She looked over at me and smiled. She had gotten the hint. She *was* a lawyer, after all.

Chapter 40

The next day, Saturday, after work, I headed for a small burger joint down the street from the drugstore that me and Anthony used to go to all the time. That was until Damian found out in grade eight and started hanging there too. I hadn't been there in a long time, and it felt weird to be back without Anthony, and especially weird to see Annie sitting in one of the booths that me and Anthony always used to sit at.

I sat down across from her. She looked annoyed.

"Took you long enough," she said.

"It was really busy today, sorry."

Plus my ankle was still messed up, but I didn't add this part. I was trying to walk as naturally as possible, even though I was sure I looked like Terry friggin' Fox.

"Do you have it?" she asked.

I scanned the place quickly for the hundredth time since walking in, but it was kind of dead for a Saturday; just a couple of dudes by a window. Definitely no Red Jacket. At least for now.

"Hello?"

I turned and looked at Annie, who had her arms crossed and was looking uncomfortable.

"Oh yeah," I mumbled, fishing out the envelope from my knapsack and pushing it across the table.

She opened it immediately and pulled out the paper. "That's it?"

"There's everything on there except for when I took my first crap," I said.

Not exactly, but enough to get this stupid adoption process underway. Not that I was going with Marla, which was the only reason I had finally decided to fill out Charlene's stupid information form. It was either that or get suffocated in my sleep by Patricia and Annie and everyone else who couldn't stand me.

"What about the picture?" Annie asked, her cheeks all red.

I dropped my head and kept it there for a few seconds. Out of all the reactions I've had to use when I'm lying, this was the best one. Especially for the hard lies, the ones to people you care about.

When I lifted my head back up, Annie was shaking hers.

"I knew I should have just gone to your house," she said. "I can't trust you with anything."

"I totally forgot."

Annie folded her arms. "Or maybe you tore it to shreds, and it's sitting in some garbage bin."

I flinched. "What kind of a dick do you think I am?"

She didn't say anything for a minute.

"Do you *want* to mess this all up?" asked Annie.

"I don't know what I want," I mumbled back before I could think.

I wanted to keep Joseph with me a little longer, and now that I had bought some more time with the ultrasound picture, that looked like it was a go. Check. I wanted to keep Marla away from him long enough so she could get interested in some other kid. Semi-check. I wanted to talk to Claudia. Hopeless. And then there was Julian. This sudden whiff of burgers made me sick.

"I want Marla," said Annie, slowly peeling off her jacket only to pull it back on again as a mom and her kids sat down at a table across from us.

"What are you staring at?" she asked.

"Nothing." I wanted her to remove the jacket again so I could look at Joseph, but couldn't figure out a way to ask this without it sounding weird.

"So, I like Marla, remember?" she said again.

I sighed. "Do we seriously have to talk about her?"

Annie looked like I had just landed from another planet.

"You make her sound like she's amazing," I continued.

"She's the best we have," Annie said.

"For now."

"She's really smart," added Annie.

"You mean she's rich."

"Isn't that a good thing?"

I shrugged. "You're just gaga over her friggin' bimmer."

"How do you know what car she drives?"

I didn't, but that wasn't the point.

Annie sighed. "Whatever she has, it's better than a bus pass."

We both got quiet, and I just felt really down all of a sudden, like after my grade six field trip—the one I had gone on alone because Anthony had come down with the flu or something. Anyways, I went and talked to no one for three days.

When I came back, my parents were all anxious to hear the great time I had, and I felt sad for them, for believing.

"What happened to your ankle, anyway?" Annie asked.

"It's nothing," I replied.

"You can barely walk."

"It doesn't matter," I said impatiently.

Annie shrugged. "Sorry for caring."

I looked around the restaurant again. No Red Jacket in sight.

"Some assholes," I finally mumbled.

Annie leaned in. "Some what?"

I sighed. "Assholes," I said, a little louder.

The mom with her kids shot me a dirty look.

Annie sat up straighter. "What do you mean?"

I ran my finger across some salt on the table until the tip was all shiny.

"I was walking home from work, and some guys came out of nowhere."

Annie's eyes got wide. "They beat you up?"

I shrugged. "Kind of."

"What did they do?"

"Just stuff."

No friggin' way was I about to tell her everything.

She leaned forward and looked deep into my eyes with her sad ones. "That sucks," she said.

For some reason that I couldn't guess if someone had a gun to my head, I added, "And Claudia doesn't wanna talk to me anymore."

Annie started playing with the string of the hood of her jacket. "That's your girlfriend?"

I realized then that I had never really mentioned her to Annie before.

"Not anymore," I answered quietly.

I looked away, somehow sensing that if I looked at her any longer, I'd start crying or something, even though I wasn't sure what the hell I'd be crying about.

"I think Julian's fucking with me," I said.

"What do you mean?" she asked, letting go of the hood string to rub her stomach.

"I don't really know," I answered.

Annie didn't say anything.

"How's Anthony?" she asked, after a minute.

I looked at her, confused. "Anthony?"

"Tammy says he's kind of a loner."

I couldn't help but notice that Annie's belly rubs were getting a little more intense. I felt a headache coming on.

"Tammy?"

"My friend," Annie replied quickly, without looking at me. "The one that had the HIV rumour."

"Oh, right," I replied, like it was all coming back to me.

"She used to go to your school."

Used to. So that was why I hadn't seen Tammy in a while.

"Which school does she go to now?"

"Somewhere in town," replied Annie. "You used to tease her."

My tongue felt as heavy as metal. "I never did anything."

"Yes you did," Annie answered. "At the pool, remember?"

I paused long enough to gather my thoughts. "The pool?"

Annie stared at the table. "What did you think I meant?"

I shrugged. "I barely remember that summer."

She frowned, and the vein down the side of her forehead was suddenly showing.

"I mean, I remember some stuff," I mumbled.

She acted like she hadn't heard. "She only hung with us a couple of times. But she liked you."

I stared at this big drink someone was carrying on a tray. I imagined what it would be like to dive right into that cup and forget that I ever supposedly knew Tammy.

For some reason that I couldn't understand, Annie just kept talking. "She had long hair, but she chopped it all off just before school and dyed it black."

She had laughed a bit at Brian's party too, but I had to stop my brain from figuring out whether the two were a match.

"I don't remember," I said quickly.

My head was really hurting now. On top of that, for some reason a guy that had just walked into the restaurant reminded me of Anthony, and I realized I hadn't spoken to him since running into Red Jacket. I pictured him cooped up in his house all alone watching *The Usual Suspects* or something, and I just wanted to kill myself.

"This all sucks," I mumbled, rubbing my temples.

"Tell me about it," Annie said. She started fanning herself with her hand.

"Why don't you just take off the jacket?" I asked.

Even though there was no one around us, Annie glanced around like the place was packed. She shook her head.

"Is it moving more?" I asked.

She shrugged. "I guess."

I felt this strange jealousy come over me. "You don't sound like you care."

Annie stared at me. "Holy shit, are you gonna tell me this is a gift from god or something?"

I suddenly felt like putting my head on the table, even with all the dried up ketchup drops covering the surface like a case of bad acne. "Forget it."

Annie clasped her hands together. "Make the next four months disappear, and I'll forget about everything."

"We should give this baby to someone who will appreciate it," I said. "Someone who deserves it."

Annie looked really sad all of a sudden and looked down at her stomach.

"Someone like Marla," she whispered.

"Someone better," I replied.

Annie sniffled a bit.

"Who's better?" she asked, wiping her eyes.

I looked down at the table, but there was no salt left to wipe up.

"Me."

I felt Annie freeze in front of me. "What?"

"Us," I added quickly, not sure whether that sounded better. Hell, I wasn't sure what I was saying anymore. Or maybe I did, but I had no clue where the words were coming from, unless I had somehow rehearsed them to the ceiling before going to bed last night. And even if I had rehearsed them, I wasn't sure whether they were coming out right. Or whether a friggin' burger joint was the best place to blurt them out.

I looked up and saw the palest Annie I had ever seen, and wondered whether Joseph was suddenly getting a shitload more blood than he needed. That couldn't be good. Annie unzipped her jacket and sat back, clutching her stomach. I pictured her fainting and cracking her head open on the brown-tiled floor of the restaurant.

I tried grabbing her hand, but I couldn't get a hold of it.

"Don't touch me." Her voice was cold.

"Did you hear what I said?" I asked.

"Fuck off."

The words hit me like bricks. I wanted to say them right back, but Annie got up at that moment and walked towards the door. I got up and followed her, my crippled ankle barely able to keep up.

"Isn't this what you wanted?" I asked as we stepped out.

Annie didn't stop walking, but I could see her shaking her head till I thought it would do a three-sixty, like that girl in *The Exorcist*.

She had turned down Langdon in the opposite direction of the drugstore, past a coffee shop and Laundromat. I followed without a clue where we were going, but I was quickly getting the feeling that it didn't matter.

After a block, Annie stopped and turned to me.

"You know what I want?" she asked. "You really wanna know?"

I looked up and down the sidewalk. "Can we talk without yelling?"

"To not be pregnant," she said, like she hadn't heard me.

"*You* were the one who didn't want an abortion," I said, even though I now liked thinking about Melanie and her friggin' clipboard as much as I liked thinking about Red Jacket's laugh.

"He's going to a really nice home instead," Annie said.

I thought of my kitchen that had this nice butter smell all the time, and the big wooden key-chain hanger by the front door.

"My home is nice," I said.

Annie started crying. "Jesus Christ, Kye, should we get married too?"

I took a deep breath.

"You don't have to take care of it if you don't want," I replied. I looked out onto the road at all the tires spinning like mad, and pictured myself getting chewed up by the rubber.

Annie shook her head and clutched her stomach. "This is getting better by the second."

"I just wanna see him," I said. "Like, really see him."

"You'll see it in the hospital."

"I wanna see him when he smiles, and with stupid overalls on," I continued. "Not when he's a slimy alien."

Annie looked at me like *I* was the slimy alien. "Fuck, Kye, it's not a library book."

"Don't you care?"

This pained look came over her face, like I had just hurt her in the worst way possible. "Is that what you think?"

"I'm sorry," I said. "You're just kind of—"

Annie moved in closer. "What?"

I shrugged. "I don't know," I said. "Kind of cold."

"Well, I'm not cold," she shot back. "I'm actually hot."

She tugged at her jacket. "Hot from hiding under this since September."

I looked down at the sidewalk and dug the toe of the shoe on my good foot into a deep enough crack.

"I've cared more than you all along," Annie continued. "And now look at you." Disgust filled her face. "You want the baby. I can't fucking believe it."

"I just wanna help," I said quietly.

"Then give it to Marla."

I leaned against a lamppost to give my foot a break, and looked up at the clouds. Their weird shape made me think of Joseph. I pictured him lying in Marla's arms, her bracelets digging into his bony head.

"Please." Her voice was trembling.

"I don't know what to say," I finally replied to the sky.

"How about *yes*?"

It sounded simple enough. So why couldn't I spit it out, especially now that Annie was bawling her eyes out?

"I need time."

"We don't have time."

We still had more than four months, but I didn't really want to think about Joseph being born. Not without me. But then when I thought of being there, of standing next to Annie as the doctors and whoever pulled him out, I got all cold and just wanted to go home.

I looked at Annie. She was a mess.

I looked away. "I just can't say yes right now."

I expected her to cry harder; hell, I was even bracing myself for a scream. But she just stood there, with her bangs shaking back and forth in the wind, like she was still trying to take it all in. She pulled her hood on, and we just stood there a second.

"I hate you," she finally said.

Then she turned and ran faster than I had ever seen her run before. I didn't even bother to try catching up with her. But I didn't watch her, either; I didn't want to. Instead, I looked up at the laundromat sign, then inside at this couple opening up their detergent. They looked young, but older than me and Annie. I wondered if they had a baby, and if that was why they were there together at that moment, scooping white soap out of a box. I looked down the street again just in time to see Annie disappear down a side street.

I took a deep breath and started limping back up the street towards home. I pulled my hood on, in case Red Jacket and the others were on the prowl. I had even put on another jacket that morning, one they wouldn't recognize, just to be safe.

Chapter 41

Monday, ten thirty in the morning. I put my granola-bar wrapper in the toilet and flushed. The last time I had hidden out in the washroom was back in seventh grade, when Anthony had taken off for a vacation in the middle of February and left me with no one to sit with in the caf. I ate lunch in the washroom every day that whole friggin' week. I gave him such hell after he came back all tanned and stuff that he hasn't gone on another vacation since. I like to think it was for me, but his mom just probably doesn't have that much money.

The first thing I saw in the mirror when I came out of the stall was a shitload of granola crumbs on my shirt, which I quickly brushed away. Not like Claudia was waiting for me outside to give me a big kiss or anything. Still, I had to be as invisible as possible, not look like a messy two-year-old.

So far, the day was turning out alright, even if it was only morning break. I had managed to avoid the first two periods, including English, which meant no stupid chats to watch between Claudia and Ryan what's-his-fucking-face. The other class I had missed was math, which wouldn't have been a big deal, except that it was at the other end of the school, and showing myself to three quarters of the student population didn't exactly go hand in hand with being invisible.

French was next, and that class was by the grade seven lockers, so that shouldn't be a problem. Even better, I could cut through the library to get there quicker. All I had to do was get my books.

I could hear voices in the halls and the slamming of lockers, and decided there was enough going on to distract anyone from noticing me slipping out of the bathroom. At least I wasn't limping so much anymore. When I got to the door, I looked down once more at my shirt for any crumbs; then I took a deep breath and stepped out.

My eyes focused on the only locker I cared about; mine. And the person standing beside it, pacing. Anthony. What the fuck?

The only reason I had decided to come to school at all that morning was that my plan was to avoid him and Julian. The reasons were the same and somehow very different in a strange sort of way. I didn't trust Julian, and I had a pretty good hunch that Anthony didn't exactly trust me.

I slipped back into the bathroom, pretty sure that he had spotted me. I looked around, measuring up my millions of escape options, which included some urinals, three sinks, and two stalls. I wanted to bang my head against the wall. The first class of the day that I could safely go to, and Anthony had to mess it up for me. Jesus Christ.

Some dude walked in at that moment. I had seen him around, but he had no clue who I was, thank god. When he walked up to a urinal, I could see him kind of glancing back at me like *Are you just going to stand there?*

I slipped back into the stall I had left minutes ago, realizing only after I closed the door that this was even weirder. But it was too late now, so I just sighed and dropped my head, thinking about how the hell I was going to manage to skip school for the rest of my life.

I waited about thirty seconds after the dude had left before unlocking the stall door.

"Kye?"

My finger jammed the lock back into place. Having Anthony stand at my locker had been bad enough. Having him on the other side of a vandalized metal stall door was more than I had bargained for. The day could not turn out any worse than it just had. Even if I were to discover that Red Jacket went to Fincher and he and Julian both decided to take me behind the school and kill me. Dr. Jacobi always tells you to think about the worst possible scenario with your fears, and up until five minutes ago, that was it. Now my best friend was talking to my stall door like a mental patient, and I couldn't come out.

"You're gonna be late for class," Anthony said.

I could feel my legs starting to shake, but I didn't say anything, somehow telling myself that as long as I kept my mouth shut, he wouldn't know for sure that I was in that stall. Now who was the mental patient?

"You don't have to worry about going to the locker," he added.

"I'm not worried," I said without thinking.

So much for keeping my mouth shut.

Even Anthony must have been surprised, because he didn't answer for a second.

"Julian was looking for you," he finally said.

Great.

"Not in a bad way," Anthony added.

Christ, could he read my friggin' mind or something?

He got quiet after that, and I could hear small random noises from beyond the bathroom. The shutting of one last locker, some kids horsing around as they scrambled to class, a teacher's voice.

Then, I heard the stall door next to me close, and when Anthony spoke next, his voice sounded an inch away, even though it was so low I could barely hear it.

"Is it true you're gonna keep the baby?"

"Who told you that?" I asked.

"Julian and Claudia," Anthony replied.

My heart dropped. "What, are they a couple now?"

"So it's true."

"I never said that."

"So you don't know yet?"

"I have to get to class," I said.

"Me too," said Anthony.

I heard him unlock the stall door and walk out.

"By the way, I got your books for you," he said. "French, right?"

I didn't say anything, too taken aback that he still remembered my locker combination.

"Anyways, they're by the sink."

It didn't take me long to realize he was gone. The air felt chilly again and just different, and I somehow knew that all I had to do was whisper and I'd hear my echo bounce off the bathroom walls. There was a time when I could have rattled off Anthony's locker combination without thinking, and now all I could do was trace a sad, depressing *33* on the stall door. Beyond that, it was a blur.

I turned around and bent over the toilet.

Chapter 42

I shut the door behind me and glanced at the grandfather clock my parents had inherited from some ancient aunt. Three thirty. Not bad. I had managed to kill a whole six-and-a-half hours at the bus terminal without running into anyone. Facing that patch of ground where I had pushed Annie hadn't been easy, but it sure beat the memories from the mall.

I camped out around the public phones that nobody ever used, right by a big jeans advertisement of some wide-eyed half-naked chick, and a snack bar that ate up the ten bucks I had started the day with.

I was glad to be home. I leaned against the wall while my heart found its place back in my chest. I wondered if Joseph's heart could beat that hard. I hoped so. A heart was friggin' important.

I had walked out of Fincher that morning with nothing but the French books Anthony had left by the sink. I hadn't even stopped to get my jacket. I just left without a clue whether I could ever go back. Now I just wanted to sit in a really hot bath or something. I looked at my hands. They weren't as red as five minutes ago, but my fingers were too numb to undo the laces of my shoes, so I managed to just pull them off. Plus if I kept my hoodie on, I felt alright, even if my parents always say I look like a gangster with it on.

Speaking of which, a noise came from the kitchen; it was them. I would have started crying if I hadn't started wondering what the hell they were doing home so early.

As if they hadn't already heard me come in, I slowly tiptoed down the hall towards the kitchen, thinking of any really old relatives that could have died, or the chances of both parents losing their jobs on the same day. When I got close enough to hear my mom's voice, I stopped to try and make out the words, but all I could tell was that she was worried. Then again, what else was new?

"Kye, is that you?" she called out.

I took my time before actually entering the kitchen, as though this was the critical step to convince them that I hadn't been there all along, eavesdropping.

My mom looked up and gave me a small smile, and my dad just nodded. Neither of them seemed to notice that I was shaking like a friggin' icicle.

"Sweetheart, take that hood off," my mom said. "You look like a gangster."

I decided to ignore her. I didn't want to imagine what my ears would look like if I took it off. Probably all frostbitten and stuff.

"Grab a seat, Kye," said my dad.

I hopped over to the table. Okay, so I overdid this just a little, especially since my ankle had pretty much healed up. But judging from my dad's voice, it was going to be all downhill once I sat down, so a bit of extra sympathy wouldn't hurt.

My mom, like a champ, jumped out of her chair. "Oh Kye, is it still hurting you?"

"A bit."

She wrapped some ice in a towel for me, and I patted my ankle while my dad looked at me like I deserved pain from here to friggin' eternity. His glare was rubbing off on my mom, who sat down again almost guiltily without asking whether I wanted something to drink, even though what I really wanted was a sandwich or something. But nobody looked in the mood to make me one of those either.

He looked down at my foot. "Put lots of pressure."

I nodded. Any more pressure and I'd block circulation to my ankle, and they'd have to amputate.

"Annie's having some trouble at school," my mom suddenly said.

I looked around the kitchen, half-expecting to see Annie emerge from the pantry or something, all dolled up in one of her shapeless sweaters.

"What kind of trouble?" I asked, even though I had a pretty good idea it didn't have anything to do with not fitting into her chemistry lab coat.

"She's getting teased," my dad replied, speaking to the big flower at the centre of the tablecloth. "A lot."

I moved the ice around my ankle. "That sucks."

"Patricia called us up last night," my mom said. "Apparently the poor girl had a nervous breakdown."

My heart lodged itself in my throat.

My dad rolled his eyes. "Not exactly, Helena."

"She's severely depressed," my mom added defensively.

"She's being severely *teased*," he corrected her.

"Horribly," she added, shaking her head.

My dad sat up a little straighter. "But we've come up with a solution."

"She'll be going to *your* school," my mom blurted out almost proudly, like they had found the cure for cancer or something.

"In January," my dad added, like we shouldn't get too excited just yet.

Mom touched her forehead like she was the biggest bimbo. "Of course."

My dad nodded. "This is good news."

I rubbed my ankle, thinking about how I'd have to break it to stay home for the first couple of months after Christmas vacation, while Annie got comfortable sitting behind Claudia in class, her stomach getting bigger by the second. And Julian. A jolt of pain shot up from my ankle to my crotch. Fucking good news indeed.

"Patricia will be making the request with the school," my dad continued. "We can discuss this plenty more in the coming weeks."

Or not.

"Annie's been skipping school," my mom said. "Did you know about that, Kye?"

She was worried that I did, and that Patricia would come over and whip us all with her long ponytail.

I thought back to Annie's muffin crumbs as I said, "No."

They both shook their heads. I didn't know whether it was because they felt sad about Annie or because they sensed I was lying, but it didn't really matter.

My dad pulled his chair closer to the table.

"Right now we have to focus on Marla," he said.

"Isn't she nice, Kye?" my mom asked.

I shrugged. "She's okay."

"She's certainly capable of raising a child," my dad added.

"Sure," I mumbled.

My dad frowned. "Sure what?"

I folded my arms. "She's nice."

He looked at my mom like everything was settled.

"But so is seventy-five percent of the planet," I added.

"Pardon?" my dad asked.

"Nice," I replied.

He gave this little laugh like I was the world's biggest retard.

"Well, that may be," he answered, "but not everyone is willing to take in a child."

Mom's eyes were tearing up. "I think she could make a wonderful mother."

"You guys make her sound like fucking Mother Theresa."

My mom gasped. "Kye!"

"Sorry," I mumbled. "But seriously. Jesus Christ."

My dad ripped his glasses off so hard I was sure he had broken them. "That's enough."

I sat back in the chair, my heart pounding. I had never really sworn at my parents, but that was only half the reason that my hands were shaking. I could sense I was getting ready for something, I just didn't know what it was. Like that time I was ready to take a swing at Damian's head at afternoon recess on the very last day of elementary school. The sun was so hot that I should have taken off my jacket, except I had my balled up fist stuffed in the pocket as I tried figuring out the best way to make it land on Damian's face. And then the bell rang.

"Marla's not the only person who'd make a great mom."

The voice brought me back to reality, and it took me a second to realize that it was mine.

My dad put his glasses back on and massaged his chin the way he does when he has to think something over.

"Is there someone else you were thinking of?" mom asked.

She looked at my dad when she asked the question, which is what she does when she's nervous about the answer to something. I was too.

"It's a he," I blurted out, feeling myself get hot.

My tummy also started cramping, even though all I had had to eat that day were two chocolate bars and a bag of chips. Okay, three chocolate bars.

My dad cocked his head to one side. Christ, I just wished he would say something, sort of like how Annie wanted me to say yes about Marla.

"I suppose single fathers can make good parents," my mom said slowly.

"I suppose." My dad didn't sound convinced. "Who is he?"

"He's nice."

This didn't exactly make my dad look super impressed.

"Charlene never mentioned anything about a man," he said.

"You're sure he's single?" asked my mom.

"Yeah." After last weekend, I wasn't sure of anything.

My dad sighed impatiently. "Would you like to tell us who he is?"

What I really wanted was to run upstairs and grab those papers off my desk with all the numbers on them, even though my legs were shaking so badly under the table, I doubted I'd have made it out of the kitchen. It was too bad, because I couldn't even remember the cost of diapers at that moment, except that they were pretty expensive. Well, at least at the drugstore. Maybe they sold them in bulk or something.

My mom leaned closer to me. "Sweetheart?"

Plus, it would have helped to have Joseph's picture next to me to help my parents imagine what life could be like with him. I tried imagining their reaction. Would they start hugging me? Would my mom pull out a paper and start making shopping lists for bottles and baby food?

My dad shook his head. "I'm almost wondering whether this person exists."

I almost laughed. "So am I."

The phone rang.

My dad sighed. "Let it go to voice mail."

But mom was already picking it up. "Hello? Hi Patricia, we were just thinking of you."

She gave me and my dad a lame-ass wink.

Then her face got very pale. "Oh."

I could see from my dad's face that he had completely forgotten about our conversation and was now fixated on my mom, who had both hands clutching the phone like she was in an arm wrestle with it.

"Oh my god," she whispered.

My heart raced. Oh my god what? Had something happened to Joseph? I felt a sickness in my stomach.

"Yes of course," was all she said before hanging up the phone. Her eyes were glued to the floor. She couldn't look at us, and I could barely look at her. I started tapping the table nervously, trying to figure out what could be so wrong, and all I could think of was Joseph. That he wasn't in Annie's stomach anymore; that the picture upstairs was all I had left.

"Helena, what's wrong?" my dad asked.

My mom lifted her head and looked through us. "Annie's gone."

Even though I knew what I had heard, I still wanted her to repeat it. But I also didn't. My head suddenly felt like it weighed a ton, and I had to place it on the table. Normally my dad would have said something about hair not having a place on the kitchen table, but when I had the nerve to look at him, all I saw was this faraway look in his eyes, and then I closed my own.

Chapter 43

"Are you sure she's gone?" my mom asked.

Patricia stood there with shaking hands that she kept hiding by crossing her arms. Her face was whiter than snow. Was my mom blind? Maybe she was just saying that to fill the awkward space between us, that moment between walking into the house and getting on with finding Annie. The door had been unlocked, and we had just let ourselves in, somehow knowing that this was one of those exceptional days from hell where you didn't care who walked into your house.

I scanned the hallway for signs of other people—grandparents and aunts coming out of the kitchen or living room. I had never thought of Annie's extended family, but the silence echoing through the house gave me my answer. There was no one.

"Do you want some tea?" my mom asked.

Patricia just put her hair behind her ears, but my mom took off for the kitchen anyway, like she knew the place, leaving me in the hallway with Patricia. She didn't look at me, which only made me feel weirder. I wished that Annie would appear to make this all easier, but there wasn't a sign of her anywhere; not a pair of shoes in the hall, not even a similar feature on Patricia's face, and I suddenly felt like we were in the wrong house.

I stuffed my hands in my pockets, and Patricia leaned against the wall, her eyes fixed on something over my shoulder.

My mom stepped out into the hallway. "Where are your cups?"

Patricia walked off to the kitchen almost energetically, like we were all there for fucking tea time.

I gripped the banister of the stairs, scanning each step for something that Annie could have dropped on the way down; something that would make the climb worth it. Nothing. At least the stairs were carpeted. Less chance of Patricia hearing them creak as I dared to go where I didn't have a right to.

When I got to the doorway of Annie's room, I froze. I would have never dreamed that it was as girly as it turned out to be. Or pink. The canopy bed, her dresser, the friggin' drapes. Even the pouf by her bed looked like a giant wad of bubble gum.

It was weird being in her space, or what had been hers. Now it looked and felt abandoned. Everything seemed neat enough. The drawers on her dresser were all closed without anything embarrassing hanging out, like a bra or something. The bed spread didn't have a single bump, and even her laptop was still on her desk, the screen a dead grey. No sign of Annie anywhere. I tried imagining what she might have thought of in her last minutes there, standing in the doorway like I was, giving everything one final look.

I looked over my shoulder back into the hallway, waiting for either Patricia or my mom to run up the stairs and pull me away from Annie's world. But no one appeared, so after a few seconds, I walked far enough into the room to reach the closet. It was closed, and when I put my hand on the knob of the door, my heart started going nuts.

It seemed like forever before I managed to slowly pull it open. I stood back for a second, like I was waiting for the monster that we're all scared of when we're little to jump right out. When it didn't, I reached out and ran my fingertips over her clothes, pushing hangers this way and that.

I looked for something she might have worn recently, like some humungous jeans or something, but all I saw was skinny stuff. My heart started speeding up again as I stepped deeper into the closet, almost killing myself on this pair of green flip-flops on the floor.

They were just sitting there, like she had thought about putting them on today and then changed her mind at the last minute, even though it was November. I pulled them out and held them for a second, my fingers tracing the small purple sparkly beads along each side. I tried to remember whether I had ever seen her wear them at the pool last summer, but the only image that kept coming up was Annie in front of that laundromat, her jacket wrapped tightly around her and tears dropping off her chin.

I tossed the shoes back into the closet and tried shutting the door, but one of the flip-flops was blocking it. I didn't want to touch it again, not even with my foot, so I left the door open just a bit and turned to her nightstand.

It seemed bare from where I was standing, but I walked over anyway, keeping my eyes peeled. For what exactly, I'm not sure. I don't want to say a note, because that's pretty cliché. But I still wanted a sign of something that I could bring downstairs to Patricia and finally be the good guy.

I took a deep breath and pulled open the upper drawer. Empty. I yanked open the bottom one a little too hard and almost pulled it right out. There was nothing but a box of Kleenex anyway. I slammed my fist into the pink bedspread. What the fuck?

And then I saw the knapsack. It was tucked in a corner by her dresser, and I couldn't have gotten to it faster if I had flown off the bed. The zipper wasn't closed up completely, and I jammed my hand as deep into the bag as I could stuff it. Nothing. I then turned to the side pocket. My fingers reached down and pulled out a couple of black hair elastics. I dug in again and felt something else. Like paper, only different; smoother, glossier.

Even when I pulled them out completely and knew for sure that this was the discovery I had been waiting for, and that discoveries weren't just big in movies but in real life too, I didn't pause before looking at them.

Not to take in the twenty or so Barbie dolls sitting on Annie's dresser, and count how many blondes there were versus brunettes. Not to read the quote on this black and white poster by her bed. I didn't take any time at all before looking down.

The pool. Annie. And Julian. Annie and Julian. I squinted hard to see if I was anywhere; anywhere that could explain why I wasn't in focus with them, with her wet hair pasted on her forehead, the glint from her earrings, and his tongue on her cheek. Annie doesn't mind. She's laughing, and he is too. But all I saw was this fat dude in orange swim trucks standing off to the side of the pool, ready to dive in.

I took a deep breath and looked away for a second, but when I looked back, they were still there, their cheeks golden brown from hours in the sun. Not that stark white that could at least tell me that this picture—that everything—had happened at the very beginning of summer; long before that night when I pulled Annie away from the pool ladder.

When I tried taking another breath, it practically hurt. I crouched down on the floor, trying to wrap my head around what I had just seen; Annie's teeth all lined up in that smile, her head bent at this thirty-degree angle, a few strands of her hair mixing with his. It was all less believable than Annie being gone, and suddenly I wanted to find her even more. To hear that what I had just seen was a misunderstanding, that I would've been in the picture too except I was in the bathroom or getting a popsicle from the snack bar. That it was all an accident.

But their pose in the second picture seemed anything but. It was all so natural, right down to the nonexistent space where their noses touched. Her eyes were closed, and she looked all relaxed. Like she was used to being that close to him.

"That's her old knapsack."

I looked up to find Patricia standing in the doorway. She was still crossing and uncrossing her arms. I sat down on the carpet, sliding the photos under my leg.

I think Patricia kept talking. Her mouth was moving, but I didn't hear a word. I was thinking about Joseph. My Joseph. I gulped hard. It might have sounded right fifteen minutes ago, before unzipping Annie's knapsack. Now the words felt empty and strange, like they were in a foreign language or something.

I focused back on Patricia, only because I thought she had whispered something but I had missed it. She leaned against the doorway like she needed help keeping herself up. I felt bad for her, and for a second I forgot about everything. At least Joseph was protected in that embryonic sac or whatever the hell it was called. Patricia had to picture Annie sitting in some sketchy bus station.

"How do you know she's gone?" I asked.

Patricia's face changed for the first time since I had arrived. "Excuse me?"

I looked away, guilty.

"Her middle dresser drawer is empty," she said after a minute.

I thought of those muffin crumbs again. "Did you try the mall?"

I couldn't tell whether Patricia heard me; she just dropped her head in her hands.

"We were going to get through it," she whispered.

Then she looked up at me, and I thought about the last time I saw Annie; how the vein in her forehead had looked ready to pop out. Like Patricia's in that moment. My cheeks felt hot, and a guilt as heavy as a rock was in my stomach.

I stood up, suddenly overtaken by this second wind that had come out of nowhere.

"We'll search everywhere," I said.

I looked at Patricia, hoping that she'd have some kind of idea as to how to go about this, but in that minute Marla appeared in the doorway. She must have just arrived because her cheeks were frozen red, and her jacket was still on. Mine was downstairs, even though I should have just run in, too focused on finding Annie to take it off. I suddenly felt ashamed.

"What's the plan?" Marla asked, putting her arm around Patricia. I wanted Patricia to shrug it off, but she didn't—like the two had known each other for eons. Maybe another history I didn't know about. I could have punched them both.

"Kye wants to search the whole town," Patricia said.

They both stared at me for a second.

Then Marla smiled. "I'll go with you."

"I can go alone," I mumbled, completely forgetting that I didn't have a friggin' driver's license. Marla didn't throw this in my face, though, which I suppose made her a decent human being, but whatever.

I practically pushed my way out of the room, old boobs rubbing my arms on either side.

My mother was sitting in the kitchen all Zen-like, her nails scratching her teacup. The sound hurt. "We have to go look for Annie," I said.

She looked up but didn't move.

I walked over and started pulling on her arm, like I was five years old and wanted to go home. That was kind of how I felt.

She finally did stand up, but only because Patricia had walked into the kitchen. My mom pulled out a chair as Patricia eased herself into it really slowly, like if she did it any faster, all of her bones would collapse into a pile on the kitchen floor. My mom gave me this look, and I knew she wasn't going anywhere. I sighed and walked to the front door to put on my shoes. Let them all sit there with their fucking tea.

"Any ideas where to look?"

Marla again. Couldn't she just leave me alone?

I nodded.

"And a car wouldn't help?"

I hated when adults pulled that shit, asking questions that they perfectly well knew the answers to. I would have given Marla the most hateful look I knew how to give, if I hadn't needed her stupid car.

* * * *

Marla's car had leather seats and that new-car smell. I slid in and started rubbing my hands.

There must have been a thousand buttons on the dashboard, and they all lit up like Christmas lights. Marla started turning dials everywhere with the intensity of a pilot.

"You should be warm in a second."

I kept to my side and stared out the window. Within a few seconds it felt like I had third degree burns all over my ass.

"Seat warmers," said Marla.

I just nodded as she backed out onto the road.

"So where do we go first?"

"The mall."

Patricia might have already tried there, but maybe she hadn't thought of checking the bathrooms.

I hopped out of the car as it came to a stop in front of the main entrance, and ran inside before Marla had a chance to insist on going with me.

In no time at all, I was standing by the first-floor bathrooms. The exact spot where I had run into Annie. Even though I knew they had been swept up a long time ago, I scanned the floor for the muffin crumbs.

I suddenly realized Marla could have been some use after all, and I regretted leaving her in the parking lot. How else was I going to find out whether Annie was in there?

At that moment, the bathroom door was yanked open and a large lady with a hundred earrings forming a half-moon along her earlobe emerged. I thought about asking her to check for me, but she was already giving me this weird look.

It didn't seem like I had a choice. It was either open the door and run in and out myself or give up. I took a deep breath and pushed the door open wide enough to see this old lady at the sink washing her hands. She looked up at me through the mirror, and my heart started beating faster, but I couldn't turn back now.

"Annie?"

My voice gave off this echo that sounded louder than it was, and I backed away until the door closed on my nose, and I was once again on the other side.

Through the door I could hear someone repeating the name a couple of times; it was probably that old lady. A few seconds later, she came out shrugging her shoulders.

"I don't think your friend is here," she said.

The other bathrooms upstairs were easier, because nobody was there. I stood around what seemed like forever before deciding to walk in. The stall doors were all open, but I made a quick run up and down just to make sure. No Annie.

From there I decided to check out the food court, hoping that maybe she had decided to grab some food or something. But after a few minutes the smells were getting me pretty hungry, and I didn't have any money with me. Anyways, stuffing my face with Annie and Joseph missing felt more wrong than murder.

When I got back outside, my heart was pounding as I tried catching my breath and come to terms with the fact that there was now one less place to look for Annie. Marla's car was right by the door, where I had left her. I suddenly felt self-conscious walking towards it, imagining Marla studying me critically through the window, even though it was pretty dark and I could practically hear Dr. Jacobi saying that Marla couldn't see anything.

I climbed in and shut the door.

"Nothing?" asked Marla.

I shrugged. Even shaking my head no felt impossible for some reason.

The car started moving, and soon we were on the road again.

"Where to now?" asked Marla.

"The park," I mumbled.

"Which one?"

If she had to come along, why couldn't she at least know where I was talking about?

"Just go back towards Annie's house," I said. "I'll tell you when to turn."

"We'll find her," she said.

"I know."

When we got to the park, Marla looked hesitant.

"It's kind of dark," she said.

"She might be there," I answered, unsnapping the seat belt.

"Is that your school?" Marla asked, nodding across the street.

I didn't say anything, and just got out of the car.

The swings had been removed for the winter, and even the picnic table by the small-kids' stuff looked like no one had sat there in months. Still, for some reason, the whole place seemed frozen in time, like nothing had changed since that lunch hour in September.

"Does she like this park?" called out Marla from a couple of feet behind. She probably wanted to know whether we had ever met here to discuss the baby. Or her.

I just ignored her and walked over to the bench, where Annie had sat during our conversation. I looked hard for an outline of her body against the wood, for something. I checked behind the bench, even though it would have taken a miracle for her to hide there and not be seen.

After a few minutes, and with my nose starting to get cold, I turned and headed back to the car, brushing against Marla on the way. I didn't say anything, but I didn't have to. I could hear her following behind me, the little gravel stones moving under her feet.

"I'm sorry we didn't find her," she said when we got back into the car. I think she was saying this as much to herself as to me. For the first time that night she seemed a bit down, not as cheerful. Maybe it was finally hitting her that Annie could really be gone, but I didn't want to think about that.

She started the car and took off down the street, as I watched the park and Fincher fade behind me.

When I couldn't see either of them anymore without craning my neck, I said, "There's still lots of places to look."

"I guess it was all getting to be too much," Marla said, like it was her turn to ignore me.

"It isn't over," I shot back.

She eased the car to a stop at a red light. "It must have been a lot for you too."

"It's a friggin' baby, not an *it*," I said.

The light turned green, and we took off again in silence.

"I know it's a baby," she said after a minute or so. Her voice had lost some of the friendliness that had been annoying the shit out of me since laying eyes on her for the first time in Charlene's office. I'd have to be careful if I didn't want to freeze my ass off walking the rest of the way home. We were about five minutes away from Patricia's, but the trees and houses in the dark only looked half familiar.

I wasn't ready to go back there, to face my mom sipping her tea, and Patricia's white hands.

My heart almost stopped as we passed Hedgerow. It was a long street, but I had lived here long enough to know that it led straight to Einstein—Julian's street. I looked back, and thought about going there now. Ringing the doorbell and telling him that Annie was gone. Watching his face change as he took in the news. Or maybe watch it stay stone-still and cool, like he always looked. Like he already knew everything.

I leaned my throbbing head against the window. It felt cold and good.

Marla turned onto Annie's street.

"We aren't finished," I mumbled, but my voice sounded weak and faraway.

"It's too dark, Kye," she replied.

I wasn't used to hearing her use my name. It felt weird.

"But we can still look," I said a little desperately.

But I had no clue what to say after that. I just stared out at the passing houses, each one different but the same. Some recycling bins were already out. People getting ready for the next day. How did they do it?

Suddenly, my whole body lurched forward as the car came to a stop.

Marla's hands were still on the steering wheel, but she was staring at it like she had woken from this dream and couldn't figure out what she was doing behind it.

"Her house is further down," I said.

"Was it going to be me?"

The question came out in one of those whispers that you hear loud and clear.

"I don't know," I mumbled, after a minute of not saying anything.

Her face and eyes looked really grey in the moonlight that streamed through the car and I instantly felt guilty. It wasn't the answer she had been hoping for, but "maybe" sounded way too hopeful, even as I tested it out then, nice and softly, under the collar of my jacket, my warm breath brushing my chin.

Suddenly, I saw a figure up ahead, on the sidewalk. It was walking towards Annie's house.

My heart started pounding. "There."

Marla saw what I did, and the car took off, slowly. It took us all of five seconds to catch up. As we got closer, I put my nose up against the window, but I could already tell it wasn't her. The hair was longer, and her hips were too narrow, almost like a boy's. There was no way that Joseph would have had any room. I gulped hard and looked away.

The house was just ahead now. I saw my mom's car first, parked right alongside Patricia's old Nissan. I thought of walking in there and shaking my head at Patricia, her tired eyes not even blinking as she looked away from me, unsurprised at my failure.

"We'll go back out tomorrow morning," I said.

"You have school," said Marla.

I shrugged. "So?"

Marla parked the car, but we sat there a minute, neither of us saying a word. Then, we slowly undid our seatbelts.

Before I could open the door, Marla touched my shoulder. I turned around, caught in this weird stare of hers, like she had something super important to say before we went back into the house, back into a reality where Annie was gone.

"Don't mess up school," she said.

I felt anger rise in me. So now she had a right to be my friggin' mother, all because she had driven me around a little? I looked down at the floor, when what I really wanted to do was destroy this fucking car. Bust the windshield and cut up all the nice leather seats until all the interior stuffing was floating around like balls of snow.

I wondered whether she could read my thoughts. She was looking at me, I could feel as much. I pictured her eyes looking the way eyes do when they're a hair away from crying. I had gotten to be an expert at knowing that look.

"My last mess-up almost got you a baby," I mumbled.

Then I stepped out.

* * * *

"So, mom says she's gone."

"They don't know that for sure."

"Do you miss her?"

"I miss him."

"What are you going to do?"

"When are you back again?"

"Just under three weeks."

"What would you do?"

"I don't know, Kye."

"I figured."

The End

(Even though my parents keep calling it a new beginning)

Chapter 44

The light's hurting my eyes, and for a second I think that I'm home again, under the covers, and any minute my mom will be coming through the door and yanking up the blind to hint at me that I should have been out of bed a long time ago. To help her chances, she'd have a promise of macaroni and cheese or something else cooking downstairs for lunch.

But these lights are just from the hallway or from the caf a few feet away, not sure which. Right now I have bigger questions, like figuring out who the hell won the War of 1812, and the exam is in twenty minutes.

At least, that's my guess. I would check my cell, but it's sitting in my bedroom, still uncharged from the night that Annie went missing, when it lost all its juice. I could walk over to the clock above the bathrooms down the hall, but that would take me further from the gym, which is where I'll have to be soon, sitting at one of those rickety old desks with a pile of papers in front of me, ready to totally fail grade ten history.

Unless I can figure out these notes, but Anthony must have the crappiest handwriting on the planet, a fact that I had totally forgotten about when I saw the pile of photocopied papers sitting in my mailbox on Sunday. I couldn't believe it either—all I had done was leave a mumbled message with his mom that probably missed the essential facts. Like in my mad dash to my locker on Friday, December fifth, at four o'clock in the afternoon, when the only people left at school were teachers and janitors, my history books were the only ones I hadn't stuffed in my knapsack while my mom waited in the car outside.

I lean my head against the wall and take a long, last sip of my juice box. I've been doing nothing but drink since I got here, which means the chances of having to pee during the exam are at Richter-high levels. Richter scale, named after Charles Richter. Now, if only I can remember names like President James Madison and Isaac Brock. But now all I can think of is that if I really *do* end up having to take a piss during the exam, everyone will definitely notice me then, which makes me wonder whether hiding out in the grade seven hallway is worth anything.

It's a three-foot-wide space between two sets of lockers, and my ass fits into it just fine, even if it is numb as hell. Maybe my parents are right about my losing weight. These jeans are definitely loose, but I can still keep them up without wearing a retarded belt like my dad was trying to push on me this morning.

Still, I remind myself that I'm separated from my fellow classmates by no less than two hallways, a whole cafeteria and like, two dozen classrooms. That's all it takes for me to feel good again about where I am, and thank god for that, because I sure as hell am not interested in talking to anyone, not even to myself, even though my parents are half-convinced I'm crazy. All because I've refused to go back to school since Annie "disappeared".

That's what the cops are calling it, so my parents are too. I don't know what Patricia thinks, but I haven't seen her since that night. I know she's spoken to my mom a bunch of times on the phone, and I keep meaning to go over and see her, but I can't quite yet. I'm scared she'll use that word too—*disappeared*, and I don't think I can hear that from Patricia. I myself don't call it anything at all; it's easier that way.

I look back down at Anthony's Swahili code for the hundredth time and try to ignore the sound of footsteps that have just invaded my hallway. Probably some kid who doesn't want to be noticed either. The footsteps are getting closer pretty damn quickly, and I'm wondering whether I should move or something.

"Yo, dude."

The first things I see are the sneakers, all colourful and tall. I wish I could just keep looking at them, but I find myself drawn to his face, curious about what he looks like and how much of what I see will look like the photos from Annie's knapsack.

Even though it's only been a week, it seems like his hair has gotten longer, but the rest is all still there. The green eyes behind those Hugo Boss glasses, the beauty spots around his nose. The only thing different is the pimple, smack in the middle of his forehead like a bull's eye. I've never seen Julian with a pimple before. I also haven't seen him alone in the longest time, and there are no signs of Peter or anyone else in sight. When our eyes meet, he gives me the kind of smile I've seen him give the mean teachers that no one likes. Phony.

"I knew I'd find you," he says.

My body stiffens, and I want to crawl even further back into this space between the lockers and prove him wrong, but the wall's digging into my back as it is.

I look back down at those sneakers. Man, they're big enough to walk on the moon, and I suddenly wonder whether they also have the power to pick up my BO, like those dogs at airports going around sniffing people's bags. I managed a shower this morning, much to my parents' joy, and I put on like, a million coats of this shitty deodorant. Still, after sitting in bed for a week, I can't be sure of anything. Like how to continue this conversation that already seems to be dying.

"You ready for the exam?"

I nod and look back down at Anthony's notes.

"Me too," he says.

"You're always ready," I say back.

I follow the long blue lines along the sides of his sneakers as he tries to kick an eraser on the floor. He misses completely and rams his foot against the trash can in the corner.

"You suck," I mumble.

He laughs. "At least I don't swim like a girl."

"I don't swim like a girl," I say to the floor.

"And I can play softball," he adds.

I slowly stand up. I haven't used my legs a whole lot lately. Once I feel steady, I try and look at him, but his eyes are kind of going everywhere.

This weird silence comes over us, and I suddenly realize how thirsty I am, but my juice box is empty. The straw hangs limply over the side, all sad.

"Any news on Annie?" he suddenly asks.

I can tell he wants to look at me because he knows it's the polite thing to do, but he only gets as far as my cheek.

I can't be bothered to guess what he's thinking. Maybe a week ago I would have tried, but now I know that if I do, I'll just get this ache in my chest that will never go away. Not after Christmas break, not after anything.

His eyes are still on my face, and normally I'd worry that I have some big orange streak on my face from the pasta I'd had for lunch, but I don't even care about that. I know I'm ugly.

Nothing could make him flinch. Except maybe the word *disappeared.*

"She might still come back," is all I say.

I stuff my head in my pencil case and start rummaging like mad through my two pencils and eraser, like I'm about to spend a week in the wilderness or something and I'm checking on my supplies one last time. He's probably thinking I'm crazy, or high or something for believing anything other than the obvious. That the police and my parents are right.

"We have to go." he says with a sigh.

I shrug but gather up my crap and start following him. I can't remember when I last followed him anywhere. The rows of lockers we're passing are all blurry, and the gym feels miles away. The bright orange doors are just ahead, and I know we'll be there sooner than I could ever want.

I want to say something before we reach them. Something smart and witty, like he always does, but nothing comes to friggin' mind, not even a lame-ass joke. And now we're here, and we're both blending in with the crowd of students waiting. I don't look at any of them, but I can feel their confidence. They know the War of 1812 and whatever else will be on this exam. They know it all.

People are brushing against my arms, and my hand accidentally touches the back of someone in front of me. It's a girl, but she's not Claudia, so I don't look at her.

There's a universe of sneakers around me. They're all flashy like his. I keep my eyes down, and it feels good. It feels like old times, back in grade seven, before *him*, before everything.

He's no longer beside me, and I don't know if he said anything before disappearing into the crowd or whether he just ducked out, pretending that he never knew me, that that gym class in grade nine never happened.

I want to find him and tell him that I could have lived without ever being on his stupid softball team. I could have survived being the loser just fine. I don't even need Anthony, and good thing too, because he probably doesn't need me anymore either. He's probably kissing ass with someone else, solidifying his connections for after Christmas break.

I don't know where I'll be then. I don't even know where I'll be two hours from now, after this exam is over. Probably back in my bedroom, mulling over all the answers I got wrong and maybe consoling myself with a movie. I haven't watched one in a while, and I think for a second about what I could be in the mood for, but nothing comes to mind.

I've stopped in front of a desk with an old lady behind it. She's grinning at me like I'm her grandson or something, and I wonder whether I was smiling without even knowing it. Now I'm just staring at this red scarf tied around her neck and the foundation over her cheeks that's cracking like the top of my mom's baked cakes.

"Nice to see you, Kye," she says, like I'm a friggin' celebrity.

I guess I've given her my name, and now her eyes scan the long sheets in front of her, looking for it. She finally crosses it off, and I turn to find a seat.

I don't know where Anthony is, and I don't dare look beyond the first row of desks. There's one right in front of me that's free, which is a friggin' miracle, except that there's still a shitload of people that have to sit down, which means they're all going to pass by me. Time to rummage through the pencil case once more.

"Hey Kye."

That's Sandra, waving at me from two rows over. A nice enough girl, who happens to be standing right in front of Claudia. My heart speeds up for a split second, until I realize she's walking over to the other side of the gym, probably to avoid me. She looks good, as always. Jeans and this thick, woolly sweater that I just want to wrap myself in. She stops at this guy Richard Long's desk and giggles. She probably wants to go out with him.

Damn, is my mouth dry, and I already need a bathroom break. This young-looking teacher I've never seen before has just updated the time on this gigantic easel at the front of the gym. I still have a couple of minutes before the doors close and I'm trapped.

I pick up my knapsack and pencil case and head towards the doors.

I wonder whether the scarf lady is asking me where I'm going, or whether I got out before she could notice that I had too much stuff with me to ever go back. I start walking down the hall. It's pretty much empty, except for a few stragglers who are just making it in time. One of them is Daniel Kidd, and he ignores me. Big surprise there, since he's said about ten words to me since we started high school. Not that I care anyway.

I make it out the side door and it's fucking freezing.

I zip up my jacket to my chin, but it does no good. I stuff my hands in my pockets and keep walking, wondering why I am here and not taking a whizz like I had planned. There's no point in going back now, and besides, the sun is starting to warm my head a little. If I close my eyes I can feel it on my eyelids, and I imagine being in bed with the sun streaming through the window like it always does.

My mom probably cleaned my sheets today. It will be all nice and fresh, with that fabric-softener smell—even better. I want to be there now, but when I open my eyes, all I see is some old dude hanging up Christmas lights around his porch. It sure doesn't feel like Christmas.

I've almost passed the park, but I keep my eyes straight ahead. No point now in glancing over and remembering shit that isn't worth remembering anymore.

I get to the bus stop and sit down on the bench. It feels like someone just put an icicle up my ass, but I stay put and open my knapsack. I haul out Anthony's notes and look them over. I won't be needing them anymore, but I can't chuck them, even though they're only photocopies. I just can't do it.

Then my cold fingers slowly slide the plastic bag out. The envelope's still open, and I glance inside one last time. I don't bother pulling the pool pictures out. I've looked at them enough to remember every detail on my deathbed. I take a deep breath and a quick look around, but everybody is still in school, so I pull out the picture of Joseph. I don't look at that one either. I just hold it in my hands like that for a minute or so, trying to imagine what it would feel like to hold him for real.

Then I slide him back in and lick the envelope, forgetting what my mom once said about that stuff being poison. Suicide by mail. For the first time in days, I want to laugh.

I look at the address. I was surprised that he was listed. I guess his five-hundred-grand-a-year dad isn't so impressive after all. Nobody is, really. I wrote the address really clean and big, too. No mailman could have a doubt about who's meant to get this envelope. I get up and open the mailbox and just stand there a second. The hand holding the envelope is getting closer to frostbite by the second. I look up and down the street, almost like I'm expecting somebody, like I'm giving

Annie one last chance to appear and tell me not to do it. That Joseph is alright.

I don't even feel the envelope against my hand as it slides off and into the dungeon of the mailbox. I stick my face in after it, but can't see a thing.

I turn and walk away. It'll be a while before I reach home, but for some reason walking feels right. The old dude has his lights almost up now. I see what looks like a wreath sitting on his car.

I keep walking. My cheeks feel sticky and wet. It's probably the cold getting into my eyes and stuff. I wipe the tears away with the back of my hand, but I feel new ones coming on. I want to go back to the mailbox and shake it like an animal until Joseph falls out again, but those things are heavier than you'd think. Last summer Julian dared me and Anthony to topple one over, but we couldn't.

I close my eyes hard and try remembering. The arms and legs standing guard against the tornado behind him, the vertebrae, and pear-shaped head. It all comes back to me, but against the sun in the sky and some kids yelling down the street, it all feels meaningless.

About the Author

I wrote my first novel, "Kimberly and the Seventh Grade Disaster", when I was thirteen years old. Good thing it never saw the light of day. In the years since, I continued writing stories, earned a degree in Creative Writing from Concordia University, read a lot of books (some over and over, like *Catcher in the Rye*), watched a lot of movies, got married and became a stepmom. *The Pool Theory* is my first novel that strangers are allowed to read.

I can be reached at:
www.alexanazzaro.com
@AlexaNazzaro

Reading Guide

1. Describe Kye's personality shift throughout the story. Does he become more or less mature with time? Why?

2. Do you think Kye is comfortable with his sexual identity?

3. Describe how Kye's history of being bullied has shaped his personality.

4. Why do you think Kye and Anthony love movies as much as they do?

5. What role does Anthony play in the group of three friends?

6. Why do you think Julian chose to be friends with Kye and Anthony in the first place?

7. Discuss the power dynamics in Kye and Claudia's relationship, and how they shift throughout the story.

8. Discuss the way Kye's parents react to the baby news. What do their reactions indicate about each one's personality and relationship to Kye?

9. Discuss the presence of adults in the novel. Do you feel they play a large enough role? Why or why not?

10. Parks figure prominently throughout the novel. What significance do they have in the story?

11. Do you think Julian had any connection to Red Jacket? Why or why not?

12. Based on Kye and Adam's phone conversations while Adam is in Australia, do you feel the two brothers grew closer?

13. What do you think Annie's summer relationship with Kye was like? With Julian?

14. Describe Kye's feelings for Annie at the end of the story.

15. Do you think Kye and Claudia ever had a chance at a real relationship?

16. Do you think Kye was sincere in his wish to be a father?

17. If you had to imagine Kye's future, what do you see?

18. Describe the experience of having this book narrated by a boy.

19. Do you feel that Annie betrayed Kye in any way? Why or why not?

20. Discuss the significance of the title of the novel.

CPSIA information can be obtained at www.ICGtesting.com
Printed in the USA
LVOW10s0909160713

342982LV00002B/29/P